Love at First Sight

NEW YORK TIMES & USA TODAY BESTSELLING AUTHOR

KELLY ELLIOTT

Love at First Sight
Book 1 Southern Bride Copyright © 2019 by Kelly Elliott
ISBN EBOOK 978-1-943633-57-9
ISBN PAPERBACK 978-1-943633-58-6

Cover photo by: Shannon Cain Photography by Shannon Cain
Cover Design by: RBA Designs www.rbadesigns.com
Interior Design & Formatting by: Elaine York www.allusiongraphics.
com
Developmental Editor: Elaine York www.allusiongraphics.com
Content Editor: Cori McCarthy Yellow Bird Editing
Proofing Editor: AmyRose Capetta Yellow Bird Editing

This book is a work of fiction. Names, characters, places, and incidents either are products of the author's imagination or are used fictitiously. Any resemblance to actual persons, living or dead, events, or locales is entirely coincidental.

For more information on Kelly and her books, please visit her website www.kellyelliottauthor.com

Love at First Sight

This book is dedicated to Alyssa Hawk.
She was a loving mother and friend and is
missed profoundly by those who loved her.

"Her absence is like the sky, spread over everything."
— *C.S. Lewis*

Prologue

"KEEP YOUR EYES closed, Chloe."

"Okay, but will you tell me what is going on?" I asked Easton, my voice laced with excitement and a bit of worry. Things between the two of us the last few months had been sort of weird. It felt like we were drifting apart. Or maybe I was drifting away from Easton, knowing that our college days were coming to end. He was going one way, I was going another.

He guided me up a step and then stopped me.

"Can I open them yet?" I asked with a nervous giggle.

Easton and I had been dating for ten months to the day. I was positive this was a surprise anniversary dinner and a way for Easton to attempt to bring us closer. Plus, it was my last night in College Station before I headed home. We had both graduated from Texas A&M and were about to start our careers. It wasn't lost on me that we still hadn't talked about how we were going to handle our long-distance relationship. Easton was taking a position with a drilling company in Houston, and I was headed back to Oak Springs to work for my family's cattle ranch, the Frio Cattle Company. It had been my life growing up, and I couldn't wait to get back. I missed the smells, and I missed my pet goat Patches most of all.

Even though my heart wanted to remind my head how much I missed Rip, I wouldn't let it go there.

Warm breath tickled my ear as Easton whispered, "Open your eyes, Chloe."

I opened them and gasped at the sight before me. Red roses filled the small private room of my favorite Italian restaurant in town. A rustic, round table held candles and two plates filled with my favorite dish, chicken fettuccine alfredo.

"Oh, my goodness. This is the most amazing thing ever!" I said, spinning around the room, then facing Easton. "You did all of this for our ten-month anniversary?"

He dropped to one knee, and my stomach fell. Oh, my God. This was not happening.

No. No. No. Please stand up.

"I did this because I'm madly in love with you, Chloe Parker, and I don't want to live without you. I would be honored if you would please be my wife."

My mind spun as I stood there, staring down at him, unable to make my mouth move. Easton wasn't my first love. He wasn't the first guy I'd ever kissed. Hell, he wasn't even the guy I lost my virginity to. He was someone I had come to care about. A friend. A lover. But did I love him enough to marry him? This was not how I had envisioned this moment. My chest rose and fell, and it felt like it was getting harder to breathe.

A single tear slipped down my cheek as I forced a smile. Easton would never know that that tear was not because I was happy... It was because I was about to let go of the past. My past. A past I had held onto for so long that maybe this was a sign I needed to finally forget him.

Forget Rip.

Forever.

Chapter 1

Chloe

SENIOR YEAR OF high school.

"Run, Rip! Go!" I screamed from the sidelines as Rip caught the pass and headed for the winning touchdown.

When he made it, I spun around and looked for Alyssa. My best friend. She was in the stands holding the sign we had made for Rip and Mike. Alyssa and Mike had been dating for two years, while Rip and I, well, we were simply Rip and Chloe. The two best friends everyone thought should be dating—but weren't. I agreed with them, although I kept that little secret to myself.

Rip, on the other hand, hadn't once hinted at wanting something more since sixth grade when he kissed me at the middle school dance, and my father unleashed on him. To this day, I blamed my daddy for scaring Rip so much that he became deathly afraid to even look at me wrong. But sometimes, I did catch him looking. And the way it made my skin flame and my lower stomach ache confused me.

"Chloe."

The sound of his voice had me spinning back around and launching into his arms.

"You did it, Rip. You won the game."

He laughed as he held me tight and then spun me around, make me laugh.

Once my feet were back on the ground, he shook his head. "Nah. It was the whole team. Hell, the whole town backing us."

Rip Myers. Always the modest one, no matter what it came to. He wouldn't brag how he had scored the most points in this game, or how he had won a full-ride scholarship to three different colleges who wanted him to play football, as well as a baseball scholarship to the University of Texas and Texas A&M. He would play off the fact that he was most likely going to be the class valedictorian, with me trailing in second place. I was okay with that, though.

Leaning up on my toes, I kissed him on the cheek. "Congratulations, Rip."

His cognac-colored eyes looked down at me, almost making me dizzy with such an intense stare. "You know how much you mean to me, Chloe? Right?"

I nodded.

Leaning down, he brushed a soft kiss to my forehead before being pulled back and tackled by all the other players.

My heart pounded as I laughed and tried to forget how his kiss had burned into my skin. How every touch, caress, and look he gave me burned into my very soul.

"I don't get it."

Lori Rhodes stood next to me. She was the captain of our cheerleading team.

"What don't you get?" I asked, reaching down and picking up my pom-poms before walking with the rest of the team over to our coach. The football team would be presented with the state championship trophy and she would want us all to be ready to take a picture for the *Oak Springs Gazette,* our local newspaper.

"Everyone knows Rip likes you and you like Rip."

I rolled my eyes. "We're friends. Best friends, and we always have been."

She scoffed. "He runs by everyone, including his coach, after that touchdown to get to you. *You,* Chloe. He looks at you like you're the best thing since apple pie, and you do the same. It's obvious the two of you want to be together."

4

Peeking over my shoulder, I watched as the entire football team continued to celebrate. Focusing back ahead, I shrugged.

"We're just ..."

"Friends. Is that why every girl who tries to go out with Rip is met with utter devastation when he only goes out with them once or twice and barely even kisses them?"

My blood boiled any time someone talked about Rip going out with a girl. Especially when the girl in question was doing the talking. *Rip's a great kisser! Rip took me to make out point, and we danced under the stars.*

Ugh.

I'd had to listen to it for the last four years of high school and was tired of acting like it didn't affect me. The only thing I did know for sure was that Rip was still a virgin. I knew it because he told me. A small part of me was hoping that maybe, just maybe he was saving himself for me, like I was for him. I would never admit that to anyone, though, not even Alyssa.

"From what I've heard, he's a good kisser," Lori said. Then she tossed her head back to laugh, turned and walked backwards. "I will say, if you don't go for him soon, I may have to take a shot at him."

I swallowed hard and forced a smile. "Don't let me hold you back."

Lori smirked. "Oh, you wouldn't be able to."

She turned and started walking faster, leaving me lagging behind. I wasn't alone for long, though. Rip ran up next to me, draped his arm over my shoulders and launched into the plans we had for our fishing trip tomorrow.

Later that night, at Mike's field party, Rip and I sat on the back of his tailgate talking. He'd had a few too many beers and was asking me if I wouldn't mind driving him home. Since I knew he always got loose lips when he was drinking, I decided to probe him for some answers.

"Rip, do you ever get tired of people asking us why we don't date?"

The beer paused at his lips for the briefest of moments before he took a long drink.

5

Without looking at me, he said, "Nah. I'm not bothered by it. They're just jealous."

I laughed. "Of what?"

"That I have a pretty girl on my arm all the time."

Smiling, I bumped his shoulder. "Is that all I am to you?"

"Hardly, Chloe Cat." He turned and looked at me. "Do you get bothered by it?"

"Nope," I lied. How I thought I would be able to share this was beyond me. That's when I saw Lori walking up. I held my breath as she made her way to Rip. My eyes roamed her way-too-tight shirt that showed practically all of her breasts, and her super tight, super short skirt.

"Hey, Chloe."

"Hey, Lori."

She turned to Rip and ran her tongue along her bottom lip. I rolled my eyes.

"Congratulations on winning the game, Rip."

"Thanks, Lori."

"I was wondering if you might want to," she looked my way, then back to Rip, "spend some time together. Alone."

Rip smiled, and his gaze raked over her body. I swallowed hard and looked away. If he went off with her I was going to have to leave. There was no way I could handle it.

"Thanks, Lori, but I'm talking with Chloe right now."

The corners of my mouth threatened to spread upwards.

"She won't mind. Will you, Chloe?"

I could either say I didn't mind and push Rip right into Lori's arms, or I could be a bitch.

When she tilted her head with that look only she could give, I had my answer.

Bitch, it is.

"Actually, I do. We were in the middle of talking about the plans we have for leaving early in the morning. Rip was asking me to drive him home, so if you'll excuse us, I'm sure you won't have a problem finding another guy to be...*alone* with."

Lori's mouth dropped open, and Rip tried to hide his beer-induced laugh but failed.

Turning on the heels of her boots, Lori walked away.

"Damn, Chloe! If I didn't know any better, I'd say you were jealous."

"Hardly. I simply saved you from getting some weird sexual disease from her."

Rip watched Lori walk away, his eyes clearly on her retreating ass. Maybe he had wanted to be with Lori. My heart dropped to my stomach at the thought.

Jumping off the tailgate, I said, "I'm ready to leave now. Are you about done?"

"We can leave if you're ready to."

I held out my hand. "Want to give me the keys, or would you rather I call Lori back over? I didn't mean to send her away if that was what you wanted."

Rip jumped down, stumbling a bit. He placed his hand on the side of my face. My stomach fluttered when he rubbed his thumb over my cheek.

"Lori is definitely not what I want."

My breath caught in my throat. We stared at each other for what felt like forever. Finding my voice, I whispered, "What do you want?"

His eyes went to my mouth, and then just as quickly back up to meet my gaze. He smiled, both dimples displayed on that handsome face. "I think I want my bed so I can get some sleep, or we'll never be able to get up and go fishing in the morning."

Disappointment rushed over my body, but I quickly pushed it away. I jumped into the driver's seat of his Ford truck and said, "Then let's get you home."

My sunhat blocked the strong rays, but not my view of Rip while he stood at the bow of the boat. For only being eighteen, he had a body to die for. He had a broad chest and muscles that made all the girls at school stare at him. Including me. Years of sports and hard work on his granddaddy's farm and Frio Cattle Ranch had made him solid. Plus, his oldest brother, Jonathon, who was married to my Aunt Waylynn, owned a construction company. Rip had put in countless hours working for Jonathon last summer.

"I can't believe I haven't caught anything," Rip stated.

Once a month, Rip and I went fishing with my dad, Uncle Trevor, and my younger brother Gage. I was a female surrounded by a lot of testosterone...completely outnumbered but I could totally hold my own against these men.

"Dude, you're not using the right bait," Gage announced from the back side of the boat.

Rip shot Gage a dirty look. "I know what kind of bait to use, Gage."

"Don't argue, boys, you're scaring the fish away," my Uncle Trevor said, pulling his hat down over his face. He was currently sitting with his feet up and eyes closed. I think he often napped more than he fished but he would say he was "waiting for the right moment to cast his line" whenever anyone pointed that out.

Glancing over to my father, he walked up to Rip. The two of them were soon lost in conversation about bait. I sighed and looked out over the water.

My father and Rip had always been close. I knew my father had had a talk with Rip once after he caught us kissing in middle school. I wondered if whatever it was my father had said to Rip was the reason he wouldn't kiss me again. I thought I saw it in his eyes every now and then. It was how he looked at me. Or little things he said to me. Like last night. He hinted he wanted me, but then he didn't say it. It seemed like he wanted to kiss me as much as I wanted him to. Neither of us would ever make the first move, though. I knew why. We were the best of friends, what if things didn't work out?

Or maybe Rip was just curious and not serious about wanting me.

"Penny for your thoughts," Uncle Trevor said, sitting next to me.

I had to quickly change my thoughts even as Uncle Trevor's voice pulled me from them. "Rip hasn't told me what school he's going to yet."

"You hoping he picks A&M?"

With half a shrug, I replied, "Maybe. It's going to be weird if he goes somewhere else. We've always been there for each other."

Trevor nodded and looked back over toward Rip and Daddy.

"I'm sure wherever he ends up going, he'll always be there for you, Chloe."

I rested my chin on my knees. "I know."

"Things are going to change a lot in the next year, hell, the next few years."

"I know that, too. It kind of scares me."

"You ever going to tell him how you feel?"

I snapped my head to look at my uncle. "What?"

He shook his head. "I know that look, trust me. The look of wanting someone so badly but being afraid of taking the leap. I've walked in those shoes. I see it on his face as well as yours, Chloe. Someone has to take the first step."

Swallowing hard, I pressed my lips together tightly, trying to decide if I wanted to admit my feelings, and if Uncle Trevor was the person I wanted to admit them to.

"Do me a favor, Chloe Cat. Do it before y'all leave for college. Will you promise me that?"

"What if..."

He shook his head. "There is no time in this life for *what ifs*, little girl."

"Holy shit! He's got something big!" Daddy yelled out as Trevor jumped up and headed over to watch Rip reel his catch in. When he pulled up a giant bass, I couldn't help but smile. He held it while Trevor took a picture. Then his eyes met mine, and I smiled even bigger, giving him a thumbs up.

"Way to go, Rip!" I shouted and snapped a picture on my phone.

"Guess the bait I was using worked. Huh, Gage?" A shit-eating smirk went across his beautiful face.

9

My father looked proud while Gage shot Rip the finger, then changed the bait on his line to what Rip was using. They quickly got back to fishing after Rip let the bass go in lake.

Picking up my book, I leaned back and got lost in the words, grinning. This was a perfect day for me.

And even though I was smiling at how perfect the moment was, I knew there weren't many of these days left for us in the coming months.

Chapter 2

Chloe

"**H**EY, CHLOE."
The whispered voice came from behind me.

Turning, I saw Alyssa handing me a piece of paper. A note from Rip.

I couldn't help the silly smile on my face. Glancing around the room, I moved my hands toward my lap so I could read the note. Rip was the only person I knew who still wrote notes on paper instead of sending a text. He only did it with me, though, and it made me feel special. I had a shoebox at home filled with notes from him that I'd kept as mementos, among other things that Rip had given me since we were younger. Inside that box was the very first flower he ever gave me, pressed between the pages of a little Bible my grammy had given me when Daddy and I first moved from Oregon to Texas.

That's where I was born...Oregon. Daddy never truly told me why he left Texas to move to Oregon, though. That's where he met my biological mother, who I haven't seen since I was five and never care to see again. Even now I can remember the mean words she would say to me. Those words still had an edge to them that tore at my heart.

Once we moved to Texas, though, everything changed for the better. I found my very best friend—second to Rip—Patches. He's a goat my granddaddy gave me. And my father married his high school sweetheart, Paxton. In my mind, she is my one and only mother, and I love her so much.

Glancing down, I read his note.

Dear Chloe Cat,

I've got an early Christmas present for you. Meet me under the bleachers after school.

Love always,

Rip

My thumb ran over the words, *love always*. I smiled and folded the note, slipping it into my back pocket.

"What did it say?" Alyssa asked.

I glanced over my shoulder and grinned. "He has a Christmas present for me."

She returned the grin. "I hope it's his dick in your va-jay-jay!"

"Oh my gosh! Shut up!" I whisper-shouted. "You are insane!"

We both started to giggle until Mrs. Hathaway cleared her throat.

"Chloe, Alyssa. Is there something you'd like to share with the class? Perhaps something that has amused you?"

"No, ma'am," we said in unison.

Facing forward, I placed my hands on my burning cheeks.

When the teacher went back to writing the math problem on the board, Alyssa leaned forward and whispered, "You know, if you told him you wanted him to take your virginity, he would."

I waved her off and glanced around the room. It wasn't a secret I was a virgin. A silly fool who was holding out hope that the man to experience sex with me for the first time would be my very best friend.

Alyssa's comments really threw me for a loop. The rest of the day I couldn't stop thinking about Rip. Thoughts of him filled almost every free moment. We passed each other in the hall four times during the school day. Every day. We sat next to each other every single day at lunch with the rest of our friends. We had one class together, the last class of the day. French.

It has always been my dream to go to France some day, and when I decided to take French instead of Spanish, Rip did the same just because he wanted to make sure we had at least one class together. Alyssa also took it. My insides melted whenever Rip spoke French in class. A few times I caught myself daydreaming he was making love to me in France for the very first time as he whispered *Je t'aime* in my ear.

When I walked into French class today, Rip was sitting on the corner of Miranda Williams's desk. The way they were smiling at each other instantly made me jealous. Quickly recovering, I walked to my desk and sat down. Miranda laughed at something Rip said, causing me to look again. This time she saw me watching them. She placed her hand on his leg. Rip slid off her desk, then leaned down and said something only she could hear.

I looked away, opening my book and quickly acting like I hadn't noticed the exchange.

"Hey, Chloe Cat."

Ignoring Rip, I kept writing notes.

"Chloe?"

With a quick glance, I smiled. "Hey, Rip."

"How's your day been?"

"Fine."

He sat down next to me, his normal seat in class.

"Just fine? Did you get my note from Alyssa?"

"Yes. I don't know why you couldn't just ask me in class."

My words were cold and bitter, and I regretted them the moment they were out. How was it that just a little bit ago, I was grinning from ear to ear as I read that note, but now I was feeling a mixture of anger, sadness, and love?

"I thought you liked getting notes from me."

I looked at him and then at Miranda. "I'm sure I'm not the only girl who likes getting notes from you."

I sighed, pissed at myself for being jealous, and for showing my jealousy.

"Chloe..."

"It doesn't matter, Rip."

He went to reach for my hand, and I pulled it away.

"Talk to me. What is wrong?"

When I looked over at Miranda again, she was watching us. *Bitch.*

I gathered up my books and stood. "I feel like I'm coming down with something."

As the teacher walked into the classroom, I headed out and said, "I'm not feeling well. I'm going to the nurse."

Not even giving the teacher time to respond, I picked up my pace and headed to my locker.

Stupid. You're so stupid. He's not yours, Chloe. He was never yours.

I threw my books into my locker and grabbed my backpack and purse. Slamming the door shut, I made my way to the exit. I never skipped class. Ever.

I pushed the door open and headed to my car.

"Chloe!" Rip shouted from behind me.

I nearly wanted to cry for being so childish and stupid. Why couldn't I simply tell him how I felt? I hated this game. Hated it. Uncle Trevor's words were bouncing around in my head, reminding me that I would always feel this way if I didn't tell him.

"Not now, Rip."

"Stop!"

"I'm going home."

"Will you fucking stop walking away from me and tell me what in the hell is wrong with you?"

Stopping, I spun around and glared at him.

Internally, I screamed at him.

I'm in love with you, you stupid, blind fool!

Rip jogged up to me and stopped. "I'm sorry, I didn't mean to curse like that. *Please* tell me what's wrong."

I shook my head and looked away. "I'm having a bad day, that's all."

He pushed a piece of hair behind my ear that had fallen from my ponytail. "Will you tell me what's wrong?"

Tears stung at the back of my eyes because I couldn't tell him I was insanely jealous that he was talking to another girl. I couldn't tell him that it was me who loved him, me he shared Saturdays fishing with, me who should be on his arm and not just because we were friends.

But I told him none of that.

"It's stupid and childish. It doesn't really matter anyway. Why don't you go back to class? You can sit with Miranda."

There. I did it. I showed what a jealous fool I am, and I regret nothing. Well, that's partially not true.

He pinched his brows. "Anything that makes you upset matters, Chloe. And why would you tell me to go sit with Miranda?"

Pressing my lips tightly together to keep from crying, I turned away from him.

He placed his finger on my chin and turned me until I was looking directly at him.

I swallowed hard. "I don't know why I said it. I guess because I saw you with her when I walked into class. If you're dating her, that's fine. Honest...like I said, I'm having a bad day and want to be alone."

When he smiled, I felt my knees go weak. "I'm not dating her. I don't want to date her. What you saw was her trying to make a move on me when you walked in to the classroom. I leaned down and told her it would never happen."

I felt like a fool. "Why wouldn't it ever happen?"

He shrugged. "She's not my type. Listen, I still have that Christmas present for you. Want it now?"

I felt my cheeks go hot.

"If you want to give it to me now."

He reached into his back pocket and pulled out an envelope. When he handed it to me, I felt giddy and warm inside, and that was before I even knew what the precious container held.

"What is this?" I asked.

"Open it and see."

I still felt foolish for how I had acted earlier, but I pushed it aside, and opened the envelope. I stared down at two tickets as I slowly pulled them out. Then my eyes jumped up to meet his.

"Rip, these are tickets to see *Tartuffe* in Austin."

He flashed me a bright smile. "In French."

Staring back down at the tickets, I covered my mouth.

"I wish I could take you to see a play in France, but I'm little short on cash right now, saving up for the future and all."

My gaze jerked back up to him. "This is... Thank you, Rip."

I threw myself at him, and he wrapped me in his arms.

"Has your day gotten better, Chloe Cat?" he whispered against my ear.

"So much better."

"I hate seeing you upset."

Squeezing my eyes shut to hold back my tears, I whispered, "I'm sorry."

Rip continued to hold onto me in the middle of the parking lot of our high school. I didn't want him to let me go. I wanted to confess to him right then and there that I wanted more than our friendship. I wanted *him*.

"There isn't anything I wouldn't do for my best friend."

My smile faded briefly before I withdrew. Maybe that was all I truly was to Rip. His best friend. I wasn't ready to accept that role in his life, though. My heart was still holding out hope for something more.

"It's on Christmas Eve! How exciting," I said.

"I've got the whole thing planned and have already asked your folks if we can stay in Austin for the night. They agreed because Mike and Alyssa are going, too. The girls can stay in one room and boys in another. I gave your father my word y'all would be okay and nothing inappropriate would go on."

I smiled. "Sounds amazing."

Hugging him once more, I kissed him on the cheek.

"I think this is the best present I've ever gotten besides Patches."

Rip laughed. "Damn, I don't think I'll ever be able to top Patches."

"No, I don't think so." I wanted to add, *Unless the present of your heart was finally mine*, but I kept that locked deep inside.

"Come on. Let's head on over to Lily's Place and grab a few shakes and split a piece of cheesecake. I'm starving."

With a nod, I replied, "I'll meet you over there."

As I walked to my car, clutching my present to my chest, I realized now we were both skipping class. With a smile on my face, I slipped into the car and started it.

All thoughts of how silly I'd acted were gone, and I was looking forward to hanging out with Rip alone.

Chapter 3

Rip

I SAT ON the bed of my truck and watched as everyone gathered around the massive bonfire. It had become a tradition: every year on New Year's Eve, we lit a bonfire at the Parker Ranch and celebrated. Chloe's grandparents were pretty chill about it. They had one rule—no alcohol—and pretty much everyone respected it. A few jerks would try to take some out to pass around, but Chloe wouldn't have it. More than once I'd seen her toss a bottle or two into the bonfire, causing it to ignite even higher, usually making everyone cheer.

"How was the play?"

Turning, I saw Miranda walking over to me. *Good Lord. Why can't this girl take a hint?*

"It was great. Chloe enjoyed it, so that's all that matters."

She laughed.

"Oh, yes. *Chloe.* You know everyone thinks you two have a friends-with-benefits thing going on."

"I don't really care what everyone thinks." I just wanted Miranda to go away, but I didn't want to get rude to accomplish that.

She shrugged. "Maybe not. But you know how people talk and how twisted stories can become. What are you doing tomorrow night? Maybe you and I could hang out."

"I've got plans."

"With Chloe?"

Squinting at her, I replied, "No, with my father. We're going hunting."

"What about when you get back?"

I felt Chloe's stare. From across the flames of the bonfire, I turned and looked directly at her. She was standing next to Alyssa and Lucy. I couldn't help but remember how she had reacted that day last month when she thought something was going on with Miranda and me. I had replayed it over and over in my head. Had she been jealous, or was she really just having a bad day?

God, women were frustrating as hell. A part of me wanted to admit to her how I felt, but I wasn't sure if she felt the same. And what if she did and things didn't work out? I'd lose my best friend and I couldn't gamble that.

"Well?" Miranda asked. My gaze was still locked with Chloe's. She tilted her head and raised an eyebrow, as if to silently ask me if everything was okay.

"Sorry, Miranda. Like I told you that day in class, I'm not interested."

She sighed in frustration. "Listen, Rip. You either go public with this weird, twisted relationship with Chloe, or everyone, including me, are just going to assume you're gay."

I looked at her and laughed. "Did you ever think for one minute that maybe I'm not interested in anyone here in Oak Springs, Miranda? Hell, half of y'all have slept with most of the guys in town, and the other half have slept with guys from other schools. If I'm interested in taking anyone out, I will."

Her mouth dropped open and her cheeks flamed up like the bonfire. "You're a real asshole, do you know that?"

"And yet you keep coming back around like a bee to honey. Asshole, huh? I've been told that once or twice."

Miranda folded her arms and shook her head. "You're a real prick. Whatever. It's your loss."

"And somehow I'll learn to live with it." *God, she forced me to be rude on New Year's Eve. What a way to start off the new year.*

19

She stormed off to stand with her friends. Most of them were cheerleaders. Even though Chloe and Alyssa were cheerleaders, too, neither of them had gotten sucked into that group of bitches. I was glad; everyone standing in that circle was fake, but Chloe and Alyssa weren't.

"Looks like you pissed off one of the Barbie dolls," Mike said with a chuckle as he punched me in the shoulder.

"Yeah, they don't like being turned down...repeatedly," I replied to my best friend. Well, best friend after Chloe. Mike had no issues coming in second to Chloe.

"Alyssa and I are thinking of going camping next week for a few days with a few other people. You and Chloe want to come?"

I shrugged. "Maybe. I need to check with Jonathon. He might need me to help him build some cabinets."

Chloe and Alyssa walked up to us, lost in conversation.

"I wonder if we can make it happen?" Alyssa said as they came to a stop in front of us.

"Make what happen?" Mike asked.

"Chloe wants to study abroad in France. I'm wondering if we can both do that at the same time."

"That would be fun," I said.

With a nod, Chloe replied, "It would be."

"Maybe some French guy will sweep you off your feet, Chloe, while you're over there," Alyssa said.

Chloe giggled. "Maybe."

"Oh, it's a shame they stopped doing the love locks on the bridge in Paris. How romantic would that have been?" Alyssa was in her own little world now, and it was starting to piss me off.

Jealousy mixed with rage and raced through my veins. I looked away, not even wanting to think what college was going to be like. Once Chloe was able to get away from this small town, would some guy catch her eye? Of course. The thought made me feel sick.

"I was telling Rip it might be fun to go camping next week."

Alyssa jumped and clapped her hands. "Oh, that would be fun. Chloe, can you go?"

"I can't next week. I'm helping my father and Uncle Trevor on the ranch. Daddy wants me to start taking on a bigger role. The plan is for me to work there each summer, starting when I graduate from high school."

A part of me was relieved Chloe wouldn't be going camping. It was selfish as hell, but the thought of her hanging out with some of these guys, yeah, it made my blood boil.

"Hard to believe they're grooming you to take it over some day," Mike stated.

"They know how much I love it. I mean, I'll do the business side of things, and Gage will handle the daily running of the ranch once he gets his degree and Uncle Trevor steps back some. That won't be for years, though. He loves that place too much to not stay involved."

I smiled. Chloe's father and her uncles Mitch, Trevor, and Wade, lived for that cattle ranch. Her other two uncles, Cord and Tripp, worked the ranch every now and then, but Cord owned a local bar on the square called Cord's Place, and Tripp was a lawyer, married to Harley, the town vet.

"Yeah, that is years down the road. Gage is still in middle school," I said.

Chloe laughed. "Yes, I know. According to him, he's not going to college. Everything he needs to learn he can learn from my uncles, or my dad."

"He's probably right," I said.

Glancing at the ground, Chloe nodded. "I'm worried he's going to be lost when I leave, though."

I reached for her hand and squeezed it. She had no idea how lost I'd be when she left, too.

"He's gonna be fine, Chloe. We'll all be fine."

I wasn't sure if I was saying that because I needed to hear those words, or because she needed to hear them.

The sinking feeling inside my gut told me once we left for college, everything, including everything between us, was going to change.

Chapter 4

Chloe

I SAT IN the stands and watched as Rip hit a homerun. Jumping up, I cheered for him as Jonathon and Rip Senior did the same. My father walked up with a bunch of hot dogs and beers.

"Shit! I missed a homerun, didn't I?" he asked, handing Rip Senior and Jonathon their food.

"Sure did. That's my son!" Rip Senior cried out while Jonathon rolled his eyes.

"Dad, what did Rip say you needed to stop doing?"

Rip's dad sank back down on the bench. "Calling out *'that's my son.'*"

We all laughed. My father handed me bottle of water as he said, "Looks like we're going to have to be road tripping it when he plays for A&M." He turned to me and winked.

I smiled. My father treated Rip like his son and never missed his football and baseball games. Once upon a time, when I was much younger, I was open about my crush on Rip and it drove Daddy mad. Now I keep it to myself—ever since the time he caught us kissing. Yeah, that had been my idea, but that wasn't my last kiss. I had been kissed by a boy or two in high school. Nothing that sparked a flame inside of me. I also wasn't the least bit interested in dating anyone in school. The idea of being with someone other than Rip wasn't even a thought in my head. My life revolved around a very tight circle of people—and goats—and I liked it that way.

Rip was running back to the dugout and glanced up at us. I waved and he waved back before the other players all started to congratulate him.

"That boy will be snapped up within weeks of heading to college."

All of a sudden, I picked up on some chatter that had me on high alert. My gaze moved to a few women sitting below us on the bleachers. They were mothers of two of the other players on the team. I had no idea who they were because Rip played for a select team. There were guys from all around the area who played with him, all from different schools.

I tuned into their words. "Mary has the biggest crush on him. Look at her down there."

Following their gaze, I saw group of girls younger than me standing above the dugout, trying desperately not to act like they were looking at the boys. I couldn't help but smile in relief because I initially thought Mary was someone our age who could possibly catch Rip's eye.

They soon drifted off into another conversation about redecorating or something, so I tuned them out. I let my thoughts wander as I looked at Rip in the outfield now. Chewing on my lip, I made a mental list of pros and cons in my head for telling Rip how I really felt about him. Did I tell him now? Prom? Maybe graduation. Or did I wait until we were away from the watchful eye of my father and freer to do things while at college?

In the end, I decided I'd have to be patient and wait. If Rip was afraid of making a move because of Daddy, he wouldn't be once we were in College Station and on our own. That is, if he decided to go to A&M. If not, I'd have to tell him before we left for college.

With a wide smile, I dared to let myself believe that soon I would have Rip Myers all to myself.

SPRING BREAK SENIOR YEAR

"Come on, Alyssa! Just do it!" I said with a laugh.

"I can't!" she cried as she swung from the rope swing over the water and then back.

Laughing, I shook my head. "It's spring break. You know you have to jump in at least once. It's tradition!"

She was now back on solid ground, holding the rope and gnawing on her lip.

"Come on, Alyssa! Do it!" I shouted. "Do it! Do it! Do it!"

"Stop peer pressuring me, woman!"

"Hey, Chloe!"

Turning around, I found Justin Rivers walking over to me.

Crap. Crap. Crap.

He was going to ask me to prom again, I just knew it.

I smiled and waved. I was not looking forward to hurting his feelings, but everyone knew Rip and I went to all the school dances together. That was Rip's idea, not mine. If he had wanted to ask someone else, I would have dealt with it, but he always asked me, and I always said yes. Except this year, he hadn't asked yet. Alyssa said he probably assumed I knew we were going together, but then Rachel said he had hinted about asking her.

Ugh. Why do I have to have feelings for Rip? My life would be so much easier if I wasn't in love with him.

As Justin got closer, my heart sped up a bit. If he asked, maybe I should say yes.

The only problem was, I didn't want to say yes to Justin. I wanted to say yes to Rip.

Chapter 5

Rip

CHLOE STOOD ON the edge of the river, chanting for Alyssa to let go of the rope swing. Mike laughed as he came and stood next to me.

"Why does she do the rope swing when she is deathly afraid of it?" he asked.

"Beats me. It's your girlfriend. Why don't you ask her?"

He laughed. "I've long ago stopped trying to figure out Alyssa. I love her, weird quirks and all."

I nodded.

"Listen, Rip, I know you say you and Chloe are friends only..."

"We are."

"I know. I know. Just hear me out, okay. I heard Justin Rivers asking her to prom."

I screwed up my face. "What? Why the hell would he ask her? He knows we always go to prom together."

"Rumor has it, you asked Rachel."

"Lewis?"

He nodded.

"No, I didn't."

"Well, Alyssa said Rachel was bragging in gym class to everyone that you were going to be asking her."

25

I rolled my eyes. "Goddamn it."

"Did you? Hint that you might ask her?"

"No! I was in her mother's flower shop asking about flowers for my mother's birthday. Rachel asked me if I had a date for prom and I... Oh, shit." My entire body sagged.

"What?"

"I winked and told her not yet. I guess she could *take* that as a hint."

Mike shook his head.

"What did Chloe say? To Justin," I asked.

"She didn't say anything, according to Alyssa. I think she was stunned he asked."

"Asshole. We both know why he wants to ask her."

"Yeah, he wants in her pants, like every other guy in Oak Springs. You know the only reason they've stayed away is because they're afraid of you, especially after you beat up Mark for making that comment about Chloe's ass during sophomore year."

I laughed. "He deserved it."

Mike chuckled, too. "He did, but that scared the shit out of everyone. I sort of feel bad for Chloe. I mean, maybe you should ask Rachel and let someone else take Chloe."

I shot him a dirty look. "I've taken Chloe to all the school dances since middle school. She's my girl, and no one else can have her."

Mile's frowned. "That's what I mean, Rip. You want her all to yourself, but you won't give her what you should. You."

I rubbed the back of my neck in frustration. "You don't understand. If something went wrong..."

He let out a gruff laugh. "What could go wrong? Everyone sees the way you two look at each other. Rip, you admitted it to me, you love her. Why can't you tell her?"

"I can't. I just can't, Mike. If it ruined our friendship, I don't think I could handle it. She means everything to me, and I'd fuck something up and hurt her. I can't risk hurting her."

Mike shook his head and looked around. "What if someday she gets tired of waiting for you and moves on? Finds someone? Hell, gets married? *Then* what are you going to do?"

I swallowed hard, not wanting to think of that day.

He sighed. "Well, you better do something soon. Justin's here, and he's walking right over to Chloe."

My heart raced when I saw Chloe wave to Justin and smile. I pushed past Mike and started toward Chloe. She was up next on the rope swing and was about to walk away to talk to Justin. I ran and grabbed her, throwing her over my shoulder before launching us off the cliff together. Chloe screamed and all I could hear were a few guys calling out my name. I was sure Justin was going to be pissed, and I didn't care.

When we landed in the water and came up, Chloe screamed again.

"Rip Myers! The water is freezing and I wasn't ready!"

Laughing, I took her hand and made her swim out to the small rock we always sat on together. We'd been swimming out to this rock for as long as I could remember. After I climbed up, I sat down and she sat between my legs as we watched our friends jumping into the water.

"You excited about the baseball game next week?" she asked when she couldn't take the silence between us any longer.

"Yeah. I guess so."

"Have you made a decision yet?"

I'd been offered three football scholarships and two for baseball. All the schools were breathing down my neck to commit to them. I hadn't told anyone yet, but I had chosen Texas A&M to play baseball for them.

"Yeah."

Chloe turned and faced me. I could see the worry in her eyes. She was going to A&M, and although she had never come out and told me, I knew she wanted me to go there.

"I think I'm going to play baseball."

Her breath hitched. "Baylor or A&M?"

Smiling, I replied, "A&M, of course. I can't leave my Chloe Cat."

Chloe screamed and threw herself at me, nearly knocking us both off the rock and back into the water. Wrapping my arms around her,

I glanced up and saw Mike staring down at us, with Justin standing next to him. The smirk on Mike's face spoke volumes.

Fuck 'em all. It was always going to be Chloe and me.

Always.

When Chloe pulled back, we were inches from each other. God, I wanted to kiss her. Hell, the first day I ever met her in kindergarten I wanted to kiss her. The one time I did allow myself to go through with it, though, her father threatened to kill me.

"Chloe?" I asked, my voice sounding breathless all of a sudden.

"Yeah?"

"Will you go to prom with me?"

A wide smile broke out over her face. "I wouldn't want to go with anyone else, Rip."

I placed my finger on her chin and lifted her face, my eyes trained on her soft pink lips.

What would she do if I kissed her?

Her tongue swept quickly over her lips.

Leaning in, I moved at the last moment and kissed the side of her mouth, then leaned my forehead to hers. She closed her eyes, and we stayed like that for what seemed like forever before Mike called out to us.

"Rip! Chloe! Let's go!"

Taking her hand, we jumped back into the water. Chloe climbed on my back and we laughed and joked the entire swim to shore. Both of us ignored what had almost happened. We were good at letting those little moments when it seemed like we both wanted more slip on by without a word of acknowledgement.

Chloe grabbed a towel and started toward my truck, while I dried off at the water's edge.

"You did that on purpose."

I looked up and saw Justin standing there. "I did what on purpose?"

"You knew I was going to ask her to prom, and you made sure I wouldn't be able to do that."

Grinning, I stood and walked over to Justin. "What made you think we wouldn't be going to prom together anyway?"

He shook his head. "You're going to make damn sure no one else can have her, aren't you?"

Leaning in closer, I got in his face. "You're damn right I am. She's mine. Don't forget that."

"You want to fuck her first that badly and you'll keep the rest of us away by acting like a dick. Got it."

My fist came up, all on its own, and punched Justin. He stumbled back and tripped over a log. He ended up going into the river. Everyone turned toward the commotion, including Chloe.

Mike was right there, pulling me back by my arms.

"You ever talk about her like that again, and I will kill you."

"Rip!" Chloe shouted, running over to us. "What is going on?"

Justin stood and rubbed his jaw. "I'm not the only one who thinks it, Rip."

"Fuck you, Justin!" I shouted as Chloe stood in front of me. When her hand landed on my chest, I felt like I couldn't breathe. Her touch instantly calmed me down, while at the same time, it drove me insane.

"What in the world was that about?" she asked, looking from me to Mike.

Jerking my arm free, I answered. "Nothing. He was being a dick. Let's go."

Placing my hand on Chloe's lower back, I guided her away from everyone and over toward my truck. Justin was about to keep running his mouth when I shot him a warning look. He stopped himself and laughed. When a few other guys fist bumped him, I knew he was right. I'd lost a few friends over Chloe. Most of the guys in school thought we were already sleeping together. I didn't give two shits what they thought about me, but I cared about what people thought of Chloe, and she wasn't that type of girl to hop from bed to bed with any of these dicks.

Chloe is mine.

When I sat down in the truck, I let my words replay in my mind.

Chloe is mine.

Hitting the steering wheel, I shouted out a few curse words.

Who in the hell am I kidding?

"Rip, you're scaring me. Why are you so angry?"

I looked at her. "You ever want something so badly that it fucking scared you?"

Her mouth dropped open, before she replied, "I mean, I've wanted something badly but never enough that it scared me."

"Well, I do, Chloe. And if I allow myself to have it, I'm going to ruin everything."

I hit the steering wheel again. "Damn it!"

"Rip, is this about the scholarships? If you're picking A&M just for me, I don't want you to do that."

Trying to get my breathing under control, I dropped my head back against the seat and laughed. A sort of maniacal laugh, actually. This whole thing was so messed up. I needed to either tell Chloe how I felt or let her go. I couldn't keep things going the way they were.

"It's not about that, Chloe Cat."

"Okay, then what's it about?"

I shook my head as she reached over and took my hand. Closing my eyes, I squeezed her hand. "Nothing. I'll figure it out."

"Rip, I'm here if you need to talk."

My head lifted off the seat, and I turned to face her. "There isn't anything I wouldn't do for you. I need you to know that."

She smiled, and my heart felt like it jumped in my chest. "I know. We did the whole blood oath in fifth grade, remember?"

Laughing, I nodded. "I remember. My mother was pissed I got blood on her suede sofa."

Chloe giggled. "I forgot about that part."

With a long, deep exhale, I turned the truck on and pulled out of the parking lot. "Come on, I need to get you home. I promised your dad you wouldn't be late for family dinner night."

"Family dinner night at the Parker house. I don't know why my grandmother insists on keeping them up. It's a total nut house!"

"Is Patches still on lockdown?"

Chloe and Patches were thick as thieves. At times, I thought Patches truly believed he was human. And he lived for annoying

Chloe's Aunt Waylynn, who also lived on the ranch with my older brother Jonathon in one of the guest houses. They were married with two kids. Liberty and Hudson. It was weird to think Liberty and Hudson were my niece and nephew, and Chloe's cousins, too. We were already sort of non-blood related, which was crazy.

She chewed on her lip. "Yeah. He got into the house the other day and ate all of my grandmother's plants. It was hours before anyone noticed he was in there."

I laughed. "Who found him?"

"Me! And thank God. He was laying on Granddaddy's favorite chair. You should have seen him, Rip," she said, laughing harder. "He was sound asleep and the chewed-on remote was sticking halfway out of his mouth!"

"That damn goat. Your daddy says Patches is never going to die because you spoil him so much."

Her arms wrapped around her body, and her smile faded. "I'm not sure what I'll do when he does."

"I promise you, when that time comes, I'll be there."

I could feel her eyes on me. "You swear, Rip. No matter what, you'll be there for me?"

Stopping at a red light, I faced Chloe. "I swear on my life."

Chapter 6

Chloe

"**H**E HASN'T BEEN able to keep his eyes off you all night."
I turned to look at Alyssa. "Yes, he has."

She rolled her eyes. "Chloe, the moment Rip saw you in that dress, he couldn't form words. Prom is almost over. Are you going to tell him?"

Chewing my lip, I shrugged.

Rip and Mike had been talking to the DJ before heading toward us.

"They're going to play the last song, Chloe. Just do it."

Stopping in front of me, Rip looked into my eyes. "You look so serious."

I shook my head. "Just can't believe prom is almost over."

He took me into his arms. I laughed. "Um, Rip, there is no music."

The way he smiled made my heart leap. An old song from a group called the Dixie Chicks started to play. It was a song that Rip's mother, Kristin, loved. I wanted to sing the words to him because I wanted him to do the very thing they sang. *Cowboy, take me away.*

Rip and I started to two-step, which was not easy to do in heels. A part of me wondered if Rip had asked the DJ to play the song.

When he held me closer I felt my heart jump to my throat. I rested my head on his chest and prayed the moment wouldn't end.

When the song finally did, I looked up at Rip. He leaned down and for the briefest moment I thought he was going to kiss me. My breath caught in my throat as he looked down to my lips, then back to my eyes.

"Chloe," he whispered.

Swallowing hard, I opened my mouth to tell him I loved him. That I wanted more than just a friendship, but the fire alarms went off, most likely a prank, but everyone panicked as teachers and administrators ushered us out of the ball room. Rip had a firm hold of my hand as we quickly made it out of the building. My one chance to tell Rip how I felt slipped right through my fingers.

The rest of the night our entire class was locked in at Main Event where everyone spent the rest of the night acting like middle school kids. We played laser tag, climbed ropes, played video games, and avoided talking about our futures.

I stood in the middle of the apartment I was sharing with Alyssa, a huge smile on my face.

Alyssa walked in and dropped a bag.

"That's it. The last of my stuff."

She walked over to me and laced her arm in mine. "We are officially college students."

We both giggled like silly girls.

"Finally! On our own," I said.

"Not yet you aren't," my daddy said from the doorway. I headed over to him, taking one of the bags he was carrying.

"Okay, well, sort of on our own."

Alyssa's parents walked in with my mom.

"This place is so adorable. I'm glad we decided to rent you an apartment rather than have you stay in the dorms," Darlene, Alyssa's mother, said.

"I agree. I like the security here, as well." Alyssa's father, Walter, added.

My mother opened the refrigerator and sighed. "We need to go grocery shopping."

"Paxton, I think the girls can go on their own," Daddy said.

"They won't know what to buy!" my mother argued.

"Mom, Alyssa and I know what to buy. I know how to cook. I learned from the best."

She sighed, wiped a tear away, and leaned into my father. "I thought I was ready for this day. It appears I'm not."

"Don't cry, Mom!" I said, making my way over to her. "It's going to be fine. I've got Alyssa with me, and Rip and Mike aren't that far away."

Rip and Mike had moved into off-campus housing in an apartment they shared with two other guys. All of them played sports. I already knew Mike would most likely be here all the time with Alyssa.

"What are your plans for the rest of the day?" my father asked.

Shrugging, I replied, "Probably go to the grocery store and then go visit Rip and Mike."

Darlene and Walter came out of Alyssa's bedroom.

With a sad smile, Darlene said, "Well, it looks like the girls have everything. This is your new home for the next four years, girls. Enjoy it."

Alyssa hugged her father as I looked around our little apartment. Our parents had bought us basic furniture since it came unfurnished, and now it was time to make it our own.

"I see a trip to Hobby Lobby in our future!" I said as I gazed at the empty walls.

"I see someone sitting down and looking at her budget. You're not on an open-ended account, ya know."

With a grin, I hugged my father. "I know, Daddy. Thank you for everything and thank you for taking us to lunch."

My father kissed the top of my head and hugged me tighter. "I love you, Chloe Cat."

"I love you, too, Daddy."

Then it was my mother's turn.

"I'm going to miss you so much. The house won't be the same." Tears started forming in both of our eyes. I needed to get the focus off of me, stat.

"You'll make sure Patches is okay?" I asked.

She pushed a stray piece of hair behind my ear. "Of course I will. Gage and Patches will both miss you so much."

I wiped my tears away. "I'm going to miss them, too. I'll miss everyone."

My parents wrapped me up into another hug.

"Okay, we better do this before it keeps getting harder," Walter said as everyone made their way outside.

Alyssa hugged her folks once more, as did I. We stood there and watched as they drove off. When they turned the corner and were out of sight, I wiped the tears off of my cheeks.

"And suddenly I don't want to be on my own anymore," Alyssa whispered next to me. Turning, I pulled her in for a hug.

"Come on, let's start unpacking things."

After we both unpacked our clothes, we met in the kitchen to start putting all the food-related items away.

"So, are you really finally going to tell Rip how you feel? Now that you are both at college, and the whole telling him at prom didn't work out," Alyssa said, leaning against the counter, eating an apple her mother had left.

Letting out a long breath, I nodded. "Yes. As scared as I am, I know it's time."

She smiled. "He likes you, too, ya know. Mike tells me all the time how frustrated he gets with Rip because he won't tell you."

A bout of nerves hit me. "What if he really does only want to be friends?"

"Then it's his loss, but I don't think that is the case. Maybe now that we're not around our parents and everyone from Oak Springs, he'll finally take the chance."

Alyssa was right.

"Come on. I told Mike they needed to treat us to dinner!"

Two hours later, Rip and I were in the living room of the guys' apartment. Mike and Alyssa were in his room watching a movie on their own.

"Want something else to drink?" Rip asked, getting up and heading into the kitchen.

"No, but I do want to talk to you about something."

"Okay. I'm all yours."

I smiled; if he only knew.

He stared at me as I fought to keep my breathing under control.

"I want more."

He drew his brows in and asked, "More of what?"

"You. Us. More than friendship."

My heart raced as he stood there, staring at me like I had magically grown two heads in the last thirty seconds.

"I want us to date and see where this goes. You have to know I feel more than just friendship toward you. I love you, Rip. I've loved you since the first day I saw you in kindergarten."

He continued to stare at me. Something that looked like conflict flickered in his eyes.

I could now hear my own heart beating in my ears. With each passing moment, the longer he stood there staring at me, the more I regretted my decision to tell him how I really felt. Maybe Mike had been wrong. Maybe Rip didn't actually like me more than just as best friends.

But what about all the signs he gave me? I was so confused suddenly.

"Rip, will you please at least say something?"

After drawing in a deep breath, he walked up to me. He cupped my face in his hands, and I felt my entire body warm with his touch.

Kiss me. Please kiss me.

He leaned down as I lifted up on my toes. Our eyes were locked, and I was positive Mike and Alyssa could probably hear my heart beating. It pounded in my chest.

Rip was within inches of kissing me. His hot breath danced over my lips. Then he pulled back and rested his forehead against mine.

Just like he always did before it seemed like he was going to kiss me.

I clutched onto his arms, trying not to let my legs go out from under me.

"Chloe Cat, you have no idea how much I treasure you."

Smiling, I squeezed his arms.

"I want to kiss you, and I want to tell you that everything will be okay between us, but what if it isn't? What if we lose what we have and can never go back to that place again?"

My eyes burned while I fought to hold back my tears.

He was rejecting me.

"I never want to lose you as a friend. You mean the world to me, and I love you, too. I just can't risk losing you like that."

Dropping my hands to my sides, I stepped away from him. His eyes looked as if he was also holding back tears.

"I see. So you're not in love with me enough to be with me, but you love me enough to keep me by your side all the time? Want to explain why you kept me so close all through high school?"

"Chloe."

"No, Rip, there were so many times I looked into your eyes and it felt like I was looking into my own soul. I thought you wanted to be with me."

He raked his fingers through his hair but said nothing. His silence was my worst enemy.

I laughed, causing him to jerk his head to look at me. I'd taken a gamble and lost. What else could I do but laugh because the only other option was to cry, and I'd already given Rip every other part of my heart, so why not my dignity, too.

Turning away from him, I threw my hands up in the air. "I can't believe this. I had it all wrong."

"Chloe, no, you didn't have it wrong. It's just..."

I faced him again. "You want me all to yourself and no other man can have me. Not even you. Is that it, Rip? God forbid you take a chance."

He looked at the ground.

"I'm going to ask you once more, and if your answer is still no, I will never bring this up again."

"Chloe, don't do this to me. You sprung this shit on me our first fucking day in College Station."

I stared at him. I'd waited all through high school for this day. I deserved an answer and wouldn't leave until I had one.

"Do you want something more than friendship, Rip?"

When he didn't answer me, I walked over to the sofa and picked up my purse.

"Chloe. Chloe!"

I opened the door and headed down the steps. I soon heard Alyssa behind me.

"Give me your keys. I'm driving," Alyssa said.

"Chloe, stop for one damn minute and talk to me," Rip called out.

Handing her my keys, I covered my mouth to keep my sobs from rushing out. Once I was safely in the car and she had pulled away, I let myself cry.

Alyssa reached for my hand and squeezed it. "At least it's over now. You have his answer and now you can move on, Chloe."

I stared out the window and nodded as I wiped away my tears. "Yeah, but will it ever be over?"

Chapter 7

Chloe - Present Day

EASTON GAZED UP at me, waiting for my answer. My mind swirled with memories of me and Rip. High school dances, fishing trips, memories of laughing with my best friend. The man I had always imagined would be down on his knee asking me to marry him was now back in Oak Springs, living his life. Without me.

That dreaded day came back in an instant. The day I told Rip how I really felt. After he rejected me, I pushed it out of my mind and pretended nothing had ever happened. Rip tried for almost three months to talk to me about it, but he eventually gave up and went along with the charade. He pretended it hadn't happened either. Soon he started dating, which forced me to start dating. He had moved on, so I needed to move on, too. Keeping up the farce that was the Rip and Chloe show.

And now here I was, with Easton asking to marry me. I had two options. I could either say no, and keep dreaming of a life with Rip that would never happen. Or I could move forward and marry Easton.

My heart screamed for me to say no. My head was also in agreement. So when I heard my answer, I felt the room spin. "Yes," I whispered, as more tears fell. They didn't feel like happy tears, though. It didn't feel how I had imagined it would. Excitement and joy. Immediate plans for the future. This felt like me trying to run away from the past. I loved Easton, but was I in love with him? My heart and head knew the answer, but my mouth apparently overrode those feelings.

Easton stood and spun me around while we both laughed. When he put me back down, he placed a beautiful solitaire diamond on my finger.

"You just made me the happiest man on Earth, Chloe."

Framing my face in his hands, he said, "I could feel you pulling away from me. I knew what I had to do to bring you back to me." He bent to kiss me.

"Excuse me? You only asked me to marry you because you felt me pulling away?"

Easton laughed nervously. "Of course not, Chloe. You know what I meant."

Did I? It was then everything else ran through my mind. The things I should have been thinking of before I just rushed and said I would marry him. Instead of thinking of Rip and his rejection, I had more important things to think about.

He's moving to Houston. I'm moving back to Oak Springs. How in the world is this going to work?

"Listen, I know you're heading back to Oak Springs tomorrow morning but let me go with you so I can be there when you tell your folks. They're going to be so surprised!"

Smiling, I nodded. My parents had met Easton a few times. I wasn't sure how they felt about him. My mother was pleasant; my father acted like he was a bug that needed to be stepped on and then scraped off the bottom of his boot. Of course, once I had started dating, everyone kept reminding me how they always thought Rip and I would end up together. Even my own parents.

Yeah. So did I, but that didn't work out as planned.

I couldn't keep my thoughts together. "They would love that. I know they're planning a big party for me tomorrow night. A welcome home sort of thing."

Easton's expression lit up. "That's perfect, it can be our first party as fiancés. Heck, it can even be our engagement party."

I chewed on my lip. Now would probably be a good time to bring up the fact that we were going to be living almost five hours apart from each other.

"Are you all packed and out of your apartment?" Easton asked.

"Yes, I didn't have much to pack up. Alyssa and I sold all the furniture since we're both moving home with our parents for the time being. Alyssa is hoping to get a nursing job close to Oak Springs. She and Mike are planning a wedding for next spring, so I'm sure I'll be busy helping her with that."

He looked down at me with love in his eyes. "And when would you like to get married, Chloe?"

Panic seized my chest and nearly took my breath. "We have plenty of time to decide on that."

"My mother will want to know a date fairly quickly."

I nodded. "Oh, okay."

"Let's tell your folks first, then I'll call mine. I already told them I was heading back to Oak Springs with you for a few days."

"Perfect, okay. That's great." I was babbling like a fool.

Oh God, what have I done?

"Come on, let's eat. Our food is getting cold."

Easton talked the entire meal. About his new job, about finally being out of school. He even asked me a few things about what type of wedding I wanted.

My head was spinning. Excitement and pure panic sat in the pit of my stomach. Why was I all of a sudden feeling so conflicted? Was Easton just assuming I was going to move to Houston? Surely, he remembered my long-term plans to take over the ranch from my family. It's why I went home every summer to learn the ropes over break.

"Easton, I think with the excitement of you asking me to marry you and me being caught up in the moment, we forgot to talk about a few things that are pretty major."

"I know," he stated, reaching for my hand and playing with the ring. "You want to be in Oak Springs, and I need to be in Houston."

It wasn't lost on me how he stated I *wanted* to be in Oak Springs, like that was optional, and he *needed* to be in Houston.

"Well, it's not only that I want to be there, my life is there. The ranch, my family. My job."

"Rip."

I rolled my eyes. "Easton, we've had this conversation a million times. Rip and I are only friends. And I have hardly spoken to him since he moved back to Oaks Springs."

"Yeah, besides the daily texts the two of you send back and forth," he reminded me as he dropped back into his seat. "I know the whole story. Best friends since kindergarten, he's like a brother to you. All I'm saying is the way he looks at you like he wants you, and the way he looks at me like he's ready to kill me, says he thinks your relationship is very different than the way you see it."

I scoffed. "Trust me, he doesn't. I already told you, there is nothing between us and there never will be."

"I still don't like the way he looks at you."

Sighing, I placed my fork down and let out a frustrated sigh. "Are we really going to talk about Rip when we have a much bigger item to discuss? You assume I'm going to be the one to move."

"Chloe, what in the hell am I going to do in Oak Springs? I have a degree in petroleum engineering. I've already been offered a job."

"I already have a job, as well."

He laughed. "Working on your family's ranch?"

Folding my arms across my chest, I glared at him. "You mean one day *running* my family's ranch. Are you degrading the business my family is in?"

"No. Chloe, you know I'm not doing that. I'm just saying you're going to work for your family. I'm going to work for a top oil and gas company and I'll be starting out at $140,000 a year. What am I going to do in Oak Springs for that kind of money? Work on the ranch?" He let out a sarcastic laugh.

My chin wobbled, and I looked away.

"Jesus, I'm sorry. The last thing I want to do is fight."

I swallowed hard. This was going to be a battle I knew I would not be able to win. Facing Easton again, I took in a deep breath and let it out. A part of me knew I had rushed into answering him. I should have asked for time to think about it. Let the idea of leaving my family and moving so far away sink in.

"I'm not asking you to move to Oak Springs. What I am asking is for you to be patient with me. I don't want to move to Houston until after we're married. I'd like to at least be home with my family for a while. My mother and Alyssa can help me plan the wedding."

"It will be hard not seeing you, but I'm more than happy to let you have that. I'm guessing you'll want to get married in Oak Springs. I'm perfectly fine with that, too."

A sharp pain hit the middle of my chest. "No," I quickly said. "I think we should do it halfway between Houston and Oak Springs."

He smiled. "You're sure? I figured you pictured a country wedding growing up."

"Yes, when I was little, but I let that dream go a long time ago." *The night I told Rip I wanted more from him, to be exact.*

Easton tilted his head and regarded me for a few moments before he said, "Okay. Then somewhere halfway. I'm sure we can find a beautiful venue to exchange our vows. Now we just need a date. My mother will be hoping for a wedding close to Christmas."

"Christmas?"

"Yeah, she loves decorating for Christmas and thinks a Christmas wedding would be amazing."

I smiled as I thought of Rip's mom Kristin. She was fanatical about decorating for Christmas. Trees started going up at the end of September and it was all set up by the day after Halloween.

"That's seven months away, Easton. And don't you think I should be the one picking out a theme?" I said, hearing the doubt in my own voice.

"You can pick out the theme. And, what if it is seven months away?"

"Well, I mean I don't think we can plan a wedding that quickly."

"I think we can. Besides, I want you in Houston so I can be with you. If that means we have to hustle a bit more to plan a wedding, then we will."

My mouth dropped slightly as I let his words settle in. Immediately a clock started ticking in the back of my mind with the timeline he envisioned.

"Did you want a long engagement, Chloe?"

"Yes. No, wait. My goodness you just asked me only moments ago and now we're talking about a wedding in seven months in a location I don't know, and I haven't even told my parents. Easton, you have to slow down a bit."

He leaned forward and took my hands. "I'm sorry. I'm just excited is all."

"I am, too, and still a bit shocked. Things between us felt like they were ending only a few days ago and now we're...engaged."

He nodded. "It was just stressful with the end of school, I get that. I've been busy and not giving you the attention you needed."

If only I had believed that were the reason. Maybe we truly were growing apart. Or maybe I was letting those old feelings resurface now that I was heading home. What would I find when I got back to Oak Springs?

Rip. And he would probably be dating someone.

I closed my eyes. *It's time to move on, Chloe.*

"Let's finish up and then go back to your place. Has Alyssa already left for Oak Springs?"

Picking my fork back up, I nodded. "Yes. She and Mike left earlier today."

"Perfect. It will be me and you alone for the evening."

"I only have a blow-up mattress left at the apartment."

He winked. "That's all we need to celebrate."

I waited for the warm feeling in my belly to consume me like it used to when we first started dating. But nothing came. And that filled me with something I couldn't put a name to—anxiety or maybe dread. I think I was too stubborn to admit what I truly felt. But excited wasn't it.

Chapter 8

Rip

DIGGING THE HOOKS into the hay bale, I picked it up and tossed it onto the back of the trailer. The faster I moved, the more my mind stayed busy.

"Rip, this isn't a contest. Slow the hell down before you hurt yourself," Trevor called out.

When I wasn't working for my brother Jonathon, I was helping Trevor, Mitch, and Steed out on the ranch. Knowing Chloe was fixin' to be home any day had my stomach in knots. The last four years had been a living hell for me. Chloe tried to act like that fight never happened, but I relived it every damn day since she walked out the door. Regret was my new best friend, seated alongside whiskey.

My heart slammed against my chest as I fought the urge to tell her how much I loved her. My mind wouldn't let my heart win.

Her face looked defeated as she said, "I see. So you're not in love with me enough to be with me, but love me enough to keep me by your side all the time. *Then why did you keep me so close all through high school?"*

"Chloe."

"No, Rip, there were so many times I looked into your eyes and it felt like I was looking into my own soul. I thought you wanted to be with me."

Fuck, if she only knew how much I wanted to be with her. Make her mine. Take her to my room and spend the next week in there with her, learning what she liked, learning the sounds she made when we kissed, when we touched, when we made love.

Then she laughed. It wasn't her normal, sweet, warm-my-insides laugh. It was cold and meaningless.

I looked at her, willing myself to tell her the truth.

Chloe turned from me and tossed her hands into the air out of frustration.

"I can't believe this. I had it all wrong."

"Chloe, no, you didn't have it wrong. It's just..."

She spun around and shot me a glare. Anger filled her eyes and there wasn't a damn thing I could do to take it away. I knew I was ripping her heart out.

"You want me all to yourself, and no other man can have me. Not even you. Is that it, Rip?"

Guilty, I glanced at the floor.

"I'm going to ask you once more, and if your answer is still no, I will never bring this up again."

My eyes met hers. "Chloe, don't do this to me. You sprung this shit on me our first fucking day in College Station."

"Do you want something more than friendship, Rip?"

Yes! Fuck yes! I'm scared shitless! Give me a minute to process this!

My silence was her answer. She made her way over to the sofa, grabbed her things and headed to the door.

"Chloe. Chloe!"

Alyssa stopped me before she walked out the door. "I thought I knew you, Rip Myers."

The door shut, and I nearly let my legs buckle.

"Do you have any idea what in the hell you just did, Rip?"

I didn't even bother trying to hide the tears that slipped free.

"I just let the most amazing thing in my life walk away from me."

"Rip, go after her. Take a chance, damn it. If it doesn't work out, you won't lose her as a friend."

My feet stayed planted in the same spot until Mike shouted my name.

"Rip! Go!"

Moving as fast as I could, I ran out the door and tried to flag Alyssa down, but they were driving off.

I was too late.

Leaning over, I dragged in a few breaths, and each one burned like hell. When I finally managed to walk back into the house, I caught Mike's eyes.

He shook his head and walked away. It was the last time we ever talked about what I'd done.

"Rip? Rip!"

The shout pulled me from the memory. I found Trevor staring at me. "Sorry, I got lost in a memory of something."

He gave me a look that said he understood. "You need to take a break? You've been busting your ass all morning."

"No, I'm good."

We normally used the machines to gather up the hay bales, but Trevor thought some manual labor was needed today. It was an unseasonably cool day for May and it looked like a storm was fixin' to blow in. I was still sweating my ass off, though. Of course, I'm sure my hangover wasn't helping.

"You boys in the mood for a party?"

I looked up to see Steed on a horse.

"What kind of party?" I asked.

"A welcome home party for Chloe."

I wiped my brow and smiled. "She here yet?"

He returned the smile, but something wasn't right. It was almost like he couldn't look at me. "She's about an hour or so away. Mom, Paxton, and Waylynn are cooking up a feast. Alyssa and Mike will be there. I know Chloe would love to see you there, too, Rip. Especially since y'all haven't seen each other in a few months."

I nodded. Our friendship had survived that dreaded day. Only because Chloe chose to pretend it never happened. She still came to all my games and cheered me on. She came to parties with me as long as Mike and Alyssa were there. Anything that would keep us from ever possibly being alone. It was hard because I had tried like hell to get Chloe to talk to me. To talk about that day. I needed to tell the truth. She had come out of nowhere and admitted her feelings. To say I'd been scared shitless was an understatement. I tried for three months to talk to her about it before I finally gave up.

Then I met Heather. She had come on to me pretty hard one night at a party, and I had been truthful with her and told her I was in love with Chloe. She knew the whole story and didn't care. Heather and I hit it off and dated for a while. She was the girl I lost my virginity to. She was the girl who made it her mission to make me forget about my first love. It would never happen, and she and I both knew it. We hooked up off and on over a few years. It never amounted to anything. It was just physical. I couldn't do more than that, not when my heart was already owned by one girl.

Heather was Chloe's cue to move on and start dating, as well. She dated a few guys here and there. One she saw pretty regularly for a few months, and I knew that was the guy she lost her virginity to. It nearly gutted me when I overheard Alyssa telling Mike that Chloe had finally had sex with someone. I walked away, almost physical ill. Then she met that asshole, Easton. I fucking hated the guy from the moment I met him. They had been dating for almost a year. Their relationship was one of the reasons I busted my ass in an attempt to graduate early. I couldn't stand to see him hanging on her. Kissing her. Touching her. I had to get away from College Station as soon as I could.

I balled my fists even now just thinking about the asshole.

"Rip? You're going to pop a vein. Jesus, what are you thinking about?" Steed asked.

My eyes bounced from Steed to Trevor and back to Steed. "Nothing, sir. Sorry. Yeah, I'll be there. What time?"

"Six."

"We're almost done so we'll have plenty of time to get there," Trevor said.

After Steed rode off, I went back to grabbing the bales and tossing them onto the trailer, faster and harder than before. I was pretending like each hale of bay was that dickhead, so my energy knew no bounds.

"Stop for a second, will ya?" Trevor said, pulling off his gloves and tossing them onto a bale. "Sit down."

I did as he asked, taking the time to reach for my water.

"I have a feeling I know what you're going through."

"What do you mean?" I asked, wiping the sweat off my brow with my shirt sleeve.

"If I had to guess, I would say you got scared."

I laughed. "Trevor, what in the heck are you talking about?"

"It was Chloe who told you how she felt and you told her you didn't feel the same. Am I right?"

My smile faded.

He nodded. "But you did feel the same, didn't you?"

Swallowing hard, I took another drink of water.

"Steed didn't want to tell you because he knows it, too."

With a confused look, I asked, "Knows what?"

"That the two of you should have ended up together. That one of you most likely felt too afraid to move past friendship."

"Steed thought we should be together? He said if I ever kissed his daughter he was going to twist my balls so hard I would talk like a girl the rest of my life. I was just a kid when he told me that shit, so I believed it."

Trevor's head tossed back in a laugh. "Oh, man. I'm going to remember that one for Aurora. With her being a freshman in high school, I know the boys are coming."

I slapped Trevor on the back. "Hate to break this to you, but I'm sure she's already had her first crush."

He gave me a look that made me tremble.

"Okay, well, should we finish up?" I asked.

"No, I wasn't finished. Like Steed, there were a lot of us who thought you two would end up together. But I think you need to be prepared for tonight, Rip."

"Why? What's tonight?"

"Easton will be with her."

My stomach felt like someone had forced me to drink lead. I swallowed hard and tried to shrug it off.

"Well, they have been dating for a while, so it would make sense that he came home with her to celebrate her graduation."

He nodded. "I just didn't want you to be caught off guard when you saw him."

I stood, finished off my water, then put my gloves back on.

"If Chloe is happy, then I'm happy."

Trevor stood. "Is that why you get lost in a bottle of whiskey every week at Cord's Place?"

Glancing over my shoulder, it was my turn to shoot the dirty look. "I'm good, Trevor. Like I said, I'm happy for Chloe."

"You dating anyone?"

With a half shrug, I replied, "I haven't in a few months. Don't mean anything."

We worked for a few minutes before I said, "And I did feel the same. She totally caught me off guard, and I wasn't ready for it. I mean, I was, but I also wasn't."

He nodded. "I get you, believe it or not. I understand what you're saying. Let me give you one piece of advice, son, then I'm going to let this go. If you love her, if you want more than friendship with her, you better put your fucking fighting gloves on and be ready to take it to the mat for her. Don't let her walk away this time."

I stared at him. He knew something I didn't. When he went back to work, I stood there another few moments. His words settled into the middle of my chest.

Take it to the mat for her. Don't let her walk away this time.

I shook my head and got back to work. With each hay bale, I tried to think of some reason I couldn't be there tonight. In the end, I knew I had to be. It was Chloe, after all. And I wanted to be there to welcome her home. Easton or no Easton.

I'm ready to fight for her.

Chapter 9

Chloe

I STOOD IN the middle of my room and smiled. It was familiar and made my nerves ease up some. Daddy had moved us into one of the guest houses on my grandparents' ranch when we'd moved to Texas. My Aunt Waylynn and Uncle Jonathon also lived on the ranch in another house that they had remodeled and expanded after they adopted Liberty and Hudson. Liberty was fifteen and Hudson thirteen. Liberty was a mini-me of my Aunt Waylynn. She had no issues telling you how it was, or least how she saw it.

Easton was staying up at the main house on the ranch, which was owned by my granddaddy and grammy. He was only staying for tonight, then heading back to Houston early in the morning. When Easton asked to stay at my grandparents' house, I was confused. Maybe he thought my father would want it that way. I didn't argue, though.

"Getting settled in?" my mother asked me from the doorway.

"Yes."

She walked into the room and smiled. "Chloe, are you okay? You seem so distracted."

I reached into my pocket and pulled out the diamond ring I had slipped off before I got out of my car. I knew Easton was wondering why I hadn't announced it right then and there, but I needed to take a few moments to myself before I started to tell my family.

My mother gasped as she watched me slip it onto my finger.

"Easton asked you to marry him?"

I smiled and nodded.

Then she frowned. "You said yes?"

"You sound disappointed."

"No. I'm...in shock, sweetheart. He's not..."

I raised a brow. Was she about to say he wasn't Rip?

Clearing her throat, she went on. "I mean, he lives in Houston and..."

Her words stopped short when it hit her. Covering her mouth, she turned away so I wouldn't see her cry.

"Oh, Momma, please don't cry."

"I'm happy for you, sweetheart, it's just...I need a moment."

And this was why I hadn't broken the news right off the bat. I knew what was going to happen.

"I know."

She faced me, taking my hands in hers. "I *am* happy for you, *if* you're happy. Are you happy? Are you sure about this? You haven't been dating him very long, and just a few weeks ago you said you thought things were ending."

I drew in a deep breath. "I am happy. I'm feeling a bit torn. I love Easton, and I want to, well, I want to marry him."

Her head tilted to the side. "I feel like there is a *but* in there somewhere."

"There is. Like you said, things seemed off with us, but maybe it was the stress of school ending and knowing we were going our separate ways. And if I marry him, I'm leaving home. For good."

She drew me into her arms and hugged me. "Oh, Chloe Cat. You have to do what is right for you and your heart. Have you told Alyssa? Rip?"

I drew back and looked at her. "Only you know so far."

"Well, this is a shock, and if it is truly something you really want, I'll support your decision."

The doubt in her voice was palpable.

I nodded. "Daddy is going to be so upset. All those plans we had for me working with him on the ranch. I'm letting him down."

"No! You are not letting anyone down. You are living your life. Your father knew there was always the chance you might do something different. Will he be upset? Of course, not because of the job, because you're our daughter and the thought of you moving away..."

Her eyes filled with tears again.

"I need to tell Daddy. Easton wants us to announce the engagement at the party tonight."

Wiping her tears away, a look of worry crossed her face before she forced a smile. "Okay. We can do that. All your friends and family will be there. It will be the perfect place. Do we have a date?"

"Easton wants it close to Christmas."

"Christmas! That's only seven months away!" she shouted.

"I know. We did decide we would have the wedding somewhere between Oak Springs and Houston. I just don't know where."

She narrowed her eyes at me. Had she heard the disappointment in my voice?

If I was being honest with myself, I had always dreamed of having my wedding here on the ranch. This was where my life started all those years ago, and this is where I wanted my life to start with the man I love. I guess I'd have to move on from that dream as well.

She nodded, her mind probably already swimming with ideas.

My mother was actually my kindergarten teacher when we first moved back from Oregon to Texas. She and Daddy were high school sweethearts. Things went wrong between them, and I still don't know what it was about to this day, but I figured that was their story to tell when they were ready. If they wanted to share it with me and Gage, they would. But she wasn't my biological mother. She adopted me right after she and Daddy got married. Then Gage came along.

Gage.

The thought of leaving him made me feel ill. The thought of leaving Oak Springs and everyone here had my head spinning.

"Well, if we are talking about a wedding that soon, we have some planning to do."

There was a knock on the door, and I looked over to see my father standing there.

"Planning for what?" he asked.

I took a deep breath and held up my hand, showing him the ring. "Easton asked me to marry him."

For the rest of my life, I will never forget the look on my father's face...and the moment of silence while he digested the words I'd just said.

"Is that so?" he said, walking into the room. "Boy didn't even have the manners to ask for your hand?"

I laughed. "Daddy, he isn't a country boy."

"No, he is not. I suppose you'll be going to Houston to live with him."

My gaze dropped to the floor for a moment. "Not for awhile. I told him I didn't want to leave Oak Springs until after we were married."

That seemed to make my father happy for a brief moment. Then the frown appeared on his face again. "Do you have a date?"

I swallowed hard. "Close to Christmas. That's when Easton would like it."

He nodded.

"Steed, I believe you should be saying something to Chloe."

"Right. Sorry, baby girl."

He walked up and hugged me tightly. "Congratulations. I always thought it would be..."

My mother cleared her throat and stopped my father's words instantly.

"Thought it would be what?" I asked.

"Nothing. Nothing. Listen, we best get cleaned up and get up to your grandparents' place. We've left Easton all alone up there with your granddad. Lord knows what he will do or say to the boy. You know how your granddaddy feels about city folk."

I giggled.

"Finish getting settled in and then we'll drive up, Chloe Cat," my mother said as they left my room and shut the door.

Taking in a deep breath, I pulled out my phone and called Alyssa. "Hey! You back?"

"Yes. How are things going?"

"Great! I got a job at the elementary school as the school nurse! I cannot believe that position came up."

"Oh, wow! Alyssa, that is amazing!"

She squealed on the other end of the phone. "I know! Are you glad to be home?"

Falling back onto my bed, I sighed. "So glad. Easton is here too."

"I figured he would go back with you for the graduation party. Cracks me up your grandparents had to throw you a party *the day* you got home."

I smiled. "I haven't even seen Patches yet."

Alyssa laughed. "Sneak away tonight and you can see him. I'm sure Waylynn will have him locked up tight. Rip said she asked him six times yesterday to check the barn latches."

The mention of Rip's name made my heart skip a beat. It always had, and I had come to terms with the fact that it always would. No matter what, Rip Myers would always be my first love.

"Patches is determined, and where there's a will, he'll definitely find a way." I laughed but my heart really wasn't in it.

"Maybe you can go dress shopping with me next weekend. We need to think about maid of honor dresses."

Pulling in a deep breath, I said, "Yeah, about that. Guess you'll need to shop for one, too."

There was silence on the other end of the line.

"Oh, no."

Why was everyone having this reaction?

"He asked you to marry him, didn't he?" A sense of doom and gloom echoed through the phone.

"Yes, and why do you sound like it's terrible?"

"I can give you a number of reasons why it's terrible, Chloe Parker, and you know every single one of them. The major one would be you moving. Chloe! Do you really love this guy enough to give up everything and move to Houston? What about your family, what about the ranch, what about—" She didn't even finish that sentence because, after all, she was my best friend and knew the truth.

I don't know the answers to any of her questions.

"Alyssa, I wouldn't have said yes if I wasn't sure."

"Are you sure you didn't say yes for any other reason?"

"Like what?" I asked, anger laced in my voice.

"Rip?"

"Rip?" I asked with a laugh. "Why would I say yes to Easton because of Rip?"

"Let's see. Did any or all of these things go through your mind before you answered him? Oak Springs. Working for your dad. Leaving your family and friends behind. Coming around on holidays or maybe just once or twice a year. Living in Houston. *Or* did Rip pop into your mind along with that day he rejected you?"

"He did, and you know it."

"Chloe! Come on, did you really say yes to Easton because you love him enough to leave your life behind?

"For fuck's sakes, Alyssa," I said, standing up. "I love Easton."

"Do you love Rip?"

"Yes. I will always love Rip as my best friend. That will never change."

"So if I stood before you right now..."

"My mom is yelling for me, we have to leave. I'll see you in a little bit."

"Chloe Parker!"

Hitting End, I blew out a breath. I walked to the window and stared out at the large live oak I'd grown up with. Remembering how I'd snuck out to go to parties with Alyssa, climbing down this tree. Wrapping my arms around my waist, I stared out over the countryside. All the dreams I had growing up included this ranch. The plans that I had to take over from my dad. The dreams of raising a family here. All of it came flooding over me, and I wanted to sob.

A knock at my door startled me.

"Chloe?"

Spinning around, I wiped my tears away and looked at Gage.

"Gage!" I rushed over and threw myself into his arms. I might have been six years older than him, but he for sure was not my *little* brother. At seventeen, he was already built with a broad chest like my father and muscles like Rip's.

I didn't want to acknowledge I had just compared him to Rip and not Easton. Nope, wasn't even going to give it a second thought.

"I missed you so much," I sobbed into his chest. He held me tight and didn't say a word. He always knew when I needed that extra-long hug.

When I took a step back, I forced a laugh. "Sorry. I don't know why I'm crying."

There was a look of disbelief on his face.

"What's wrong?" I asked.

"You're leaving? Dad said you told Easton you would marry him."

With a grin, I replied, "Yes, I accepted his proposal."

Gage shook his head. "But why? Chloe, everyone knows it's supposed to be you and Rip."

My mouth dropped open. "What makes you say that?"

Then he rolled his eyes. "Don't be so stupid, Chloe. Even Dad was hoping you two would figure your shit out eventually."

"Dad said he thought Rip and I would be together?"

Gage scoffed. "*Everyone* thought that. Obviously, everyone but you and Rip. I mean, why Easton? He's such a douche."

I smacked Gage on the chest. "He is not, and don't say things like that. He's here."

"Not here in our house, so I can say it."

"Gage, I love Easton."

"Enough to leave all of us?"

"That's not fair."

He looked down at me. "You're right. It's not fair. It's not fair to any of us."

He turned and walked away.

"Oh, my word." I said, rubbing my temples.

My mother returned. "He'll be fine. He's a bit upset. He always planned on it being you and him on the ranch together."

"This fall he'll be in College Station, so what does it even matter if I'm here or not?"

She raised a brow. Her mouth opened to say something, but Daddy's voice cut her off.

"Let's go or we'll be late, ladies!" my father called out.

My mother kissed my cheek. "You might want to change, sweetheart. We'll be downstairs, ready to go when you are."

Before she had a chance to walk away, I grabbed her arm.

"Mom, is it true what Gage said? Was Daddy really thinking Rip and I would end up together?"

She chewed on her lip and looked down.

"So it is true."

When her blue eyes met mine, she sighed. "Oh, Chloe, honey, everyone thought you two would end up together. You were always inseparable, and you always had such a crush on him. That wasn't a secret."

"He didn't feel the same way about me."

"Are you talking about what happened back in your freshman year of college? He was probably confused and scared."

"So, what? You're saying he did love me but couldn't admit it?"

She simply shrugged. "Did you two ever talk about it again?"

Guilt hit me like a knife to the chest. "No."

"No?" she asked, her brow raised in a judging way.

"I mean, Rip tried to talk to me about it, but I told him I wanted to forget about it. Move on. And he did. He started dating Heather."

I spit her name out like it was poison. My mother laughed.

"And that made you start dating I take it?"

"Yes. I'm okay with us being friends, Mom."

Her hand came up to my face, and I leaned into the warmth.

"Are you? Is he?"

I frowned. Before we could say anything else, my father yelled upstairs.

"We need to get going, girls!"

"I'll change really quick." My voice sounded weak, and I hated that. Hated feeling confused over my own emotions. It felt like I was a pot of water, and I was fixin' to reach my boiling point.

She nodded and rushed down the steps.

Glancing through my closet, I found the blue and white dress I bought a few months back in a little boutique on the square here in Oak Springs. It was long and free-flowing but hugged my curves in the slightest way. Slipping on my cowboy boots, I grabbed my phone, and headed downstairs.

Everyone was already in the truck waiting for me. My hands shook as I reached for the door handle. What was I nervous about? Telling everyone about the engagement? Or knowing Rip would be there tonight? Maybe he would have a date, and everyone would see he'd moved on.

Just like I had.

Chapter 10

Chloe

THE MOMENT WE walked into the kitchen, I couldn't help but laugh. Easton stood at the sink, attempting to peel potatoes.

"Son, have you never peeled a potato?" Grammy asked, taking the potato from his hand and gently pushing him to the side.

"Um, no, Mrs. Parker."

"Melanie, Easton. Just call me Melanie."

"Mom, what in the world are you having him peel potatoes for? All the food is done," my father said as he walked in and kissed my grandmother.

She gave my father a wicked smile. "I needed to see the boy's cooking skills." Then she turned and faced me. "After all, my granddaughter can't be expected to do all the cooking after she gets married."

My smile faded instantly, and I looked at Easton.

"You told my grandparents?"

He shrugged as if it wasn't a big deal.

"Oh, hell," Gage whispered from next to me.

Anger built in my veins—that pot was getting hotter. "How could you, Easton?" I asked, staring at him. My entire body was shaking.

"Sweetheart, maybe he thought you might have already told them?" my mother gently pointed out.

"We were going to announce it after the dinner. I told you I wanted to tell my parents and grandparents first myself."

Easton looked at me with apologetic eyes. "I'm sorry, Chloe. It just slipped."

"Chloe Parker, before you go tearing the boy a new one, he's right. He accidently slipped and said something. He tried to catch himself, but I'm too quick—every member of this family knows that—and I got it. Your granddaddy doesn't know yet, though."

"I don't know what yet?" Granddaddy asked, walking into the room. He smiled when he saw me and quickly made his way over to me. "My little girl is finally home."

When he wrapped me up in his arms, I nearly cried again.

Good grief, Chloe. Get your emotions together, will you?

After I got a good hug and kiss, he stepped back and I held up the engagement ring.

"Easton asked me to marry him, and I said yes."

His smile never faltered, but I saw the hesitation in his eyes for the briefest of moments. Another person disappointed.

Taking my hand, granddaddy looked at the ring. "Well, will you look at that. My little girl is going to be getting married."

"Yep," I said, glancing over to Easton and smiling. He returned my smile and mouthed he was sorry.

"Steed, go grab some of the good champagne down in the wine cellar. We are going to celebrate early," Granddaddy said.

Easton walked over to me and took my hand in his. "I'm sorry I slipped."

"I'm sorry I reacted the way I did. It was just important for me to tell them myself."

He nodded. "I get it. Listen, Chloe, I've been thinking. I know how much you love this place. I don't know if you ever dreamed of getting married here when you were little."

I grinned. "I did at one point."

There was a beautiful meadow right off the river that overlooked a good portion of the ranch on the south side. I had always dreamed that would be the spot I got married. Under the large oak tree that held so many beautiful memories. There were countless times I told my parents that that tree was where I would get married someday.

"I want to have the wedding here."

My eyes widened and my breath felt caught in my throat for a moment. "What? But, your family would have to come so far."

"That doesn't matter. You're leaving your family for me. The least I can do is let you get married at this place."

The words felt like arrows tossed into my heart. Instead of making me fall in love, they did just the opposite.

"This place?"

He smiled. "The ranch. Your home. The place you grew up."

That should have made me feel better, but it didn't.

"Do you have a special spot where you'd like to be married?" he asked.

My mother walked up and looked between us. "Did I hear you right? Are you getting married here on the ranch?"

"Yes!" Easton said. "I was just asking Chloe if she had a special spot for the ceremony."

Glancing my way, my mother grinned wide.

Before she could say anything, I replied, "I think the backyard here at Grammy and Granddaddy's place would be the perfect setting."

"Here?" Easton said, sounding a bit disappointed. "I mean, how many acres is this ranch, Chloe? Surely you have a spot you liked when you were younger."

"The south pasture?" my mother asked, looking confused.

I shook my head. "This house means the world to me. It's where my family still meets once a week for dinner. I've grown up here. It will be perfect."

Easton leaned down and kissed my cheek. "That's fine. I'd marry you anywhere, Chloe."

My heart warmed at his sweetness. I knew he meant every word.

"Easton, grab some chairs and help, will you?" Gage called from the back door.

Glancing out the back window, Easton's eyes grew big. "How many people are you expecting? There looks like enough seats for a hundred.

Laughing, I replied, "Just my dad's family is nearly thirty."

"And they have weekly dinners? Thirty people?"

"Almost thirty. You should have seen it when all my cousins were little. It was a madhouse."

"Easton!" Gage called again. I was positive that Easton suspected Gage had a serious attitude about the engagement.

"Ignore him. He's upset I'm going to be moving."

With a sad look in his eyes, Easton kissed me once more. "It's all going to work out fine, baby. I promise."

"I know," I said, not really convinced, but not wanting to give up either. I had committed myself to Easton. A part of me did love him and would figure out how to make this work. So now I just needed to convince my heart to play catch up with my mind.

He headed out back. Before I had a chance to go help, my mother grabbed me and pulled me through the kitchen and down the hall into the study.

"Mom, what are you doing?"

"The backyard, Chloe? *That's* where you want to get married?"

"Yes, what's wrong with the backyard? It has a beautiful view of the sunset, and Grammy has the spring fling dinner and benefit dinner there every year."

The spring fling was a huge dinner Grammy and Granddaddy threw after the entire weekend had been spent vaccinating the cows and castrating them. It might sound gross, but it was one of my favorite times of year on the ranch.

She looked at me like I had grown two heads. "What about the little spot you told me and your father you wanted to be married at... for years?"

I pressed my lips tightly together. "I...I changed my mind, Mom."

Leaning in closer, she said, "Chloe, if you still love Rip..."

"Mom..." I warned.

"No, this is important."

"I'm not marrying Easton in the same spot I wanted to marry my old crush."

"Is that all Rip is?" she asked, jerking her head back.

"No. He's my best friend."

She slowly nodded. "Okay. If you're sure, Chloe."

"I'm sure," I snapped.

Turning, I walked away, and instead of going out back, I headed to my father's office. When I opened the door, I stopped in my tracks. My heart leapt to my throat.

"Rip?"

He glanced up and smiled, both dimples on full display. My knees went weak, and I hated myself for that physical reaction. I hadn't seen him in months. We texted nearly every day, even if it was to just say have a good day. Seeing him tonight, though, was not what I was expecting. And I certainly hadn't planned on running into him alone.

"Hey, why do you look surprised to see me? You had to know I would be here for your party."

With a grin, I walked into the room. "Of course, I did. I'm surprised to see you in my dad's office is all."

Leaning back in the desk chair, he sighed, and dropped a pencil onto the desk.

"Your dad is trying to find an accounting error. He asked me to look at the books. I only got here a little while ago."

"Oh," I said, sitting in the chair. "Putting that accounting minor to good use, huh?"

Another smile.

"I always did like numbers."

I chuckled. "And I always hated them."

"Glad to be home?" he asked.

"So glad. I missed having you in College Station. I had to go for my Thursday morning coffee all alone."

"Why didn't Easton go with you?"

With a half shrug, I replied, "It was our thing. Didn't feel right going with anyone else."

He nodded. It looked as if he wanted to say something but stopped himself. "Things going good between y'all?"

I swallowed hard. "Yes."

"How's it going to work with you here and him in... Is it Houston?"

Glancing down at my hands, I noticed I was rubbing them together. Then I lifted my hand and showed him the ring.

"He asked me to marry him last night."

The color in Rip's face drained. He looked white as a ghost as he stared at the ring and then jerked his eyes to mine. "And you said yes."

I heard the immeasurable hurt in his voice, there was no doubt. I swallowed the lump in my throat. "Yes, I did."

He didn't say anything. He simply sat there, staring at me.

"What about you? Are you dating anyone?"

He looked away for a moment and then back at me. "No, I'm not." He stood. "Um, if you'll excuse me, Chloe. I just remembered your grandfather asked me check on the barn. Make sure Patches wasn't going to escape."

I stood, a wide smile on my face. "I'll go, too. I've been itching to see him."

Rip ran his hand through his hair. "Well, if you're going down there, then you can check on everything, and I'll help finish setting up. I already found the mistake Steed overlooked. I'm sure Easton would like to meet Patches."

A wave of disappointment washed over me.

"Okay. Sure. I'll see you at the dinner?"

"Yeah."

Rip gave me his usual parting wink. But there was definitely a wall that had been hastily thrown up between us. I watched as he quickly walked out of my father's office.

Turning back to the desk, I looked down at the papers. This was supposed to be my job. The job I had looked forward to since I was little girl. Sitting behind my father's desk, helping my family run one of the largest cattle ranches in Texas.

"Here you are! Rip said you were in here. What was wrong with him? He seemed really upset."

I spun around to find Alyssa. Her words rattled around in my chest. "I told him about the engagement. I didn't want him to hear it for the first time when we announced it later."

"Oh, shit."

Chewing on my lip, I nodded. "He seemed a little surprised, but I didn't think he was upset."

She snarled at me. Alyssa had never forgiven me for not talking to Rip about that day. She had begged me for weeks to sit down with him, insisting we could work through it. I had ignored her. My stupid pride getting in the way.

"If you didn't see him get upset, then you're blind as a fucking bat, Chloe."

I rolled my eyes. "It doesn't matter, Alyssa. He didn't ask me not to marry Easton. He didn't profess his undying love for me and beg me to be his as he whisked me off into the sunset."

"Chloe, I wish for once you would open your eyes and see what is right in front of you."

My mouth dropped open. "Excuse me?"

"Do you know why Rip left Texas A&M early?"

"Yes, he had the credits to graduate early."

"No. He busted his ass and took classes and then finished out online. He still needs two classes to graduate."

"What?" I gasped.

"He didn't tell you because he didn't want you asking why he was going back home. He had to get out of there because he couldn't stand seeing you with Easton."

"That's insane. I've dated other guys before, and he's dated other girls."

"His longest relationship was with Heather. And that was an off-and-on thing. You dated a few guys before Easton, nothing serious. Then Easton came along, and things got serious. Rip told Mike he couldn't take seeing you with him. He had to leave."

I stared at her in disbelief.

"No," I said, with a chuckle that sounded more like choking. "He knew how I felt about him, Alyssa. If he had feelings for me too, he would have told me."

"You were dating someone else, Chloe. You were happy. That's all he's ever wanted for you. He wasn't about to risk losing your friendship when you were seriously dating someone."

Turning away from her, I wrapped my arms around my body.

"I'm sorry. Maybe I shouldn't have said anything. I mean, you love Easton, right? You love him enough to marry him and move away. It was wrong of me to say anything. I'm only repeating what Mike told me, and after seeing Rip just now, I thought maybe you might have had a change of heart about him. Maybe you should stop and think about all of this. Chloe, I know you care for Easton, love him. But do you love him like you love Rip?"

Staring out the window, I saw the barns in the distance. "I need to go check on Patches, and I want Easton to meet him. I'll see you around, Alyssa."

As I walked to the door that led to the backyard, Alyssa called out after me. "Chloe! Wait. Chloe!"

I kept walking, my eyes scanning the crowd. Then I found him. Easton was talking to my Uncle Cord and Uncle Trevor.

"There's our girl!" Trevor said, picking me up and spinning me around. He set me down and kissed me on the cheek. Uncle Cord followed.

"Welcome home, Chloe Cat," Cord said.

"Thank you. It's good to be home. Uncle Cord, Mom said Maebh and Katlyn were in Ireland."

He nodded. "Yeah, they went back to visit Aedin and Aunt Vi."

Cord had married Maebh, a woman from Ireland who moved to Oak Springs years ago to open her own restaurant. Her mother had been from the area and met her father in Ireland. After she passed away, being in Texas made Maebh feel closer to her. Katlyn was their thirteen-year daughter.

"Easton, hey. I was looking for you."

Stopping by his side, I tensed when he put his arm around me. I found myself looking around for Rip.

68

What in the hell? I'm going to kill Alyssa for putting that thought into my head.

"I need to go check on the barn locks, and I really want to see Patches. Want to come?"

"Is this your pet?"

"Yeah. You do want to meet him? Right?"

"Uh...sure. If you want me to."

I pouted, and he laughed.

"Fine, I'll go meet your lamb."

"Goat," Cord and Trevor said at the same time. "Son, if you're going to marry a country girl, you better learn farm animals."

"How did you know?" I asked as I looked at Easton accusingly.

Holding up his hands, he laughed. "This one is on your dad. He introduced me to everyone as your fiancé."

"Ugh. Can I not do this the way I want to?" I said, almost stomping my foot like a child.

"Sorry, babe."

He took my hand in his. "Let's go see your lamb."

"Goat!" Trevor and Cord called out.

"Is there a difference?" Easton asked with a laugh.

"Yes!" I replied as I lightly punched him in the stomach.

We walked in silence the first few minutes before Easton spoke. "I saw Rip."

"Really?"

"He came up and congratulated me. Guess you told him. When?"

"Oh, yeah, he was in my father's office doing something for him. I ran into him there. He asked how things were going, and I told him."

"How did he take it?"

Turning to look at him, I furrowed my brows. "What do you mean?"

Easton laughed. "Please, Chloe. You can stop the whole *I'm not aware Rip likes me* act."

I jerked my hand from his. "You think I'm putting on an act?"

He looked down at me. "Yes. I do. He was clearly not himself when he came up to me. He was pissed. I saw it in his eyes."

Placing my hands on my hips, I shook my head slowly and deliberately. "First off, Easton. I don't put on acts for anyone about anything. Our freshman year of college I told Rip I wanted something more than friendship. You know this. I told you the story. He didn't feel the same. We moved on, I got over it, and here we are today. Am I going to have to defend my friendship with him for the rest of my life, because if so, it's going to get old really quick."

He looked down at the ground and kicked at something. It was then I noticed he had on loafers.

"Why are you wearing those shoes?" I asked.

"I like these shoes."

Covering my mouth with my hands, I tried not to laugh. "Easton! You're on a ranch! You should have at least worn sneakers."

He rolled his eyes and smiled at me. "I didn't realize you were taking me on a nature walk."

Taking my hand in his, he kissed the back of it. "I'm sorry. I really try not to be jealous of your friendship with Rip, and maybe he does simply care about you as a friend."

The corners of my mouth turned up.

"Come on, let's go so we're not gone long. I think we'll be eating soon."

When we walked into the barn, I took a deep breath. "Oh! That is the best smell!"

Easton gagged. "What in God's name is that smell?"

"It's called a barn, East. Animals live and eat here."

"And obviously shit here."

I made my way in and stopped at Patches' stall. He was kicking at the door, having heard my voice.

"This is my baby boy, Patches."

I opened the door and slipped inside. Patches was all over me, which made me laugh. When he pushed me down, Easton walked in and started to pull him off.

"Get off of her, you idiot!"

"Easton!" I scolded. "Do not call him that. Let him go right now!"

"Chloe, he was..."

"Greeting me. It's been months since I've seen him. Now be gentle with him. He's really old."

"He stinks."

Patches turned and stared at Easton. He looked ready to charge, and a part of me wished he would.

"You should step out of his stall, East. I think you pissed him off."

Easton looked at me like I had lost my mind.

"You're joking, right?"

When I nodded, Patches answered him with a *beeeeehhhhh*, and then came the charge.

"Shit!" Easton yelled, jumping and managing to slip out of the stall without being hurt.

Patches trotted back over to me, happy as a clam.

"Patches, I missed you so much. I'm so happy to be home. Yes, I am."

"Tell me you're not thinking of bringing him. I don't think we can keep a goat in the city."

Looking up at him, I asked, "City?"

"Yeah. My folks said they're going to start looking at houses in their neighborhood for us and send us some links."

"Houses?"

He laughed. "We are going to have to live somewhere, Chloe."

"You don't want to live a little bit out of the city? Maybe on a couple of acres?"

"No. No way am I driving in the Houston traffic to work."

Nodding, I kept scratching behind Patches ears.

"And your parents want us living by them?"

"Of course, they do. Do you have a problem with that?"

"No. Of course not." I'd only met Easton's parents one time about seven months ago. We had only been dating a few months, and they came up to visit for the weekend. They were nice, but I couldn't tell if they liked me or not.

"Your folks do like me? Right?"

Easton forced a smile. "Sure they do."

I tilted my head and gave him an incredulous look. "That was reassuring."

He laughed. "Probably just as much as your dad likes me. Or Gage, for that matter. Everyone just needs to get to know each other more. Once you're in Houston, you'll get to know my whole family."

"When will you get to know mine?" I asked, standing and giving Patches a long hug.

"I'm sure we will be coming back to visit often."

"Christmas time?"

He shrugged. "Every other, I'm sure."

Laughing, I stared at him before I said, "No. Easton, I'm not going to come home every other year for Christmas. We're only six hours away. We can find the time to visit. We can switch off whose family we spend Christmas day with, but I want to be home for the holidays."

"Mom's not going to like that. Christmas is a big deal in our family."

"And you don't think it is in mine?"

"Your family is so big. You won't even be missed."

I slammed the gate shut and jerked the latch down. "Alrighty, then. So I'm forgettable. Thanks for that."

This time I did stomp off. I was pretty sure I threw in a little huff while I was at it.

"Chloe, come on. We're arguing about stupid things. It will all work out."

"Stupid things?" I said, spinning around and causing him to nearly run into me. "Easton, we need to talk about these things. I'm giving up my entire life here to be with you. The least you can do is let me come back and spend every other Christmas Day with my family."

"*Giving up* your life? Funny, I thought we were starting a life together."

"We are, but can't you understand what I'm walking away from? My family? The job I always thought I would have? My friends? The only life I've ever known?"

"Then maybe you should have thought a little bit longer on your answer, Chloe."

Turning, he started back for the house. I stood there, staring at him. My eyes stung as I forced to keep my tears back.

"Okay, so I might be wrong here, but shouldn't couples who just got engaged be all over each other, kissing and hugging?" I smiled at the sound of my cousin Liberty's voice.

"Liberty," I said as she walked toward me. She looked like she had just gone horseback riding.

"Oh, my gosh. You are a vision of Aunt Waylynn!"

Laughing, she pulled me into her arms. "You do know I'm adopted, right?"

I hit her lightly on the shoulder. "You still look like her. A mini version."

Her eyes sparkled. "I saw Uncle Rip a few minutes ago."

"Really?" I asked, looking around. "What was he doing?"

"He was in with the horses when I got back from my ride. Looked like he was saddling up Daddy's bay to go riding."

My heart leapt a little in my chest. Oh, how I loved going on rides with Rip around the ranch. The way we would race across the pastures. Settling under that old oak tree of ours while the horses grazed, talking about all the plans we had for after we graduated college.

"Hey, are you okay? You got a really sad look on your face just now."

"I'm fine. Sorry. I guess the little argument with Easton got to me."

"He's cute," Liberty said, looking off in the direction Easton had stormed off.

"Yes, he is."

"There are way better-looking guys here, though."

Lifting my brow, I leaned in and said, "Do tell, Liberty."

Her cheeks turned pink. "I'm not talking about guys my age. I'm talking about guys like Uncle Rip. I always thought y'all would end up together."

I let out a frustrated sigh. "Well, apparently everyone but Rip thought that."

"Ouch. Watch out, Chloe. There was a little bit of bitterness in those words."

"You're fifteen, Liberty. How would you know what bitterness is?"

She threw her head back and laughed. "You have been gone awhile. I need to go so I'm not late for the dinner we're throwing in *your* honor."

"Okay, see you soon."

Liberty lifted her hand and waved as she walked off. "In case you care, he rode off toward the south pasture."

"I don't!"

"Sure. Keep telling yourself that."

I groaned and headed back toward the party. I took one quick look over my shoulder and toward the south pasture. Surely Rip wouldn't miss my dinner. He just wouldn't.

Chapter 11

Rip

CROSSING MY LEGS in the shade of the old tree and leaning back against the trunk, I tipped the whiskey flask back and drank as I stared at the swing. I had changed out the wood a few weeks ago to a newer piece.

Ranger, my brother's horse, was walking around grazing as if he hadn't a care in the world.

"You ever been in love, Ranger?"

The bay lifted his head and silently answered.

"Yeah, it does suck. What do you think I should do? Tell her not to marry him? Maybe finally confess I love her, that I've always loved her, but fucked up and was too chicken shit to make it right?"

Ranger stared at me.

I let out a grunt and took another drink. "She's marrying him."

Ranger nickered.

"My feelings, as well. I can't tell her how I feel, though. She's obviously in love with him. I mean, she's walking away from Oak Springs to be with him. If that isn't love, I don't know what is."

Ranger walked up and grazed right next to where I was sitting.

"This was our spot. We would come here and talk for hours. She told me when we were around five she wanted to get married here... to me."

Nausea hit me as I imagined Chloe standing under this tree exchanging her vows with Easton.

Fucking prick didn't deserve her.

Taking another drink of whiskey, I leaned my head back. My eyes closed, and I tried like hell to think about anything other than Chloe and that ring on her finger.

The sounds of a running horse woke me. I jumped up and whistled for Ranger. He was looking toward the north. I turned and saw someone riding up on a horse.

"Jonathon?"

He damn near ran me over before he pulled back on the reins.

"What in the fuck are you doing, Rip?"

I looked up at him in shock. "What do you mean?"

"You're out here getting drunk while everyone is back there celebrating Chloe's graduation."

"And engagement, don't forget that part."

He rolled his eyes and slid off the horse.

"How much did you have to drink?"

"Not enough."

"Listen, I may be your older brother, but I'm your friend, too. Talk to me. What is going on?"

I laughed. "What's going on? Hell, I don't know, big brother. I've fucked up my entire life."

"You have not fucked up your entire life."

"You do know that I haven't finished school. I have two classes left. Dad still hardly talks to me."

"Then fucking finish the online classes, Rip."

Rubbing the back of my neck, I closed my eyes. "Aw, hell. I'm probably going to go home."

"No, you're going to come with me and try not to act like you're drunk."

"I'm not drunk."

"Right, then you're on your way there."

When I didn't respond, he went on. "Chloe is looking for you, Rip."

I scoffed. "Chloe has Easton now. She doesn't need to be 'looking for me' anymore."

"Is that what you truly believe?"

"She's marrying him, isn't she?"

He looked away for a few moments before focusing back on me. He went to say something and then shook his head.

"What? If you've got something to say, say it," I said.

"Fine. I'll say what I should have said a long time ago. If you love her, then tell her."

"Of course, I love her. I've always loved her."

"Then tell her, Rip. Tell her before it's too late."

"It *is* too late, Jonathon! Did you not see the ring on her finger? She's leaving Oak Springs. If she didn't love the guy, she wouldn't walk away from everything she ever dreamed of. What am I supposed to do? Ask her to give him up and stay?"

"Could you for once stop and think about how maybe she dreamed of those things with you?"

I smirked and looked away.

"She's getting married in her grandparents' backyard, Rip. They just told everyone. You and I both know when she was younger all she talked about was getting married in this very fucking spot that you're drowning your sorrows in."

My head jerked back toward him. "She's not getting married here?"

"No. Why do you think that is, Sherlock?"

I swallowed hard.

"Pull your head out of your ass, Rip. If you can't be man enough to tell her the truth, then be a friend and at least be there for her."

With that, he got back onto his horse and pointed to Ranger. "That's my favorite horse you took, you asshole."

I smiled and ran my fingers through my hair.

"Get on the horse, Rip. Let's go."

I whistled the horse over, got in the saddle, and followed Jonathon back to the main barn. After taking care of both horses, we walked up to the house together.

"I know you don't want my advice, but I'm going to give it to you anyway."

With a sigh, I said, "I'm pretty sure you've been giving it to me since you rode up on the horse."

"Stop the drinking. It's not making anything better. Damn it, Rip. If you love her like I think you do, fight for her."

Fight for her. There's that fucking phrase again.

As we got closer, I saw Chloe and Easton standing there with her parents. Jonathon stopped me by putting his hand on my chest.

"Rip, you have to tell her how you feel. She might tell you it's too late, but you will regret it the rest of your life if you don't finally admit your feelings to her. I can promise you that."

Swallowing hard, I looked past him to Chloe. She was smiling with her hand clasped in Easton's.

"I'm happy to announce that I have asked Chloe to marry me and she has said yes," Easton said. I couldn't pull my eyes off of Chloe. Of course, I came back just in time to hear their big fucking announcement.

Everyone clapped, including Jonathon next to me. When Chloe's eyes met mine, I forced a smile. I knew I couldn't let her down. If she was truly happy, I would keep my feelings to myself.

She continued to stare at me for the longest time. That smile plastered onto her face. Was she happy? Was marrying Easton what she truly wanted? Her eyes said something different, and for the briefest moment, hope sparked inside of me.

People rushed over to Chloe and Easton, hugging and congratulating them. I exhaled a deep breath and made my way over to Mike and Alyssa.

"Where have you been?" Mike asked.

"I went for a ride earlier. Time got away from me."

"Well, apparently the whiskey didn't get away from you. I smell it on you, dude."

Rolling my neck to get the tension out, I looked over at Chloe again. She was talking to someone and looked up at Easton, who wrapped his arm around her. Before I had a chance to pull my eyes off of them, Chloe's gaze found mine again.

Her smile faded, and she tilted her head.

I turned to Mike. "Can you give me a ride home? I've been drinking more than I should."

"Now?" he asked.

"Yeah. I need to get home and take care of something that I told my mom I would handle."

"Now?"

"Did I stutter? Yes, fucking now, Mike."

He held up his hands in defense. "Okay, dude. Let me tell Alyssa."

Alyssa had started a conversation with some older lady sitting next to them.

When Mike stood, I handed him the keys to my truck.

I looked everywhere but over to Chloe. I swore I felt her gaze on me, but who was I kidding? Chloe had moved on.

"Ready?" Mike said, making me jump.

"Sure, yeah. Ready."

"You okay?" he asked, a slight chuckle coming out with the question.

"Yeah, just ready to leave."

He nodded, and we started to make our way through the crowd and down to the driveway. I could see my truck. We were almost there when I heard her call out my name.

"Rip! Mike! Are you leaving?"

"Fuck me, could this day get any worse?" I whispered as Mike hit me on the back. We both turned and looked at Chloe, jogging down the driveway.

"You weren't even going to say goodbye?" she said with a sad look.

"I needed to get home, and Mike is driving me."

Chloe frowned. "Why can't you drive?"

Mike and I exchanged a look. Fuck it. The truth it was.

"I drank a little bit too much."

Her eyes bounced from me to Mike, then back to me.

"Oh. Well, thank you for coming. I'm not sure where you were hiding out. I hardly got to see you. Maybe we can do lunch tomorrow?"

"I can't. I've got a full day of work. I'm helping Trevor."

She smiled. "So you'll be here on the ranch?"

Mike looked away, trying to hide the corners of his mouth that were quickly raising.

"Yeah, but like I said, I'll probably be really busy."

"I'll call you. If you can take a break, I'll bring something for you to eat. I'd like to catch up."

Goddamn it.

"Sure, you can give me a call, and we'll see. Enjoy the rest of the party."

She walked up to me and hugged me goodbye. Then she did the same with Mike. "Thanks for being here. See you tomorrow."

The moment she turned around, I started walking to the truck.

When we got in, I dropped my head back against the seat.

"Rip..."

"Please, Mike. I already got the lecture from Jonathon. I just want to *not* talk about Chloe. Please."

The truck started. "Sure. We won't talk about Chloe."

And we didn't. We didn't talk at all.

Chapter 12

Chloe

AFTER BREAKFAST I went for a quick run before heading to the main house to see Easton off.

He was sitting on the front porch swing, staring off down the long driveway.

"Hey, I heard you were out here. Ready to head on home?"

"Yeah, but I wish you were coming with me."

My face fell slightly. I didn't want to argue about this again. Easton had started in last night about why I had to stay here until the wedding. He couldn't understand how hard it was for me to leave. I needed time. I wanted to be with my parents. Spend the summer with my brother. Work for my father and start my career that, unfortunately, would be short-lived. I couldn't figure out why that was so hard for him to get.

"I don't want to fight about this again, East."

He scrubbed his hands down his face. "Why can't you come to Houston after the summer is over? Hell, if it's a job you want, Chloe, you can get one there."

"Easton."

He laughed. "I know, I know. You can't blame me for wanting you with me, Chloe. I love you. I want to wake up every morning next to you. I want you with me."

I felt sick.

Oh, good Lord. Why can't I say one word of that back to him?

"Are you okay? Your face just went completely white."

"Yeah, I'm going to miss you, too. Please be patient and let me have this time with my folks. I just want that. I'll see how things feel this September."

He smiled and pulled me to him, kissing me. He moaned as he pressed his body to mine. Two nights earlier, when he asked me to marry him, he had wanted to be together, and I couldn't do it. I was too emotional and couldn't bring myself to sleep with him. Not when I had so many thoughts racing through my mind, most of them consisting of doubt over saying yes. Easton had been understanding when I told him I was exhausted. I saw it in his eyes, the disappointment, especially since we hadn't slept together in weeks. For Easton, a marriage proposal and one night of sex would fix everything. For me, all it did was make me even more confused than I was before.

Ugh. Jesus, Chloe, get your shit together.

"That's what I wanted to hear, baby. I need to get going. I've got a long drive."

"Be careful. Let me know when you get there."

"I will," he said. I walked him to his car and waited for him to roll down the window.

Leaning in, I kissed him. "I'll see you soon."

"I told my folks you'd be down in a few weeks. They want to have an engagement party of their own and my mom's birthday is June second. I'll get you a plane ticket, so you can fly. I don't want you making that drive all alone."

A part of me was angry he would make plans without even asking me. Not wanting to start yet another fight, I smiled and kissed him once more.

"Sounds good. We can talk more about it when you get to Houston."

He winked and pulled down the driveway. I stood there, watching him until I couldn't see his sports car anymore. Then I continued to simply stare at nothing. An empty driveway. My heart was just as empty, and it wasn't because of Easton leaving.

"Chloe?" my grandmother called.

"Darling? Are you okay?" she asked, wrapping her arm around me.

"I don't know, Grammy. I just don't know about anything right now."

Stepping around, she placed her hands on my shoulders and looked me in the eyes.

"Chloe, you need to take a few days to yourself and let this all process. I didn't want to say anything, but you and Easton argued a lot last night over the simplest things. It was hard for your granddad and I not to hear you two."

"He wants me to just up and leave, Grammy. Like none of this matters to me. Why can't he understand I need some time?"

She simply smiled at me. This was one of those life lessons she was going to let me figure out on my own.

"Come on, I'm making some cookies...you can help."

We walked arm-in-arm back toward the house.

"I think that is exactly what I needed! I wanted to take some lunch out to Rip today. He mentioned working with Trevor here at the ranch."

"Yes, he was here this morning. He's with Cord and Trevor doing something with the cattle in the north pasture."

"Is Daddy here?"

"He should be in his office. Head on back first if you want. I'll get everything out and ready for our baking party."

With a giggle, I kissed her on the cheek and headed down the hallway to the side of the house that housed all the offices for the ranch. My dad had one. Trevor too, as well as Mitchell and Wade. Granddaddy still kept his office, even though he was officially retired and had handed the running of the ranch over to my uncles and dad.

My father's office door was slightly open, and he was on the phone talking to someone. I paused and lifted my hand to knock.

"Chloe was going to be taking on marketing for the ranch, but I'll most likely need to start interviewing people for it."

My stomach fell. His words made everything feel so real.

"Yes, I was looking forward to working with her, but she seems happy, and that is all I care about."

I took a step back and leaned against the wall. My heart was pounding, and it was hard to breathe. What in the world was happening to me?

"Business management and marketing, yes. I'd like to start taking a step back from work. Spend more time with Paxton and the kids. Rip Myers has been taking on some of the accounting for me, as well. The kid is smart as a whip. He is working for his brother's construction company handling most of their business and getting them up to date on some new computer programs. He's doing the same with Waylynn's dance studio, but I'm hoping I can talk him into coming to work for Frio Cattle Ranch."

It was like all the plans I had made for my future were still happening, except I wasn't a part of them anymore.

"We will figure it out, Dan. I think Chloe is staying on until Christmas. I won't have to worry about filling the new position until fall."

Placing my hand on my chest, I forced myself to breathe, but each breath was getting harder and harder.

I slid down the wall and sat.

Oh God, what is happening? I can't breathe. I can't breathe!

"Chloe!"

Over my panic, I hadn't heard Rip walk up. His voice instantly sent warmth through my entire body. Then I felt his hands on my arms, pulling me up.

"Look at me, Chloe."

I did what Rip said. My eyes met his.

"Take a deep breath in."

Shaking my head, I felt the panic returning.

"Sweetheart, look at me. Look. At. Me. *Breathe.*"

"What's going on?" my father said, suddenly next to Rip.

"I think she's having a panic attack," Rip stated.

Rip hugged me, holding me so close. "Feel my breathing, Chloe Cat. Focus on my breathing."

I took deep inhales and then exhaled, my face warmed by his breath. Soon, my own breathing began to return to normal.

"That's it. Deep breath in, then out."

"Bring her into my office."

Rip wrapped his arm around my waist, and I could not ignore the way it made me feel.

I closed my eyes and cursed myself. I was engaged to another man and the feelings Rip evoked were nothing short of sinful.

"Do you feel dizzy?" Rip asked.

"No. No. I'm okay." I sat down on the small sofa on the other side of my dad's office.

"Chloe, what happened?" my father asked.

With a shrug, I replied truthfully. "I heard you on the phone, and all of a sudden I felt this pressure on my chest, and I couldn't breathe."

He closed his eyes and rubbed the back of his neck. "I'm so sorry, sweetheart. I didn't realize you were there. Please don't worry about anything, okay?"

"You're going to hire Rip?"

"Me?" Rip asked, pointing to himself. His father's name was also Rip, so I'm sure he was confused.

My father looked at me and then over to Rip. "I was planning on talking to you about working here in the ranch office, part time, of course. I know you're working for Jonathon in the office. He mentioned you got a new accounting program they are using now."

"Are you wanting to do the same?" Rip asked.

"Actually," Daddy said, a smile on his face. "I'm looking at cutting back some hours. I'd like to spend some time with Chloe before she leaves for Houston. And with Gage leaving for college, well, I was hoping to free up my life."

"You want me to do the financial stuff for the ranch?" Rip asked, clearly shocked.

"Don't sound so surprised, son. I've seen what you can do. Why do you think I've been having so many *problems* lately? I've been testing you." Daddy grinned at Rip, letting him know that he'd obviously passed his test.

Rip's mouth dropped some as he stared at my dad. "You were setting me up?"

"Setting you up, testing you...it's all semantics."

With a lighthearted laugh, Rip replied, "Steed, I don't see the difference in that."

"It doesn't matter. You passed all the tests anyway."

I couldn't help but giggle.

Rip looked at me and then back to my father. "You really want me to work here? For you?"

"Why is that so hard to believe?"

"I don't have my degree yet."

My smile faded, and I stood up. "What do you mean you don't have your degree?"

Both of them looked at me, then looked back at each other.

"She doesn't know?" my daddy asked.

Rip shook his head, clearly embarrassed he had let that slip.

"I don't know what?"

"It's not a big deal, Chloe. I'm just a couple of classes short of graduating with my business degree and one class short of my minor in accounting."

My eyes widened in shock. "It's true, then?"

Now it was Rip who looked shocked. "You knew?"

"Alyssa told me. I thought you were done last fall and chose not to walk. Why did you leave A&M if you weren't finished?"

"It doesn't matter anymore."

"It does matter, Rip! You went to school all that time on a baseball scholarship, for crying out loud. To just walk away only needing two classes. What in the world made you—"

I stopped speaking. I knew what made him leave. Alyssa had told me.

Rip shoved his hands into his pocket and turned back to Steed. "I plan on finishing. I'm registered to take the two classes online this summer. I'll have the degree soon."

My father placed his hand on Rip's shoulder. "I don't care about that, Rip. I wouldn't offer you the job if I didn't think you could do it.

Degree or no degree, I trust you with the company and I would like to see the position move to full time when I retire if it's something you're interested in doing. I know you like working with your hands and helping your brother and Trevor out, as well. That won't be for a number of years, but at least I know you'll be well trained."

Rip grinned from ear-to-ear. "I'd be honored, sir."

The room felt like it was spinning so I sat back down. It was true. Alyssa wasn't just saying those things. Rip had left school because of me. Because I was dating Easton.

"Chloe, are you feeling okay yet?" my father asked, bending down and looking at me.

"Yes. I'm just..."

"Just what?"

Glancing over to Rip, I said, "Confused."

"Confused about what?" Rip and my father asked at the same time.

I stood. "Nothing. I, um, I need to go. I told Grammy I'd help her bake some cookies. She's probably wondering where in the heck I am."

My father cupped my face in his hands and gave me a good once over. "You're sure you feel okay?"

I nodded. "I don't really know what brought that on. I mean, I do. It's okay. I'm fine."

He gave me a gentle smile. "I'm sure it is all the changes you've got going on."

I exhaled and gave him a slight chuckle. If he only knew the thoughts running rampant through my brain and my heart since I had got back home. Instead, I just said, "Yeah, probably."

Kissing me on the forehead, he winked. "Go and have fun. I called Rip in to talk business."

"Business. Sure, of course." The feeling of being left out was new. What did I expect? I had agreed to marry Easton and that meant I would be leaving. Why would Daddy include me in any business decisions or conversations?

When I turned to leave, my eyes met Rip's. "I'll see you later?"

"I have to leave after this. Plans tonight."

"Oh, okay. Have fun, then."

He must have seen the hurt in my eyes. "If you want to come, a bunch of us going to hang out at Cord's Place. Nothing fancy."

With a smile, I said, "I'd love to go. I haven't seen anyone in forever."

"We're all meeting there around eight, if you want to join."

I tried not to let my smile slip, but I felt positive I was doing a shitty job of hiding my disappointment. Before Easton and the engagement, Rip would have offered to pick me up, and we would have gone together. That would have been a given. Now...

Things really were going to be different, not only between me and Rip, but with everything and everyone.

Chapter 13

Rip

CORD'S PLACE WAS packed, which wasn't unusual. As I made my way through the crowd, a few people stopped to say hello.

When I finally caught sight of Bobby McMillan, I smiled. Mike, Alyssa, and Chloe were really the only people I had stayed friends with since high school. Since moving back to Oak Springs, though, I'd caught up with a few friends, and we would hang out once a month or so.

Bobby held out his hand, and I shook it.

"Myers! It's good to see you. I heard the news. I'm sorry, bro."

I frowned. "What news?"

"Chloe getting married to some rich dude from Houston."

Laughing, I replied, "News travels fast."

He nodded. "We're still a small town, no matter how much they try to make us grow."

I clapped him on the back. "Gonna get a beer."

The next thing I knew, a beer appeared in front of me. And Chloe was the one handing it to me.

"Hey, thanks."

She smiled. "No problem. We just got here."

"We?"

"I came with Alyssa and Mike. I didn't feel like driving in alone."

Ouch, that jab hurt. I instantly felt like an asshole. "I should have offered to pick you up. Sorry about that. Guess I wasn't thinking clearly after the offer your dad made me."

She shrugged and took a drink of her beer.

"I can give you a ride home if you want."

Chloe grinned, and my fucking knees wobbled.

Will this ever go away? Christ.

"Sounds like a plan."

"Congratulations, Chloe. Heard you are getting married. Gotta say, we all thought it was going to be you two tying the knot," Bobby shouted.

Jesus, Mary, and Joseph...if I hear that one more time.

Chloe gave him a polite smile. "That seems to be the opinion of almost everyone in town."

I took a long drink of my beer and looked around until I spotted Mike and Alyssa dancing.

"Want to dance?" I asked Chloe before I even had time to think about it.

"Yes! It's been forever since we've danced."

We set our beers down and headed through the crowd. Once we got to the wooden floor, I took her in my arms and we started to two-step to the music. It was a fast song, so we took off flying. Dancing with Chloe had always been one of my favorite things. I couldn't stand dancing with other girls. It never felt right. They fit wrong in my arms every single time. I told myself it was because we had learned to dance with each other and that made it awkward to dance with other women.

I was lying to myself even back then.

"You know, I can't seem to dance with anyone but you," she said.

"That so?" I asked with a smirk.

She laughed. "Yeah. I often wonder if it was because we figured it out together."

Tossing my head back, I laughed. "I was just thinking the same damn thing, I swear."

The song changed, and the beat slowed. It was an old song by Elvis called "Love Me Tender." The words almost brought me to my knees. It was everything I wanted to say to Chloe...but couldn't.

"My grandmother loves this song," I said, pulling Chloe in closer to me.

She didn't say anything as she laid her head on my chest. We glided across the dance floor, neither one of us talking. Fuck. I loved how she fit against me. My heart started to beat faster as I thought about what Jonathon had said to me yesterday. I knew I would never be able to live with myself if I didn't tell Chloe how I really felt.

Before I could work up the nerve, the song changed to Keith Urban's "Coming Home." I chuckled.

"Welcome home, Chloe Cat."

A wide smile spread over her beautiful face.

She looked around before looking back at me. "Let's show them what real dancing looks like."

I took her hand and spun her around a few times. Before I knew it, people were moving out of our way as we cut up the floor. A few people cheered us as we passed them by.

This felt like home. How in the hell could she leave all this for *him*?

That was all I could think of the rest of the song.

When it ended, everyone around us clapped and whistled. Chloe did a little curtsy before we walked back to the table that now had about fifteen people from high school gathered around it. Most of them were only home for the summer, or until they headed off to start their careers.

"Hey Chloe!" Lori Rhodes said.

Chloe hugged Lori. "How have you been?"

Lori pointed to her stomach. There was a small bump there. "I'm pregnant, hence the water." She held up a bottle.

"Oh, wow! Congratulations. I had no idea," Chloe said.

Lori gave Chloe a wide, toothy grin. "We were going to be getting married anyway. So just mixing things up a bit."

I couldn't help but notice Lori's smile looked forced. Behind her stood some guy I had never seen before. Lori turned around and tapped his shoulder.

"James, this is Chloe Parker and Rip Myers. I knew them in high school, too."

"Nice to meet you," I said, reaching my hand out to shake his.

"You, as well," James replied.

"Chloe, I heard you're getting married," Lori said, a smirk on her face.

"Um, yes."

Lori's eyes flickered over to me before she looked back at Chloe. "It's nice to see you finally moved on and gave up on *that* silly dream."

My brows drew in tight, but Chloe laughed. "You never change. Do you, Lori?"

Lori gave me one last once over before she pulled her boyfriend along to meet someone else.

I shivered. "Okay, being checked out by a pregnant chick gave me the heebie-jeebies."

Chloe lost it laughing.

A group of about three girls who used to be cheerleaders came up to Chloe, and soon they were all lost in conversation.

I went to the bar and ordered another beer. Someone came up next to me, and I could feel their eyes. Turning, I found a pretty dark-haired girl waiting to order.

"Evening," I said.

"Hi."

Her cheeks flushed, and she bit down on her lip. I had to give her credit, she was turning the flirting on.

"What can I get you, Rip?" the bartender asked.

"I'll take a Bud Light and the lady will take..."

She smiled wide. "A gin and tonic, please."

When the bartender turned to get our drinks, she faced me. "Thank you for that."

"Sure, no problem."

When she tried to hand me money, I shook my head.

"My name is Valerie."

"Rip." I reached out to shake her hand.

"Are you from here, Rip?"

"Yes, ma'am."

A giggle slipped from her mouth, and she rolled her eyes at herself.

"Sorry. I'm from California, not used to seeing real cowboys. That hat makes you look like the hot cowboys we dream about back home."

I chuckled. "Thank you for that."

When the bartender came back with our drinks, I paid and faced Valerie. "You will find a lot of us here in Oak Springs."

"I know. I'm seeing that. I'm here visiting my grandparents. They moved out here from Austin. This is their retirement. The whole family is visiting."

"How do you like Oak Springs?"

"It's a charming little town. Everyone is so nice. I've had fun."

"When are you leaving?"

"Tomorrow afternoon." Her eyes turned dark. "I'm here with my cousin tonight. I think she's hoping to get lucky."

I placed my beer to my lips and took a drink. Then I looked around the bar. "Well, there are plenty of guys in here who I'm sure will be more than happy to help her out with that."

Valarie's smile faded slightly. "I'm striking out with you, aren't I?"

With a wink, I replied, "I'm afraid so."

"Well, it was worth a shot, cowboy. A guy as good looking as you surely has a girlfriend."

Not replying to her comment, I lifted my beer to take a drink. I gave her a polite grin. "Enjoy the rest of your time here."

As I made my way back to the group, I noticed Chloe looking my way. I couldn't help but wonder if she had been watching me talk to Valerie.

When I got back to the table, Chloe kept staring. She had a lost look on her face, similar to after that panic attack. When I frowned and gave her an inquisitive look, she glanced away.

Mike pulled me away some. "Dude, Butch just opened his mouth and told everyone that you're in here once a week nursing your broken heart with whiskey because Chloe wouldn't have anything to do with you."

"Are you fucking kidding me?"

"No. And Alyssa said Chloe knows you left A&M because of her and Easton."

"What the fuck is this? Take Rip down night?"

"I guess she felt like Chloe should know."

"Alyssa told her? I told you that in confidence, dude."

"And I tell Alyssa everything. We don't have secrets from each other, Rip. Believe me, when she told me she told Chloe yesterday, I was pissed."

Rubbing the back of my neck, I exhaled. "So that is how she found out."

"Yeah, and the little news about you being here drinking seems to have pushed her over a ledge. She was breathing fire. I'd avoid her if you can. Like right now, if looks could kill you'd be on the floor."

I chanced a peek, and Mike was right. Chloe was shooting daggers at me.

"How in the hell am I supposed to avoid her? We're all hanging out, and I already told her I'd give her a ride home."

Mike smiled. "You're up a creek without a paddle."

"Thanks for that, Mike."

"Hey, it's about damn time it all comes out."

"No, it's not about damn time. Chloe is happy. She's moved on. She is engaged to another man."

"Yes, but would she be if you'd been up front with her?"

"I don't play what-if games."

Mike shook his head. "You're still scared. Jesus, you're about to lose her for good, and you're still fucking scared." He tossed his hands up and let them fall to his side. "I give up, man. I don't think you even know what in the hell you want anymore."

I felt a tap on my shoulder. Turning, I found Chloe. I went to talk, but she cut me off.

"I'd like to leave now. Is your offer still on to drive me home?"

I chanced a look at the exit. If I jumped a few chairs and frantically made my way through the crowd, I could probably get away clean. Then I looked down at her.

Oh yeah, she was pissed.

"Um, of course. Let's go."

She spun on the heel of her boot and started walking off. I handed my beer to Mike.

"Looks like I'm leaving."

"Good luck, bro."

Rubbing the back of my neck, I sighed. "I'm gonna need it."

The ride to the ranch was filled with silence. Chloe stared out the window, not once looking my way. I figured the closer we got to ranch the more she'd finally say what was on her mind.

I was wrong.

When I pulled up in front of her house, she opened the passenger door.

"Chloe?"

She looked over her shoulder at me.

"Have a good night." I softly said.

Her eyes narrowed while her mouth opened slightly. Then she made a growling sound, jumped out of the truck, and slammed the door. When she got halfway up her steps, she turned and shouted, "You asshole!"

My eyes widened in shock.

"What did I do?" I called out.

When she got to the door, she shook her head and looked back at me.

"Nothing. That's the problem, Rip." She slammed the door, ending our conversation before it even began.

I looked around, stunned.

"What in the living hell is that supposed to mean?"

Chapter 14

Chloe

A S I SAT on the back porch swing, I stared down at the empty notebook. My mother had asked me to start making a list of things I wanted for the wedding. Colors, theme, bridesmaids, etc. I couldn't think, though. My mind was filled with nothing but doubt. I wasn't sure I was making the right decision. Easton and I had yet another fight this morning. His mother had taken him to look at houses. Something I said we should do together, just the two of us, when I was in town. I wanted something farther out, with at least a big yard. He wanted something completely different. If it were up to him, he would be in a condo in downtown Houston. He said that three times today on the phone. I finally gave in and told him that was fine. It was the only thing I could do to end the disagreement and get him off the phone.

Was this what my life would be like? Caving in to Easton because I was too prideful to admit I had possibly made a mistake by saying yes? Was I really going to settle?

Looking back over the months we had dated, it had never been that way. The moment he slipped a ring on my finger, I became something else to him. And a part of me—a large part of me—didn't even want the ring on my finger.

"Chloe, you haven't written a single thing down?"

I looked over to find Aunt Waylynn. Smiling, I shrugged. "I can't seem to focus right now."

"Doubts?" she asked. That was Aunt Waylynn. She was a straight shooter and didn't have time to dance around a subject. There was definitely no doubt as to how Liberty turned out the exact same way.

"Yes."

"About?"

I slowly shook my head and glanced down at my ring. "Why I said yes."

"That is one hell of a doubt. So tell me, Chloe Cat, why did you say yes?"

Letting out a deep exhale, I laughed.

Hard.

Then she laughed. Soon we were both laughing and had tears streaming down our face.

"I don't...even know...what we are laughing at!" Aunt Waylnn said.

Once I got myself under control, I let out a groan. "Oh God, Aunt Waylynn. I don't know. Caught up in the moment, maybe? Trying to make our failing relationship work? Finally ready to leave things in the past?"

"Things?"

I buried my hands in my face. "I'm so confused. I am so damn confused."

"Chloe, you need to take a deep breath and ask yourself, is this guy worth giving up everything for? I'm going to be honest, sweetheart, you don't seem like the enchanted, excited bride who cannot wait to plan her wedding and marry the love of her life."

My head snapped to look at her.

Her brow rose. "I'm speaking from experience here, sweetheart. Maybe that is the question you need to be asking yourself. Is this guy, Easton, the love of your life?" She placed her hand on the side of my face. "Listen to your heart, Chloe."

When she stood, I rose from my seat. "Waylynn, what if my heart is just as confused as my head?"

Her mouth rose slightly on one side. "Oh Chloe, sometimes you have to cut the strings to make room for what truly belongs in your heart."

I forced a small smile back. "Yeah. I guess."

After a quick squeeze of her hand on mine, she headed back into the house. I dropped the notebook onto the bench and headed to the barn. I needed a distraction and it was about time for me to see Patches anyway.

On the way down, my phone rang, and I saw it was Easton.

"Hello?"

"Hey, baby. What are you doing?"

"Heading down to see Patches."

"Jesus, Chloe, when are you going to get over this weird obsession with that lamb?"

"Goat," I reminded him, realizing that he wasn't kidding with me about whether he thought Patches was a goat or a lamb. He just couldn't be bothered to remember the difference.

"Whatever."

"Easton, Patches is my best friend. I love him."

"I thought Rip was your best friend. Come to think of it, shouldn't your future husband be your best friend?"

"Are you trying to pick a fight with me because it sure as shit feels like it!"

"No. I'm frustrated. I miss you, Chloe. I hate that you're so damn far away. Can you come here sooner? We haven't had sex in so long, not even on the night we got engaged."

My mouth dropped open. That was what he missed? Sex? "I'm sorry, I can't. I promised Alyssa we would go look at wedding dresses tomorrow. It's only been a week, Easton."

"And a week is too long not to see you. Do you miss me, too?"

"Of course, I do."

Liar.

I stopped walking. Closing my eyes, I willed the doubts to go away.

The moment I walked into the pasture, I saw Patches. He no longer moved like he used to. No more running and jumping to greet me. I dropped to my knees, giving him a hug when he made his way over to me.

"Patches," I whispered.

"Chloe, I'm talking to you."

Tears stung my eyes. I would be leaving Patches again. What if I wasn't here when he was ready to pass?

"Easton, I told you I could come down on your mom's birthday. That is in six days. Can you please stop making me feel guilty about wanting to be with my own family? I'm getting sick of it."

"Well, I'm sorry if I miss you, Chloe."

"Stop doing that. Stop with the guilt trip, East. From the moment you put this ring on my finger you have turned into someone I hardly know, and truth be told, I'm not missing that person. All I wanted to do was be here with my family. Spend some time with them. Love on Patches. Why is that so hard for you to understand?"

"I'm sorry, baby. I am. It's just hard. I didn't think it would be this hard to be apart. I felt like you were growing distant in College Station. I thought if we got engaged it would change. Maybe we would at least start having sex again."

My mouth dropped open, and I fell back on my ass. Patches crawled onto my lap and curled up the best he could.

"Wait a minute. Back the hell up. Is that why you asked me to marry you? You thought I was growing distant? You wanted sex?"

"No! I mean, that was one reason. I want to be with you. I hate knowing you're there with him."

"With him? Him *who*?"

"Chloe, I've got to run. We'll talk about this tonight."

I exhaled in frustration. He hadn't even given me time to respond.

When the call ended, I looked down at Patches. He was sleeping in my lap. I couldn't help but smile as I ran my hand over him.

"Oh Patches, I don't know what to do."

As we walked around the bridal store in San Antonio, I listened to Alyssa talk about the style of dress she wanted for her wedding with Mike. Every now and then I would smile and nod, agree with something, and give the appropriate *ohh* and ahh when I thought it was what she wanted to hear.

"Did you bring your wedding book?" Alyssa asked me as I looked at a gown.

Laughing, I replied, "No."

"Chloe, why not? That was your dream wedding planner. You wrote everything down in that thing."

I looked at my mother who casually glanced at a dress she was not the least bit interested in. She'd clearly been listening to what we just said. "That was for a dream wedding. This is reality."

Alyssa took a step closer and lowered her voice. "We need to talk. Because any normal bride would be jumping out of her skin to try on dresses, and you act like this is a punishment. Your mom is starting to catch on, Chloe."

"Catch on?"

"Yes. It may not be clear to you, but it's clear to the rest of us. You have no desire to marry Easton. *None. Zero. Zilch.*"

Her words rattled in my head for a few seconds before the sales lady walked over. "Okay, ladies, I have your dressing rooms set up with four gowns each. Let the wedding dress shopping begin!"

As I stepped into the dressing room, I let my eyes wander over each dress. The sales lady had paid attention to the dresses I looked at. I closed my eyes and pointed my finger and then took a few turns. Whichever dress I ended up pointing at I would try on.

Opening my eyes, I smiled. It was a beautiful Vera Wang gown in a soft white with a plunging V-neck bodice. I stripped out of my clothes and got the dress on. When it was time for help, I rang the small bell and the sales lady came in.

"Oh, I was hoping you would try this one on first."

Outside the dressing room, I heard Alyssa's mom, Mary, and my mother going crazy over Alyssa's dress.

Then I heard Alyssa say, "I look like a princess in this! It's stunning."

I smiled at the excitement in my best friend's voice. I didn't have the same level of excitement, and that was only becoming clearer as I stared at my reflection in the mirror.

The other sales lady said something about trying on the others before Alyssa jumped at the first dress. They all laughed. I placed my hand on my stomach and took in a few deep breaths.

"It's normal to feel nerves and not excitement."

I turned and faced her.

Jesus, even the sales lady could read me like a book.

But then a huge smile erupted on her face. "Okay, let's go show everyone!"

I stepped outside the dressing room and Alyssa, Mary, and my mother all gasped.

Gathering the full skirt in my hands, I walked up the three steps and faced the wall of mirrors. I didn't even recognize the woman I was looking at. She looked tired with dark circles under eyes that were filled with sadness. I let my gaze wander down the dress. It was beautiful, and probably exactly what Easton would want me to wear... and I hated it.

"I'm going to marry you someday, Rip."

I was on our swing while Rip sat on the ground, an apple in his mouth. He took a bite and chewed it.

"Okay, but we have to get married here. At our tree."

"Chloe, sweetheart, you look so beautiful."

The moment my eyes caught my mother's in the mirror, I lost it. Tears streamed down my face and I collapsed. The next thing I knew, four women were on the floor next to me as I cried uncontrollably into my hands.

Chapter 15

Rip

"**Y**OU'RE IN A bad mood."

"Why do you say that, Mike?" I asked as I laid back on the weight bench and put my hands on the bar.

"You keep snapping at me."

With a blank look, I opened my mouth to say something, then shut it again.

"What?" Mike asked.

"Dude, you sound like a woman. I'm snapping at you?"

"You are! I ask a simple question and you snap back."

I laughed. "Just spot me, will you?"

Mike stood behind me as I lifted two-hundred-and-twenty pounds.

"Alyssa and Chloe went wedding dress shopping today."

I grunted as I lifted the weights.

"Struggling? You're only on six reps, dude. Four more to go!"

I shot him a dirty look.

"Looking a little weak, Myers."

"Shut. Up." I grunted as I lifted for the tenth and final time.

Mike had to help me guide the weights back onto the bar. *Jesus, I am a fucking wimp.*

I sat up and tried to will the nauseous stomach away. I was running out of fucking time.

"Working out too hard?" he asked, a smug look on his face.

"Fuck you, Mike."

"Yeah, you're in a bad mood."

"Jesus Christ, will you stop already? I'm not in a bad mood. Maybe I just need to get laid."

He shrugged. "When was the last time you did? A while ago?

Looking over my shoulder at him, I replied, "No."

Mike's phone beeped in his pocket, and he pulled it out to read a text message. The goofy smile on his face told me it was from Alyssa.

"Are you going to stare at your phone like a giggly school girl or work out, asshole?"

Mike looked up at me. "She found her dress."

My cold heart melted some, and I gave him a smile. "That's great, dude."

When he laid back, I almost asked him if Alyssa had mentioned if Chloe found a dress. I decided my heart couldn't take it, and I didn't want to know.

Lifting the bar, he started to pump out his ten reps. When he was finished, he sat up.

"She also said Chloe picked out her maid of honor dress for the wedding. Alyssa seemed pretty excited about it."

"That's awesome. I'm sure they'll both look beautiful."

He wiped his face with the towel. "I'm more than sure they will."

"Listen, I'm sort of nauseous. I think I pushed myself too much. I'm going to head on out."

"Are you sure? You only have the one set to go, and we're done."

"Yeah, I've got to get going. I've got an appointment I need to get to."

"For what?"

We grabbed our water bottles and headed to the locker room.

"It's with a real estate agent."

"No shit. You gonna buy a place?"

"I'm looking at buying the old Durham place."

Mike stopped walking and pulled me to a stop. "Are you serious? Rip, you've always wanted that place."

I grinned. "Yeah, found out it was going on the market. Old man Durham passed away a few months back and his daughter doesn't want to be bothered with it. The house is still in pretty good shape. I looked through the windows. It's old, so I'm sure there are some underlying problems, but nothing I can't handle."

"Even with a newer place you will get that, though."

"Yeah, my folks are pretty excited for me."

We grabbed our gym bags and started to head out to our trucks. "How many acres of land?"

There was no way I could stop the smile on my face if I wanted to. "Two hundred and ten."

"Damn, dude! That's awesome. You gonna put some cattle on it?"

"I don't know. I'm going to talk to Mitchell and Trevor. I want to get some horses. I know that much."

Mike stopped at his truck and tossed his backpack into it.

"Dude, I want to go and look at it with you."

"Come. I don't care."

His phone rang and he answered it. "Hey babe."

While I waited for him to talk to Alyssa, I turned on my truck, texted him the address even though he knew where the old farm was located. Then I pulled up Chloe's number. We hadn't talked in almost a week, since she'd screamed *asshole* at me. She was obviously still pissed.

Me: Hey. You busy? I wanted to take you somewhere. Mike is going, too.

I knew Chloe would be over the moon if she knew I was thinking of buying the old farm. It wasn't far from the Frio Cattle Ranch. There was only one other ranch that sat between Chloe's family's property and the small farm I wanted.

Chloe: I'm sorry, but I can't. Wish I could.

I stared at her reply. Deep inside I felt like something was very wrong. Even when she was mad at me, she never responded so vaguely.

Me: Are you okay, Chloe Cat? I don't know what I did, but whatever it was, you know I would never hurt you purposefully.
Chloe: I know you wouldn't. It has nothing to do with you.

Mike tapped on the window, scaring the shit out of me. I rolled the window down.

"Shit, you scared me."

He laughed. "Alyssa can't go. They're back from dress shopping, but she's with Chloe at her place. Sounds like they are doing girl stuff."

"Did she mention if anything was wrong with Chloe?"

"No, why?" he asked, his brows pulled in.

I massaged the tension in the back of my neck. "I don't know. I've got a weird feeling something is wrong, and it's not because she is pissed at me."

With a shrug, he took a few steps back. "She didn't say. Want me to follow you?"

"That works. I texted the address just in case, but it's right down from the Frio Cattle Ranch."

He nodded. "I remember. I'll see you there."

I stood in the living room of the one-hundred-and-five-year-old farm house. It had so much potential, I could practically see it coming to life in front of me.

"Man, the bead board runs throughout the entire house!" Mike said as the real estate agent stood off to the side.

"I know. Look at the wood floors. They used wide planks and crown molding throughout."

Mike laughed. "Dude, you sound like you're looking at a woman and about to have sex."

"I feel that way!"

We smiled and walked into the kitchen. "The cabinets need replacing."

"I can make you some."

"That's exactly the answer I was hoping to hear." We laughed. After all, that's what best friends are for.

Mike was a wiz when it came to woodworking. It was no surprise he was opening his own shop. Since I'd first met him in elementary school, he had always loved making things with wood.

"Mr. Myers, what are your thoughts on the house?" the agent asked.

"I'd like to put an offer in."

She smiled. "Perfect. Do you have a number in mind?"

"Is anyone else interested in the property?" I asked.

"There is one other party, but they are from out of town so they are probably looking at multiple places."

Drawing in a deep breath, I thought about how much I had in my savings. With what my grandfather left me, and the money I had managed to save, I was comfortable going in full price and even a little above if I had to.

"I'd like to come in a little above asking."

The agent smiled and handed me a piece of paper. "Write your offer and sign it. I'll call the other agent now. Let's feel them out and then we can head back to my office."

I wrote the number down and handed it back to her. She promptly went outside and made the call.

"Wow. You're really doing this?" Mike said.

"Even above the listed price, this place is worth it. I've already run the numbers. I don't plan on flipping it, but just knowing within a year I could have a good amount of equity makes me comfortable. And with Steed offering me a position, it only helps with the decision."

"What? He offered you a position?"

I nodded. "Oh damn, I thought I mentioned it. Yeah, he wants me to come in and work part-time doing accounting. He's hoping to step back a little. Eventually, he wants me to take over that side of the business when he retires. I mean, that won't be for a good while, but I can't pass it up."

"What did Jonathon say? I thought he wanted you working with him."

"As much as I love my brother, I like the business end of things. I enjoy working with my hands and all, but running his construction company was never in my long-term goals. They already have a great girl who is handling both Jonathon's and Waylynn's dance studio financial accounts. All they really needed me to do was update things and show Mary the ropes with the new software. She's catching on fast. So if I worked part-time for Jonathon, part time for Steed, I could make this work."

He slapped my back. "Sounds like you've been thinking it over."

The screen door opened, and the agent walked in.

"I received an immediate reply. They've accepted your offer, Mr. Myers. Turns out the owner seems to like your momma."

Laughing, I turned to Mike. "Looks like I have fully entered adulthood."

Mike reached his hand for mine, and we shook.

"Congratulations, dude. I'm happy for you."

With a wide smile, I followed the agent out of the house. I was happy as hell, but a part of me felt like something was missing.

"I'll meet you back at my office, Mr. Myers, and we will sign the paperwork. You'll need to put down the earnest money and start the paperwork for the loan."

"I'll be paying cash, so it should be fast and easy."

Her eyes widened. "Cash? This is a cash sale?"

Mike chuckled as he slipped over to his truck. "I'll catch up with you later, Rip."

With a wave, I replied, "Sounds good! Thanks for coming."

Focusing back on the agent, I confirmed. "Yes, it's a cash sale. Is that an issue?"

"No! No, not at all. This process just sped up exponentially. I'll see you at the office."

I jumped into my truck and stared back at the white farmhouse. Envisioning rocking chairs and sweet tea, I smiled. The emptiness was still there, though. That nagging ache deep within me.

Blue eyes popped into my mind. Her light brown hair pulled into a ponytail and a book in her hand while she sat in a rocking chair on that very porch.

Chloe.

Was she truly happy with Easton? There was only one way to find out, and I was running out of time.

Starting my truck, I took in one deep, long breath and then headed down the long gravel drive.

Chapter 16

Chloe - Four hours earlier

I SAT ON the floor in an expensive wedding dress. Crying.
I'd reached a new level of pathetic.

"Chloe Cat! Oh sweetheart, what is wrong?" my mother said, wrapping her arms around me.

"I'll get tissues!" the sales lady said, running off.

Alyssa took my hand in hers and gave it a squeeze. "Chloe."

That one simple word spoke volumes. Lifting my head, I looked at my mother in the mirror, then turned to her. The pot had finally boiled over.

"I can't marry him, Momma. I can't."

She closed her eyes and said, "Thank you, God."

Widening my eyes, I stared in disbelief. "You didn't want me to marry him?"

The sales lady handed me a box of tissues and politely excused herself. Mary helped Alyssa up so she could change out of her dress. I knew they were giving my mother and me some privacy.

"Well, Chloe. Um, I... Okay, here is the thing. If I thought you truly wanted to marry him, yes, I would have wanted you to. Everyone saw that you didn't, though. You were the least-excited future bride I've ever seen in my life. And the fact that your daddy full on hates the man for taking you away from home, well, I can't help but be relieved."

"Why didn't you say something to me? Daddy has never liked him, so that wasn't a surprise."

The corner of her mouth turned up. "No, he never has. We didn't say anything because you needed to figure it out on your own. If your father or I had questioned you, the only thing it would have done is push you toward marrying him to prove us wrong."

"I value your and Daddy's thoughts."

She regarded me for a moment. "Be honest with me, Chloe. Does this have anything to do with Rip?"

My chest squeezed a bit. "A little, but it has more to do with leaving. Giving up my dreams for a life I know I won't be happy in…"

"Do you love Easton? You must've, sweetheart, if you said yes."

"How about I get out of this dress, and we finish this conversation later? It's Alyssa's day, really. I don't want to steal any more of her thunder."

Placing her hand on the side of my face, she gave me a warm smile. "I love you and we'll figure this out together, I promise."

I hugged her tightly. "I love you, too, Momma. So much."

The fourth dress Alyssa tried on was *the* dress. She cried the moment she looked at herself. It was perfect in every single way. I placed my chin on her shoulder as we gazed at the dress in the mirror.

"It's like it was made for you, Alyssa."

"Do you think Mike will like it?"

Smiling, I replied, "He's not going to be able to breathe when he sees you in this."

Her eyes met mine. "I'm so sorry, Chloe. If I…"

I shook my head. "Don't. I needed it. Thank you."

"It was just, well, I didn't want you to make the biggest mistake of your life, and I knew you were about to."

"Deep down I did, too. Do me a favor. Please don't tell Mike. I want to tell Rip myself and I don't want him hear it from someone else. It's about time we finally came clean with each other."

She faced me. "You're going to tell him you're still in love with him?"

I looked down and then back at her. "I'm not sure what I'm going to say. And I don't know what he will say. Knowing he didn't finish school because of me... I'm angry with him right now more than anything. And confused. If he still loves me, why didn't he tell me?"

With a half shrug, she said, "Pride and fear of being hurt are powerful emotions."

Exhaling, I nodded.

"Now that we found my dress, let's look for your maid of honor dress."

"Sounds like a plan!"

It didn't take Alyssa long to pick from the three dresses I tried on. Of course, Mary and my mother loved all three. I had my personal favorite, and as luck would have it, Alyssa picked that one. It was a curve-hugging sequined gown with thin straps. Alyssa wasn't having any other bridesmaids. Just a maid of honor, and Mike had Rip as his best man.

"Lord, you look hot in that, Chloe," Alyssa said, fanning herself.

"The nice thing about this dress is you could easily have it altered and made into cocktail length," the sales lady added.

"And they told me it would take weeks to find a dress. We found two in one day!" Alyssa exclaimed.

"Let me get out of this and then we need to eat. I'm starving."

"We're going to grab something at a drive-thru, girls, because I need to get back. Your father and I have a dinner tonight," my mother called out as she headed to the front, most likely to pay for the dress. After arguing with her about it, she told me to keep my money. I learned long ago not to argue when my mother wanted to do something.

Once we were back at the ranch, Mom pulled me into the study and had me sit down.

"Let's finish that conversation, shall we?"

I blew out a breath and dropped my head onto the sofa.

"Yes, I loved him. I don't think I was ever in love with him, though."

"Not like you are with Rip?"

I jerked my head upright. My mouth opened but nothing would come out. I couldn't even formulate a reply to that because I knew, deep in my heart, that she was right.

"Chloe Parker, you have been in love with Rip Myers since kindergarten. The only problem is, when you grew up, you stopped declaring that love."

I buried my face in my hands and let out a frustrated groan. "When Easton asked me to marry him, my first instinct was to say no. The only thing I could think of were memories of Rip. All the times he came so close to telling me how he felt, or the way he had to stop himself when I knew he wanted to kiss me. Then the memory of telling him how I felt popped up. I think a part of me thought by saying yes to Easton, I would finally give up the dream of Rip. Move on with my life rather than sitting in a holding pattern for something that would never happen."

"Chloe," my mother whispered. "Can't you see, sweetheart? Rip is madly in love with you."

Tears filled my eyes. "But he hasn't ever told me." I looked down at my hands. "I think he tried after that day, and I held him off. Now, I don't think he ever will, Momma. If he loves me like everyone says he does, why was he willing to let me marry someone else?"

My voice sounded weak.

"The last thing that boy wants to do is hurt you, Chloe. If he thinks you're happy, maybe he doesn't want to ruin that for you. You're engaged to a man and willing to leave all this behind. In his mind, that must mean you truly love Easton."

With a nod, I wiped my cheeks. "Rip was most likely the reason I said yes. But he's not the full reason I can't marry Easton. I want the life I dreamed of. I want to work alongside Daddy. Here at the ranch. I want to go horseback riding any time I want. Do you know what Easton wants?"

She shook her head.

"A condo in downtown Houston. He doesn't even like the country. He can't understand my love of Patches and thinks he's a *lamb*. He's still jealous of Rip!"

Her brow lifted. "He has every good reason to be jealous of him."

"I'd say so," I mumbled.

"Go on, keep talking."

"I'm not saying no because I'm holding out hope for Rip. I'm saying no because Easton doesn't fit in with the life I see myself living."

She pulled me off the sofa and hugged me. "That was what I wanted to hear. I know your heart belongs to Rip, and I have every reason to believe things will work out the way they are supposed to in the long run. But I'm glad you are seeing the true reason why you said yes in the first place, and you're seeing the reasons why you can't go through with it. You came to that decision all on your own, sweetheart."

Her thumb came up and wiped my tears away.

"When did you figure out I wasn't going to marry him?"

"The moment you pulled the ring out of your pocket. Then you confirmed it when you said you wanted to get married in Melanie and John's backyard! I know you love your grandparents, but the backyard? Really?"

My hand came up to my mouth, and I tried not to laugh. But soon, my mother and I were in a laughing fit. Daddy walked in and looked between the two of us.

"What's going on?" he asked.

I wiped my face and walked over to him. "Daddy, I need to tell you something."

He wore a concerned look. "Is everything okay?"

"Now it is. I decided not to marry Easton."

The look of relief on my father's face was instant. "Pinch me now as hard as you can because I better not be dreaming."

I narrowed my eyes then hit him on the chest. "Daddy!"

"Tell me you're serious. You're not marrying the douchebag?"

"Daddy!"

"Steed!"

"What? I couldn't stand that kid. It took everything I had not to tell him to take his city-ass down the road."

"Then you will be happy to know that I am going to tell him we won't be getting married and that he's not the man I see my future with."

"Damn straight, he isn't. I'm so glad you came to your senses, Chloe."

"Gee, it makes me so happy to know that everyone thought I was making a mistake, yet no one was willing to say anything..."

My father shrugged. "You would have figured it out. You're a smart woman. Besides, everyone kept saying they always assumed you and Rip would be tying the knot, so I figured that spoke for itself."

Reaching up on my toes, I kissed him, then smacked him playfully. "Point taken, Daddy."

"Will you both do me a favor. Please don't tell anyone. I, um, I want to tell Rip myself."

"Rip?" my father asked, a slight gleam in his eyes. It was hard to believe this man had once threatened to cut off Rip's balls if he ever touched me.

"And Grammy and Granddad. The family, I mean."

With a wink, my father replied, "Uh-huh."

"Come on, Steed, we need to get ready for that dinner. And I believe Chloe has a phone call to make."

I chewed on my lip.

"The sooner you do it, the better it will be," she stated.

A feeling of dread washed over me. I hated hurting Easton, but if I didn't do this we would both end up hating each other. "I'll head out to see Patches and then call him."

"While you're on the phone with him, tell him to—"

"Steed Parker!" my mother warned. She grabbed him and pulled him out the door.

I giggled, then followed them. I jumped in the four-wheeler and made my way to the main barn. A quick visit with Patches would make everything right again.

Chapter 17

Chloe

A S I WAS walking into the barn, my phone rang. My heart dropped when I saw who it was.

Easton.

I took a deep breath and answered. "Hello?"

"Hey, where are you at?"

"Walking into the barn."

"That's right. It's about that time you visit your lamb."

"It's a goat, for fuck's sake!" I shouted, a little loud.

Liberty looked straight at me as I stepped into the barn. Then she started to laugh. I shot her the finger and kept walking toward Patches' stall.

"Jesus, what is wrong with you? I can't help it if I can't keep all the farm animals straight. Chloe, you've really changed since you got home."

Liberty stopped and whispered, "He's out in the pasture. He got out earlier and ate Gram's roses."

"Thanks, Liberty."

"What?" Easton asked.

"I wasn't talking to you. I was talking to my cousin, and I haven't changed. This is me. This is who I am. I'm a country girl who loves

116

animals. I have a pet goat who is my best friend. I want to live in the country, work for my father, live in Oak Springs, and I do not want to marry you!"

My hand went to my mouth while my eyes widened in horror. Liberty, on the other hand, jumped onto a hay bale and started to clap.

"It's about time!" she shouted.

I waved for her to stop and quiet down.

"I'm sorry, what did you say last?" Easton asked.

Dropping onto the hay bale, I closed my eyes. That was not how I wanted to tell Easton.

"Easton, you had to know this was coming. All we have done is fight over every little thing."

"Chloe, you're walking away from this because we had a few disagreements?"

"I'm saying no to marriage because I should have never have said yes in the first place."

"Why not?"

Liberty put her arm around me, and I rested my head on her shoulder. It was clear she could hear Easton's voice.

"This is my life, East. Here. In Oak Springs. With my family. If I left, I would only end up resenting you and we would both be unhappy."

"So you're saying no because you don't want to leave home?"

I stood and sighed. He didn't get it at all, or he refused to get it. I slowly walked toward the barn door.

"Easton, for years I've planned on working for my family's ranch. You knew that. My dad made a new position just for me! *This* is home."

"And you don't love me enough to leave it, start a new life. Make a new home?"

"Do you love me enough to understand why I can't leave? Do you love me enough to do the same thing for me?"

He let out a frustrated sigh. "I do love you, Chloe. That's why I want to marry you. Do you not love me?"

I swallowed hard. "I do love you. But I'm not...in love with you."

"That doesn't make fucking sense."

Closing my eyes, I took in a deep breath and let it out slowly. "Easton, what I'm trying to say is I love you, and dating you was amazing, and we had a lot of fun. But you even admitted to me you only asked me to marry you because we were drifting apart. I don't love you enough to walk away from a life I have dreamed of for as long as I can remember. A life I want. Living in a condo in downtown Houston is *not* the life I want. I'd be miserable. We'd both end up miserable."

"Fine. You want a house in the suburbs, we can do that. You can even bring your lamb."

I let out a bemused laugh. "If we did that, then you would be settling. And the suburbs is not the same as land and rolling hills."

"This has nothing to do with your job and your family ranch. It doesn't even have anything to do with living in Houston. This has everything to do with Rip, doesn't it? You can't leave him."

"Why does an argument with you always come back to Rip?"

"Because your whole life revolves around him. You went to every single one of his games. You even cancelled dates so you could go and cheer on your best friend. God damn it, Chloe. You are in love with the guy, and you won't admit it to yourself. That is why you won't marry me, because of that bastard."

Taking a few deep breaths, I tried to control my temper. "I won't lie to you about Rip, Easton. Yes, I have feelings for him. He is my best friend and will always be my best friend. He was also the first boy I ever fell in love with. When you asked me to marry you, I thought that if I said yes, I would finally be able to let go of my past. Let go of Rip. That was selfish of me, and I'm sorry. But the reason I am telling you no today isn't because of Rip. This last week I realized that I can't leave Oak Springs. The future I've dreamed of, the plans I've made for my life, they're all here, every one of them... not in Houston."

"So this is it? You're giving up on us?"

"East, you and I both know deep down that this was never going to work. You asked me to marry you because you didn't want us to break up. I said yes because I didn't know how to say no."

There was a long pause before he cleared his throat. "Well, I guess it would be hard for me to win your heart not only from Rip, but your whole damn town, as well." His sharp words felt like a knife in my heart. I had loved this man. I spent the last ten months with him, but now more than ever I knew I wasn't in love with him.

"I'm sorry, East."

"Me too, Chloe. You're making the biggest mistake of your life."

With a slight shake of my head, I replied, "That is another disagreement because I think I'm saving myself from the biggest mistake of my life."

"Keep the ring. I don't want it back. Good luck, Chloe."

Before I had a chance to say anything, he hung up. Jerking the phone from my ear, I stared at it.

"He hung up on me!" I said before losing it laughing. God, it felt so good to laugh about Easton for once instead of crying.

A week had passed since I had spoken to Easton and broken off our engagement. I sent him the ring back, even though he told me to keep it. It didn't feel right. He sent me a message that he got it back. A four-word text, to be exact.

I got the ring.

I didn't respond. There was nothing to say.

"Hey, what are you doing today?" Gage asked as he hit my leg with a baseball glove when he walked by.

"Nothing. What are you doing?"

He smiled. "A bunch of us are getting together to play a bit of baseball. Girls against guys. You want to come?"

"You really want your older sister hanging out with you?"

Gage laughed. "All my friends think you're hot, Chloe. I'm positive they wouldn't mind."

With a wide grin, I stood. "Okay, I'll come. Will there be anyone I know there?"

"I'm not sure. Sometimes a few people who used to be on the baseball team in high school will come in. We play every Tuesday night."

"Okay, I'll come. I could use a distraction and a good time."

When Gage pulled up to the large baseball field, I couldn't help but smile. The memories of watching both Gage and Rip play here filled my mind.

"You seem a lot happier this week. Why is that?" Gage asked.

I shrugged.

"Wouldn't have anything to do with that loser you finally got rid of, would it?"

"Why in the world did you and Dad not like him?"

Gage laughed. "That's easy to answer. He wasn't Rip."

I stared, not knowing what to say to that. He gave me a wink and got out of his truck.

I looked around to see if there were any familiar faces. My heart nearly leapt from my chest when I saw Alyssa and Mike.

Thanks goodness I'm not the only older person here.

I jumped out of the truck and made my way to them.

"What's going on, y'all?"

Alyssa beamed when she saw me, and Mike grinned as well.

"You playing in this little game too, Mike?"

He smiled. "Any time I am asked to play baseball or football, I am there."

Alyssa and I both laughed.

Two girls walked by us giggling about something. They had to be Gage's age. "Oh my gosh, I want to squeeze his ass!"

"I want to *do* him."

My brows lifted as Alyssa and I watched them walk by. "Who are they talking about?" I asked while we watched the girls join a bigger group of high school-aged girls.

"I have no idea."

We stepped closer to listen in. How I missed the days of high school. No, that was a lie.

"He's here tonight. Wait until y'all see him play. I have an orgasm just looking at him."

I covered my mouth in an attempt not to laugh. Alyssa gagged.

"Good Lord, were we like that in high school?"

"Probably," I said.

The girls all stopped and sat down. "Really, y'all, he's six years older than you, do you really think Rip Myers will look twice at you?"

Alyssa bumped my shoulder, and this time we did chuckle. I tried not to look for Rip. Once the girls mentioned him being there, I had to quietly work on keeping my breath under control. The girls were too wrapped up in their conversation to notice me and Alyssa.

"How cute! They have a crush on Rip. Remember those days, Chloe?"

I rolled my eyes. "All too well."

"He hooked up with Morgan Hicks, you know. She's younger than him," one of the girls said.

Alyssa had already headed back to Mike, but I froze in place.

"We all know why he went out with her. She's an easy lay."

My stomach twisted.

"That was months ago. I'm eighteen, I think I've got a good shot with him. Besides, who would the hottest guy in Oak Springs want to be with other than the hottest woman?"

All the other girls laughed. "Keep dreaming!" one of them said as I picked up my pace and re-joined Alyssa.

"First up to bat is the guys' team. Girls, get into position."

"It looks like they have enough girls, Chloe. Let's go sit in the stands."

"Okay. Sounds good."

The game started, and the guys were up to bat.

"Have you decided on the wedding cake?" I asked, trying not to think about this Morgan Hicks person.

"Not even close. Mike wants to do something fun and crazy. I, on the other hand, want something traditional, maybe even French-themed."

"Why not let him pick his groom's cake and you do the main wedding cake?"

She shrugged. "I really wanted just one."

"Why?" I asked.

Looking around, she leaned in closer to me and whispered, "Do you not remember what putting Mike in charge of something is like?"

I smiled at the memory of Mike planning Alyssa's eighteenth surprise birthday party. We had it at a trampoline place. The guys had a hell of a good time there.

Trying not to giggle, I replied, "You have to admit the trampolines were kind of fun."

Alyssa shot me a dirty look. "Yeah, for them."

Focusing back on the field I stopped laughing because I saw Rip. He was talking to someone I had never seen before.

"Who is Rip talking to?" I asked.

Alyssa followed my stare. "Oh, that's Morgan. She owns a pottery studio down on the square."

"Morgan Hicks?"

"Yeah, have you met her?"

I shook my head. "No, but Rip's dated her, right?"

"Um, yeah, if you want to call a hook-up once or twice dating."

Trying to pull my attention off of them, I watched the game. I jumped and screamed when Gage hit a homerun.

"Go Gage!"

When my eyes drifted back to Rip, he was watching me. I lifted my hand and gave him a slight wave. Seeing him dressed in baseball pants, a T-shirt, and that ball cap had my mind going fuzzy, and for a moment I forgot I was mad at him. He smiled back, then turned his attention to Morgan as she placed a hand on his arm. It didn't take long for that old familiar, angry jealousy to show up and rear its ugly head.

"Chloe?"

I was still staring at Morgan and Rip when I replied, "Yeah?"

"If looks could kill, poor Morgan would be on the ground."

Snapping out of it, I looked at her. "I don't know what you're talking about."

She laughed. "Okay, if you say so. Have you guys talked at all? I know you were upset with him."

"No, I texted him earlier to see if he could meet for dinner, and he hasn't responded. Maybe he already has plans...with Morgan."

Even I could hear the jealousy in my voice.

Alyssa raised a brow. "I swear to God, you two give me whiplash and you always have."

I smirked. "You and me both."

When I glanced back to Rip and Morgan, she was laughing. My chest ached, and I couldn't help but wonder if this was what Rip felt when he saw me and Easton together. But it still didn't make any sense that he would leave Texas A&M over it. And if that was the real reason, why in the hell hadn't he just told me?

Agitation crept in even though I tried like hell to stop it. I frowned at the thought of Rip pushing me away because he was too afraid to admit his feelings for me. Claiming he only wanted me to be happy. Did he for once stop and think I might be happiest with him?

Morgan leaned up and kissed Rip on the cheek. He took a step back and looked up at me. His brows pulled in slightly, and I realized I was still frowning, possibly even giving him and Morgan a dirty look. My phone rang and I jumped, causing my phone to tumble around in my hands.

"Hello? Hello?" I said, trying to calm my racing heart.

"Chloe?"

"Hey Daddy, what's going on?"

"Baby girl, where are you?"

My breath stalled in my chest. Something was wrong.

"I'm at the baseball game that Gage is playing in. At the fields. Why?"

"Honey, you might want to head home. It's Patches."

A sob instantly slipped from my lips. "What's wrong?"

He didn't answer.

Alyssa looked at me, worry all over her face.

"Daddy, what's wrong with Patches?"

Alyssa stood, and I quickly followed her lead. She took my hand, and we started down the bleachers.

"Do you want me to come pick you up?"

My hand covered my mouth and I closed my eyes.

Patches. No. Please don't leave me.

"Chloe? Chloe!"

Alyssa took the phone from my hand, and I barely heard her talking. The next thing I knew, I was in Mike's truck.

"Gage?" I said, my voice cracking.

"I sent Mike a text to let him know what was happening. I got you out as fast as I could. You looked like you were about to break down crying. There is enough gossip going on in this town as it is. I didn't want there to be more tongues wagging."

My head snapped to look at her. "Gossip about what?"

She chewed on her lip. "You. Rip. No one knows you broke off your engagement yet. I didn't tell Mike, like you asked. People saw the way you were looking at Rip and Morgan, and then if you were to break down in tears, you would for sure be on the prayer chain in a heartbeat."

I blinked to keep the tears at bay. "Maybe I need to be on the prayer chain."

Alyssa took my hand in hers. "You don't want on the prayer chain. Trust me."

I managed a small smile. The prayer chain was a group of local women, mostly older, but some of the younger women in town were joining in on it. It was mostly a gossip mill. A way to quickly spread the word about something happening in town.

"I'm sorry I zoned out back there. I'm worried about Patches. He can't be..."

Her hand squeezed mine. "Let's just get you back to see what's happened. In the meantime, take some breaths. We'll be there soon."

I turned to look out the window. Images of Patches filled my mind. He was such a naughty little goat. Always getting into something and causing grief for Grammy, and especially Aunt Waylynn. It was like Patches knew how to push Waylynn's buttons. I smiled thinking of all the parties Patches had invaded. How many times I had batted my eyelashes so he could be a part of wedding ceremonies. I loved him so much.

"Do you remember when I asked my mom and dad if Patches could come to our elementary graduation?"

Alyssa laughed. "Yes! I also remember Patches being in almost all of the weddings—and the receptions—in your family!"

I giggled. "My aunts and uncles must surely love me because I managed to have Patches walk down the aisle many times."

"Do you remember that Fourth of July picnic when Patches chased Waylynn all around the backyard because she had food in her hand?"

We both laughed.

"He lived for tormenting her," I said. "I think he knows she has a love-hate relationship with him."

"Love? Chloe, I'm pretty sure Patches is Waylynn's archenemy."

I sighed. "I hope he's okay. He's gotta be okay."

Chapter 18

Rip

SWINGING AT THE ball, I struck out. Again.

"Dude, what is wrong with you? Your game is off tonight in a big way!" Mike said.

"I don't know. A lot on my mind, I guess."

He gave me a knowing look. When I glanced up into the stands, Chloe and Alyssa were still gone. Was Chloe upset that I'd been talking to Morgan? It certainly seemed that way.

Jerking my fingers into my hair, I exhaled with frustration.

How in the hell can she be upset with me? She's marrying someone else, for fuck's sake.

Mike's words popped back into my head. "Tell her before it's too late. Tell her how you really feel about her."

Sitting down next to me, Mike pulled his phone out and checked it. "Alyssa and Chloe left," he said.

"Did she say why?"

Mike stood, then ran out onto the field and called Gage's name. "Gage! Gage!"

He looked at him, confused.

"Gage!" Mike shouted again. I walked over as Gage jogged up to him.

"What's wrong? What is it?" I asked.

Mike looked at me and then back to Gage.

"What's up, dude? I'm in the middle of the game!" Gage said as he came to a stop.

"We need to leave. It's Patches. Alyssa sent me a text over an hour ago when they left. Your dad called Chloe, said Patches isn't doing good. Alyssa just sent another text. Patches died ten minutes ago. Chloe took off on her horse."

"Fuck!" I said, turning around and grabbing my bag. I made her a promise. I made her a promise I'd be there.

Fuck. Fuck. Fuck.

"Rip, dude, where in the hell are you going?" Mike asked, grabbing my arm.

"I need to get to Chloe."

"Let me drive. Alyssa took my truck."

Gage was already in his truck and speeding out of the parking lot. I shoved the keys into Mike's hands. "Just get there, Mike. I promised her."

As Mike drove, I stared out the window. Neither of us said a word. We both knew how special Patches was to Chloe.

"What did you mean earlier when you said you made a promise to Chloe?"

"Back in high school, before we left for college. Chloe made me promise I would be there for her when Patches finally passed away."

Mike didn't respond, but he did press down on the gas a little more.

By the time we got to Chloe's grandparents' house, Chloe had been gone for almost an hour.

Paxton walked up to us, giving Gage a hug, then me and Mike. "I don't know where she is. She jumped on her horse and took off. She didn't even put a saddle and reins on."

"Is Dad looking for her?" Gage asked.

"Yes, but she could be anywhere."

Rubbing the back of my neck, I looked at Gage. "Can I saddle up a horse?"

He nodded. "I will too."

"Mike, you stay here in case she comes back...call me," I said. He nodded.

Gage and I rushed to the main barn.

"Who do you want?" he asked as we stepped in. This was just one of a few different barns the Parkers had on their ranch. Chloe's grandfather kept his prized horses in this one, along with the horses the family rode often.

"I don't care. Just give me a fast one," I said.

Gage brought over Walter, a blue roan. I started to take him out of the barn. "Dude! Walter has never been ridden bareback. At least put some reins on him."

I let out a frustrated groan as Gage handed me the reins. I slipped the bit into his mouth, threw the reins over his neck, then jumped on him when we got out of the barn.

"Call me if you find her," I said, looking back at Gage who was saddling up a horse.

"Same. I texted Dad that we were here, so he knows we're looking, too."

I kicked Walter, and he took off. If I knew Chloe, I knew exactly where she'd gone.

Racing across the pastures, I cursed myself for not being honest with her that day she told me she wanted more. For giving up on trying to talk to her. For not telling her I loved her when she stood in her dad's office and said she was marrying that asshole. I'd never hated myself like I did in that moment.

When I rounded the bend, I saw her horse. Letting out a sigh, I brought Walter down to a trot. The old hunters' cabin was where Chloe's Aunt Amelia used to write a lot of her romance novels. She now only released a book or two a year, and the cabin pretty much sat empty. Chloe and I would come here and talk for hours when either of us needed to get away.

I slid off Walter and tossed the reins over his neck, allowing him to graze with Chloe's horse, Lizzy.

Slowly, I opened the door and found Chloe sitting on the chair. It was a small cabin with the bedroom in a separate room. The living, dining, and kitchen were all one giant space. It was dusty and looked like no one had been here in years. The last time anyone had been here was probably the night I almost told Chloe how I felt about her before we left for college.

"Chloe Cat?"

Her head lifted, and she started to cry harder. "You found me."

With a small smile, I nodded. "I made you a promise I would be here for you."

She started to cry harder and made her way over to me. When she wrapped her arms around me, I held her tight.

"It's okay, princess. It's okay."

"He's gone, Rip. He's gone."

I ran my hand up and down her back as she sobbed into my chest. There was nothing I hated more than hearing her cry. I wanted to take her pain from her. Any way I could.

"I'm here. I'm right here."

Her legs felt like they were giving out, so I reached down and lifted her. She buried her face into my chest as I walked over and sat down on the small couch. I held her, letting her get it all out. When she couldn't cry anymore, she lifted her head and our eyes met. My heart felt like it did a full somersault.

"I'm so sorry he's gone, Chloe."

Her chin trembled as her gaze moved across my face. It landed back on my eyes.

"You came. You actually came."

"Of course, I did. I promised you."

The corner of her mouth lifted slightly. "Thank you."

I brushed away her tears with my thumb.

She swallowed hard and closed her eyes as she spoke. "I made it in time. I was with him when he passed. It was like he...was w-waiting for me."

More tears slipped free and rolled down her cheeks. I used both thumbs to wipe her face again. "He loved you just as much as you loved him, Chloe."

With a nod, she pulled in a deep, cleansing breath, then exhaled. The warmth of her breath on my face had my insides pulsing with the need to kiss her. Make her forget this moment. Make her forget Easton. Make her mine.

Chloe cleared her throat. "I'm sure everyone is worried."

"Your dad, Gage, and Trevor were out looking for you."

Her eyes met mine again. "How did you know I would be here?"

I shrugged. "I know you probably better than you know yourself."

Her lips pressed tightly together before she gave me a sweet smile. "I guess you do."

Chloe wrapped her arms around her body. "I needed to be alone for a few minutes. Come to terms with the fact that I'll never see him again."

"That's understandable."

She nodded.

"I texted Gage to let him know I found you. He said he would let his dad and Trevor know. I think they were all heading back to the house."

"I feel like a silly fool for running off like that."

"Don't. You have every right to be upset, Chloe. Patches was your best friend."

"One of my best friends," she whispered.

My heart stalled. I couldn't let her marry that asshole, not without telling her how I felt.

Placing her hands over her face, she let out a frustrated growl. "Everything is changing. Why can't it just be like it was before?"

I had no idea if she was talking about us or not. This was my chance. I had to tell her how I really felt, or I might never get it out.

Walking over to her, I lifted her chin and our eyes locked.

Kiss her.

Tell her.

Do something, Rip! Now!

Her blue eyes were bloodshot, and she looked exhausted. "We should probably head back up to the house. I'm sure my mother is worried."

"Don't marry him, Chloe."

Her eyes widened in shock. "What did you say?"

I shook my head. There was no going back now. "I said, don't marry him. Don't marry Easton."

Tears filled her eyes, but she blinked them away rapidly as she took a step back. "And why shouldn't I marry him?"

"He won't ever be able to love you like I love you. No one will ever love you like that."

A single tear slipped free and trailed down her face. I watched it until it traveled the length of her cheek and dropped to the floor. Then I met her stare.

"You're telling me this now?" Her voice cracked.

I rubbed the back of my neck. Afraid to even look her in the eyes.

"Now. You decide to tell me now?"

The lump in my throat was making it hard for me to speak. I cleared my throat. "I...I wanted to tell you that day."

My voice cracked, and I stopped talking. She stared at me, disbelief all over her face. "I didn't want to ruin our friendship, Chloe. You mean the world to me, and I was scared. I was shocked you had admitted it. If you had just given me a few minutes to process it... I tried to talk to you after that. To tell you I felt the same way and explain why taking the next step scared the hell out of me. But you wouldn't let me."

"Is that why you left Texas A&M? You left because I was dating Easton?"

I narrowed my brows. "Does it matter?"

"Yes!" she screamed. "Right now, it matters. Tell me the truth!"

Her anger nearly filled the entire small cabin.

"Yes. I left because I couldn't stand the sight of you with him. Every time I saw him touch you, I wanted to punch him."

Chloe turned away and grabbed onto the back of a chair. Her other hand was over her stomach.

"The thought of losing you forever has always scared me. There were so many times in high school I wanted to kiss you, but I was afraid you would tell me you just wanted to be friends. I didn't dare believe you felt the same."

Her shoulders shook, and I knew she was crying.

"Chloe, I'm sorry I..."

She spun around and cleared her face of tears. "You were afraid? You don't think I was afraid when I told you how I felt? You didn't think we could love each other enough to make it work?"

"I...I tried to talk to you, Chloe, and you pushed me away."

"You asshole! *Now* you tell me!"

I jumped when she yelled.

"I'm sorry."

Her hands came up and covered her mouth as she cried again. When I walked toward her, she held out her hand.

"Stop! You don't get to console me, Rip. Not when it's you who is ripping out my heart right now!"

"What?" I asked, instantly feeling like someone had reached into my chest and done the same to me. I took a step toward her, and she took one away.

"It was supposed to be you! It was always supposed to be you."

My eyes burned with the threat of tears. "What was supposed to be me?"

She shook her head frantically and put her hand out again when I tried to walk to her.

"Don't, Rip. Don't you dare try to make this better now. It will *never* be better!"

"Chloe, I wanted to tell you that day. I tried for weeks to get you to talk to me and you wouldn't. You kept telling me to forget it, that it had never happened. What did you want me to do?"

"Fight for me!" she said, tears streaming down her face. "For us. I poured my heart out to you that day, and you stomped on it. What was I supposed to do?"

I shook my head. "You mean everything to me, Chloe, and what if we didn't work out?"

"Goddamn it, Rip! How could we not have worked out? I loved you, and you're telling me you felt the same."

A feeling so hard hit me in the chest, I took a few steps away from her. "Loved?"

She stared at me for the longest time, then let out a scream that I was positive could be heard by Mike all the way across the ranch.

"You jerk! You asshole! You stupid idiot!"

"I admit I am all those things. That and more."

Her hands flew up in the air. "You don't get it, Rip. You just don't get it."

She was full-on crying again, and I wanted to hit myself for making her feel this way. Especially since she was already so upset about Patches.

"It was supposed to be you for everything! For all of it!"

"Chloe, what are you talking about?"

"Don't you see? Don't you understand that every single dream I've ever had I had with you?"

Chloe walked up to me and hit me on the chest with both her fists as she cried harder.

"*You*, Rip! My first real kiss should have been with you! My first date with a man who adored me should have been you! When I lost my virginity... *God*." Sobs rushed from her body. "It was supposed to be with you!"

She took a step back and placed her hand over her mouth before she whispered, "The man who got down on one knee and asked me to marry him... It should have been you..."

She cried so hard that she couldn't speak for a moment. Looking into my eyes, she whispered, "I wanted those things with you. And now it's too late. You're too late."

I closed my eyes and tried to hold down the sick feeling. "Please don't say that, Chloe. Please."

When I opened my eyes, I felt my own tears on my face. Chloe started to walk to me, then stopped. Her fingers pressed against her lips. She shook her head, then took a few steps back.

Crossing the distance between us, I took her into my arms. She cried so hard I was positive she was having a hard time breathing.

"I'm sorry, baby. I'm so damn sorry."

Chloe buried her face in my chest for what felt like an eternity before she pushed away from me. Shaking her head, she stepped back until she got to the door. "You're too late."

"Chloe! Please don't do this. I'm begging you not to marry him."

The door jerked open, and she started to walk out, but stopped. With a slow, deep breath, she looked me in the eyes once more. "I told Easton last week I couldn't marry him."

The air in my lungs felt like someone had set it on fire. "Wh-what?" I managed.

She stepped through the door and shut it, leaving me alone in the small cabin. I stumbled back and sat on the small sofa.

My fingers jerked through my hair while I cried out, "Fuuuck!"

If she had broken up with Easton last week, why had she said it was too late for us?

I broke down and cried like I had never cried before.

Chapter 19

Rip

BY THE TIME I made it back to the barn, there was no one around. Chloe's horse, Lizzy, was put up in her stall, as was the horse Gage had been on.

I took care of Walter and fed him oats before I made my way back up to the house. As I approached, I avoided going to the back door and walked down the driveway, instead. Chloe was probably back at her house anyway.

Right as I got to my truck, Steed's voice stopped me in my tracks.

"Rip, where are you going?"

Clearing my throat, I looked at him. He was standing on the front porch of Melanie and John's house.

"I figured I would head on out."

"You're not going to say goodbye to Chloe?"

"With all due respect, sir, I don't think she wants to see me right now."

He gave a thoughtful nod and then motioned for me to join him on the porch.

My heart was hammering. Steed Parker was one man I never wanted to make angry.

"Sit down, Rip. We're going to have ourselves a little talk."

I swallowed hard. "A talk?"

"Yes, a talk. Sit."

Sitting on the rocking chair beside him, I rubbed my hands together nervously.

Steed took in a deep breath, then exhaled. "I'm going to guess you told her you loved her."

My eyes widened in shock.

"Don't look so stunned, son. Everyone in this whole damn town knows the two of you love each other. Why in the hell you're both too stubborn to admit it is beyond all of us."

I glanced down at my hands.

"Chloe told me once, right after we had moved to College Station. She said she wanted more than friendship, and I freaked. I mean, there were so many times I wanted to tell her how I felt but I was afraid she only thought of me as a friend."

"You're an idiot."

I smiled. "I know, sir. I'm stupid as a box of rocks. That day I told her we couldn't be more than friends, I was so scared of losing her as my best friend, Steed. But five minutes after I said those words to her, I wanted to take them back. Things didn't work out that way, though, and we both moved on."

"If there is one thing I've learned about mistakes in the past, if you hold onto them, Rip, they'll never let you move forward. So you messed up then, and I'm going to guess you messed up tonight."

I nodded. "She told me it was too late."

Steed tossed his head back and laughed. Hard. I chuckled too because he was laughing so damn hard, and I had no idea why.

"What's so funny?"

"Rip Myers, how long have you known my daughter?"

"Eighteen years."

"That is eighteen years you have been best friends with a Parker woman. You have been around the Parker women for *eighteen years*. Have you not learned a damn thing? From any of them?"

I lifted a brow. "Sir, I'm not really sure if there is a correct answer to that question."

Steed winked. "You have learned. Parker women are stubborn as hell. They react on impulse. Take Chloe saying yes to that douchebag, Easton."

I had to press my lips together to keep from laughing.

"They love fiercely, are devoted as hell. They believe they are right one hundred percent of the time. And most important of all, they stay angry for a hell of a lot longer than most people do."

"Great," I whispered, my fingers raking through my hair.

"I'm going to give you some advice, Rip. But first I want to ask you something."

"Okay."

"Do you love my daughter?"

My chest squeezed, and my stomach felt like it flipped over. "Yes. I've been in love with her for as long as I can remember."

"There ya go."

I drew my brows in. "I'm confused. Was that your advice?"

He nodded. "Yes."

"Um, thank you, I guess?"

Steed laughed. "I don't think you and Chloe have ever let yourselves see how in love you are with each other. Love conquers everything, Rip, when you let it take control. It is your lifeboat when the water is too deep, your safety net when you close your eyes and step off the cliff. Your blanket to keep you warm when the nights are cold and your mind is filled with worry or uncertainty. The one thing that ties you and Chloe together besides your friendship is your love for one another. Love, Rip, is the reason you face the fear. You take the leap. You vow to make it work and trust that it will."

My eyes stung as I fought tears back. I had never trusted in our love. Never had faith that it would be able to conquer all.

"What do I do to win her back?"

The corners of his mouth slowly rose. "Be patient. She's hurting right now for a few different reasons. Keep fighting for her, though. She's worth the battle."

I nodded. "Yes, sir. She certainly is."

"Now, are you leaving or coming into the house?" Steed asked as he stood.

"I believe I'm going into the house with you."

"Good. You might want to stick close by me for a bit. Chloe was in the kitchen with a butcher knife earlier. She seemed pretty pissed."

When I laughed, and he didn't, I quickly stopped. "Ohhhh, you're being serious?"

"Hell yes, I am. Did you not remember the one bit that I said was important?"

"Parker women stay mad."

"They don't stay mad, son. Angry. They stay *angry*. You'll learn the difference very quickly, I'm afraid."

"Right, right. For a hell of a long time."

He slapped my back and opened the front door. "You always were a quick learner, son."

I followed Steed through the house. It was a massive house, but it felt like we reached the kitchen a lot sooner than I was ready to. I heard voices and knew more of Chloe's family was here.

"Look who I found," Steed announced.

Everyone in the kitchen turned and looked at me. Chloe's grandparents, John, and Melanie were standing on either side of Chloe. Gage was sitting at the bar alone with Mike, and Alyssa was leaning against the kitchen sink. She gave me a sympathetic look, so I wasn't sure if she and Chloe had talked about what happened in the cabin.

Trevor walked into the kitchen and slapped me on the back. Hard.

"You stupid bastard," he said as he leaned in close to my ear.

"Trevor!" Scarlett, his wife, said as she pushed him away. "Don't let him get to you, Rip."

I smiled. At least the entire family wasn't here. I might have actually turned and ran for my life.

"Rip, sweetheart, we were beginning to wonder where you were. Thank you for finding Chloe," Melanie said, a sweet smile on her face.

Nodding, I forced myself to talk. "Of course. Anything for Chloe."

Chloe's head lifted, and our eyes met. The look she shot me made me swallow hard, and I could swear I felt sweat beading on my forehead.

"We are in the process of making chocolate chip oatmeal cookies. It always makes Chloe feel better when she bakes. Why don't you join us?" Melanie asked.

"How about if I sit here and watch. I've been cleaning Walter's shoes out and brushing him down. I'm a mess."

Melanie smiled and gave me a wink. "Of course."

I sat down next to Mike. When I glanced over to Alyssa, she was lifting her brows and motioning toward Chloe. Narrowing my eyes, I mouthed, *What?*

She sighed then rolled her eyes. I looked at Mike for help, and he simply smiled.

"Mike, Alyssa, how is the wedding planning going?" Melanie asked.

"Good! We pretty much have everything taken care of. Except for the cake."

Mike tensed next to me, and I looked at him. Were they still fighting over the damn cake?

"Y'all haven't agreed on the cake yet?" I asked.

"Well, some people can't make decisions like the rest of us can. They're too afraid to commit," Chloe snapped.

All eyes went to Chloe. Mike cleared his throat while Steed walked by and bumped me.

"Been there, done that," Steed stated, grabbing one of the just-baked cookies before he walked out of the kitchen.

Chloe watched her father and then looked at Melanie. "What does he mean by that?"

Melanie shrugged, but it was clear she knew exactly what Steed was talking about.

"I'm sure you will both work it out. Love is about seeing both sides of the story and listening to each other. Once you do that, you'll come up with the perfect cake," Melanie said.

I stared at Chloe. She was looking at the batter she was mixing. I wasn't sure if she had heard her grandmother's words or not.

"Alyssa, have you looked at cakes anywhere?"

"Yes, Mike and I agreed to go with Lucky's Cake Design. Her cakes are delicious."

"Mmm, yes, they are. Do you remember, Chloe, they made the cake for your high school graduation party?"

Chloe didn't answer Melanie. She was now staring out the back window, and I knew she was thinking of Patches.

"Do y'all remember when Patches came running full speed from the barn with his kids in tow? He was heading straight to that cake," I said with a chuckle.

Everyone laughed, and Chloe cracked a smile.

"I remember it!" Waylynn said, walking into the kitchen.

"Aunt Waylynn," Chloe said, making her way over and hugging her.

"I'm so sorry, Chloe Cat. I know how much you loved him."

Chloe wiped a tear away and stood next to her grandmother. She started to scoop the dough out of the bowl and place it on the cookie sheet. Each time she put one down, John would pick it up and eat it.

"John Parker! Stop eating that dough!"

"What? I like it."

"You're gonna get sick, Granddaddy," Chloe stated.

"Fine, I won't eat it. I will take this plate of already baked cookies and take it to the study, instead. I believe there is a baseball game on."

Melanie rolled her eyes, then looked back at me. "Keep going, Rip. It seems like that was just yesterday."

"He jumped that fence and cleared it like no other animal I had ever seen before," I went on.

"Yeah, and the little bastard distracted me while his spawn tried to take out the spread," Waylynn added.

"He wasn't stupid, that's for sure," Chloe said. There was so much sadness in her voice, it nearly brought me to my knees. I wanted to take her pain away.

"No, he wasn't," Melanie, Scarlett, and Waylynn said at the same time.

"How do you think he always knew there was a party going on?" Gage asked.

Melanie laughed. "Oh, that is simple. Any function we had, Chloe would make plans for Patches to be some part of it. I'll never forget the look on your father's face when Patches started walking down the aisle of his and Paxton's wedding."

Chloe grinned. "He loved being in weddings. I was hoping he would be in..."

Her voice trailed off.

Waylynn cleared her throat. "There will never be another goat like Patches. I don't know if that should make me happy or incredibly sad."

Chloe giggled. "He most certainly lived for tormenting you, Aunt Waylynn."

Trevor clapped his hands. "I came in here to tell you the games have started. We're playing Twister."

Mike and Gage jumped up.

Glancing back at me, Mike said, "I love this family!"

Alyssa laughed as she untied her apron and looked back at Melanie and Chloe. "I'm going to go join them, do you mind?"

"No! Go, and I think I'll join you. Chloe and Rip can finish the cookies."

Chloe went to argue, but Melanie wasn't having any of it. "Thank you for giving your grandmother a break for once, sweetheart."

Letting out a sigh, Chloe cracked a slight smile. "Of course. Go have fun."

When they all walked out of the kitchen, I looked at Chloe. She was back to focusing on placing the dough on the cookie sheet.

I attempted to steady myself before I spoke to her. When she looked up at me, I lost my breath. Her bloodshot eyes made me want to pull her to me and tell her it was okay to cry. That she could be both angry at me and sad about Patches at the same time. I wanted to hold her more than anything. When she looked away, I remembered Steed's words.

"Keep fighting for her, though. She's worth the battle."

Chapter 20

Chloe

"I'M SORRY I laid that on you today," Rip said. "You didn't deserve that."

Not daring to look at him, I shrugged.

"Do you want to talk about it? Patches, I mean?"

My gaze lifted to meet his. "I don't think so. Maybe. I'm not sure."

Rip's phone rang, and he reached into his pocket for it. "Excuse me, Chloe. I need to take this call."

I focused my attention back on the cookies.

"This is Rip."

I tried not to stare at him, but it was hard not to. My heart had been racing in my chest since I walked out of the cabin.

Rip loves me. Rip. Loves. Me.

I pressed my mouth into a tight line. *How could he tell me now? Today of all days.*

"Hey George, how is everything going?"

George? George Mathews from the bank?

"Yes. I recently started working in the accounting department at Frio Cattle Ranch. Did you need something from Steed for the closing?"

That caught my attention.

"The closing date is set already?"

He paused, waiting for a response.

"I understand that, sir, and yes, I have set money aside for contingencies. But the inspection said the house was in good shape. Anything that breaks down, I'm positive I can fix. They had it listed lower than I thought they would, so that will leave me some money to work with."

Setting my mixing spoon down, I wiped my hands on the towel and looked at Rip. He turned around and caught me staring at him.

"Wednesday at three. I got it. I'll be there. Thank you, George. I'm excited." He ended the call and put his phone back into his pocket. Then he walked over and took the cookie scoop and started to put more dough on the sheet.

Okay, so he wasn't going to share what that was about unless I asked. *Well, I'm not going to ask.*

Agitated, I said, "If you want to go join them in the other room for games, you can. I'm fine in here."

"Nah, that's okay. I'll probably just take off."

My breath caught in my throat, and I croaked out, "You're leaving?"

With a half shrug, he replied, "Well, I feel like I'm in the way here."

I chewed on my lip, tears building in my eyes once more. I had been angry with Rip but having him here with me really did make me feel better.

He took one look at me and added, "I mean, I'll stay if you want me to stay."

Our eyes locked, and I could almost see him silently pleading with me to tell him to stay.

"No, that's fine. If you have things you need to do."

"I don't. I mean, I don't have anything to do. I promised you I'd be here for you, Chloe. I don't want to leave."

This time I lost the battle and let a tear slip free. He dropped the scoop and cupped my face with his hands. I waited for him to wipe my tears away with his thumbs like he had so many times.

But he didn't.

Instead, he leaned down and kissed my cheek softly, making my knees weaken. I closed my eyes tightly when he moved to the other side and kissed those tears away.

His hand moved softly along my face and his fingers slid into my hair. "I'm so sorry, Chloe."

I opened my eyes and found him staring down at me. Was he sorry about Patches? Sorry for pushing me away four years ago? Sorry for telling me he loved me on one of the worst days of my life?

For a brief moment, I almost lifted up on my toes to kiss him.

Almost.

He let me go and backed away, his fingers running through his hair. "I didn't want to tell you that way. Not today, not when you were already so upset."

I wasn't sure what he expected me to say. When he looked at me, I felt my heart race faster.

Pulling my gaze off of him, I faced the cookies again and took in a deep breath. "I need some time to figure everything out, Rip. To process it all. I guess I'm asking you for what you needed from me that day I confessed my feelings for you."

He nodded and replied. "Okay."

"I miss my best friend."

He stood next to me, the silence between us like a brick wall.

Sniffling, I added, "I've missed you. I need my best friend back."

"I've missed you too, Chloe Cat."

Looking down, I slowly shook my head, fighting to keep my emotions in control. "Rip, I'm really confused and angry with you. I need some time to sort through all of this."

"I'd wait for you forever, Chloe."

I looked away. "I really wish you had told me that four years ago."

"If I could go back and re-do that day, I would in a heartbeat. I would tell you how many times I wanted to kiss you, tell you I loved you. But I can't, and that is something I am going to have to live with for the rest of my life. Knowing I let you down like I did. The one thing I never wanted to lose was your friendship, Chloe."

"Neither do I."

"You have every right to be upset with me, and I'll wait patiently for you."

"You? Patient?" I asked with a raised brow.

The corner of his mouth rose in that shy grin. The one that still made my stomach drop. I couldn't help but wonder if he had any idea that he would forever own my heart.

"You want to go for a drive? I have something I want to show you."

Smiling, I tilted my head. "Does it have to do with your phone call?"

His face lit up. "Possibly."

"What about all this cookie dough?"

"John will eat it."

I laughed, and it actually felt good. I was still angry, and we had a lot to talk about, but right now I needed my best friend more than I needed a resolution to this mess that was my life.

"Do I need to change?"

His eyes slowly moved over my body, causing my insides to melt. Rip had never looked at me like that so openly. I felt my cheeks burn.

"You're perfect."

My mouth opened slightly to say something, but I quickly shut it. Turning, I went about covering the dough and putting it in the refrigerator. The oven beeped, and Rip grabbed the mitts and took out the cookies. He then put the other cookie tray in and set the timer again.

"We should let everyone know we're leaving," I said, my voice shaky.

What is that about?

"Right."

Rip motioned for me to walk out of the kitchen first. As we got closer to the family room, I could hear all the laughter and talking. As much as I wanted to enjoy myself with my family, the pain in my chest was almost too much to bear. Every time I thought of Patches, I wanted to cry.

Rip and I stepped into the family room and all eyes turned to us. My mother stood and smiled. "Done with the cookies?"

"No, there is a batch in the oven someone will need to take out in about ten minutes or so. The rest of the dough is in the refrigerator."

Grammy walked toward us. "Are you leaving?"

If she thought she was hiding her hopefulness, she was wrong. I looked past her to see my mother wearing the same look on her face.

"Rip offered to take me on a drive. He has something he wants to show me and thought it might take my mind off Patches."

My voice cracked when I said his name. Then Rip lightly touched the lower part of my back, and my body did a one-hundred-and-eighty-degree turn as tingles zipped across my body.

Good Lord.

I didn't know if I should be mad, sad, or turned on. I'm a Parker woman, though, so it was possible to experience all of those same emotions in the same breath.

A part of me wanted to just go home, but I knew being alone was the worst choice I could make.

Rip must have felt my body's reaction to his touch, because he dropped his hand. Had he ever touched me like that before?

Yes. Plenty of times. Guiding me into a room. A gentle touch to let me know he was there. It had always made me tingle, but tonight, that simple touch set my body on fire. I felt the walls between us quickly crumbling, and those touches meant more now than they ever had.

"Oh, that was sweet of you, Rip. You kids be careful driving." Mom said.

Mike looked at Rip. A look passed between the two of them. It wasn't concern, more like Mike attempting to make sure Rip was doing the right thing.

Making my way to my parents, I hugged each of them and then granddaddy and grammy. "I'll just have Rip drop me off at home later."

"Sounds good. Have a good time, y'all," my mom called out as we walked out of the family room.

As we made our way out the front door and down the steps, I flashed back to the cabin earlier. Was it only just a few hours ago he told me loved me? Asked me not to marry Easton? It felt like a moment and a lifetime ago.

Rip opened the door to his truck and held out his hand for me. It wasn't anything new, something he had done since the very first time I rode with him after he got his license. I tried not to react to the way our touching hands shot a bolt of electricity up my arm and into my chest.

When he shut the door and walked around the truck, I took the time to take a few deep breaths.

"You're mad at him, Chloe. *Mad.*"

When he jumped into his seat and turned on the truck, he had a small grin tugging at the corners of his mouth. Whatever he was going to show me, he was really excited about it.

"Ready?" he asked, looking at me with pure happiness on his face.

"Ready as I'll ever be."

Chapter 21

Chloe

RIP DROVE DOWN the country road while I stared out the window in silence. I was glad for the quiet, and happy he wasn't trying to fill it in with stories about Patches. My own mind was flooded with memories of that goat. From the first time I held him, to the last time I visited him this morning.

"Tell me what you're thinking about?" he asked.

"Patches. I just loved him so much, Rip."

He took my hand and gently squeezed it. "I know you did."

I let out a little laugh. "Do you remember when you were helping Trevor paint the north barn and Patches charged you and nearly took out your knee?"

Rip laughed. "He was pissed because I had stolen your attention from him."

"He was so jealous of you. How many times did he try to take you down?"

"Too many to count. I feel like he sorta liked me, though. At times."

"He loved you. I know he did."

Rip turned down County Road 165. We weren't very far from my family's ranch.

"So, are you going to tell me where we're going?"

"The Durham Place."

It didn't take me long to figure out what was going on. "Rip! You're buying it?"

"I am."

A memory of me standing in Mr. Durham's kitchen flashed across my mind. I had been there with my father; Rip was there as well. We couldn't have been more than fourteen. I was entranced by the house.

When we had walked out, heading back to my father's truck, I looked at the white house with the large porch once more.

"I would love to live here someday."

Rip stopped next to me, his hands in his pockets as he gazed at the house. "I'll buy it for you, Chloe Cat."

I felt my heart drumming faster in my chest. Rip looked at me before focusing back on the road.

"What's wrong?" he asked.

Swallowing hard, I went back to gazing out the window. "Nothing. I'm just surprised you bought it. Did you have to use your granddaddy's inheritance?"

"Yeah, and I pretty much saved every penny from the time I was fourteen or so."

I turned to look back at him. Did he even remember that short conversation all those years ago? Is that why he started saving back then?

He turned down the dirt driveway. It didn't take long for the old Victorian farmhouse to come into view. It was exactly like I remembered it. I couldn't help but smile.

"Needs some fixin' up, but I think she'll be a real beauty once it's done," Rip said, coming to a stop, and turning his truck off.

Opening the door to the truck, I followed Rip up the steps.

"How did you know it was for sale?" I asked.

"Been watching it and had my ear to the ground. I knew once Mr. Durham died, it wouldn't be long before his daughter would want to sell."

"Did you already buy it?"

"Nah, I close on it this week. Laura Durham gave me a key ahead of time so I could start measuring for Mike to make new cabinets."

"Oh," I said, walking into the house first. My eyes scanned the living room, and I gasped. I'd forgotten how beautiful it was. Wainscoting covered the first half of the walls, topped by a chair rail. Wood trim outlined the beautiful old wooden doors and walk through. The staircase was in front of me, its impressive banister screaming for attention. Large plank wood floors spread throughout the room and into the next. My hand ran along the decorated baluster on the banister.

"My goodness, look at how beautiful it is."

"The floors are still in really good shape. I think I can sand them down and refinish them."

I nodded as I continued to follow Rip through the house.

"Here is the formal living room. The fireplace mantel is beautiful. I think it just needs a light sanding and stain."

Walking up to the large windows, I looked out. "Look how beautiful that view is. It's nothing but rolling hills."

Rip stood next to me. "Yeah, it's a beautiful piece of property." He headed out of the room. "The pocket doors are sticking, but I can fix that easy. Look at the ceiling here in the dining room. Look at the beams."

I looked where he was pointing. "It's beautiful."

"The trim in this house is beautiful. I'm so glad they never painted it white."

Hearing the excitement in his voice made me smile.

When we walked into the large kitchen, I scrunched up my nose. "Oh wow, this is...old."

Rip laughed. "It's a total gut job in here. Start from scratch. I can see a large island in the middle, though. There's plenty of space."

"I'm sure you'll make it beautiful."

He tilted his head for a quick moment before he started walking again. "There is a room here that I thought would make a nice office, maybe?"

Looking around the large room, I noticed another window that looked out over the hill country.

"I could see that."

"Come on. Let's head upstairs."

"How many bedrooms does it have?"

"Five."

"Wow."

When we reached the landing, I marveled at the space. I could already picture what it would look like with furniture placed about, wall hangings, the homey touch that a country farmhouse should have.

"So the two bedrooms in the front of the house could be gutted and made into one large master bedroom and bathroom."

We walked into the room, and I sucked in a breath. Floor-to-ceiling windows sat in a large bay area to the front of the house. The view was stunning.

"It faces the west, so you could be on the porch watching the sunset, or up here, in the bedroom."

I felt my cheeks blush as I thought of lying in a bed with Rip watching the sun sink in the sky.

"If we designed the bathroom right, the tub could look out the windows, as well."

"We?" I asked.

Rip shrugged, then said, "I guess me and Jonathon."

I tried not to let it show how that made my chest ache. For the briefest of moments, I thought he might have meant me and him. By the way he was looking at me, I think he wanted to say that as well, and was tiptoeing around the *us* in this scenario. Or maybe it was wishful thinking.

We walked into another room.

"The rooms all look to be in good shape. Just some cleaning and paint," I said, walking to a large picture window. No matter what side of the house we were on, the views were stunning. There is nothing like a Texas hill country view.

"Yeah, the bedrooms will be the easiest to do."

"What do you envision this room?" I asked.

He walked up next to me and leaned against the window frame. "What do you see it being?"

Turning to face him, our eyes caught as we stood there staring at one another.

I slowly lifted my shoulders before letting them drop. "I don't know."

He broke the connection and looked out the window. For a few seconds he seemed lost in thought before he finally spoke. "Guess I picture it as a nursery or something."

My eyes were back on Rip as he continued to stare over the countryside. I had to place my hand on my lower stomach to settle the nerves that had suddenly appeared.

"A nursery?" I whispered.

Rip pushed himself from the window. "Yeah...or something."

Swallowing hard, I replied, "It would make a beautiful nursery."

He nodded, then lifted his hand and tucked a loose piece of hair behind my ear. "You have to know the reasons why I bought this house, Chloe."

"Tell me," I breathed, my mouth suddenly too dry.

Rip took a step closer, and my knees felt wobbly as my stomach fluttered. When I looked up at him, our eyes met once again. The dimples in his cheek were on full display for me.

"I bought it for you, Chloe."

Whoosh. The air in my lungs vanished. Once I found my voice, I said, "Even though I was engage..."

I let my voice trail off.

"That day you looked back at this house, and you said you wanted it. I told you I would buy it for you."

My body instantly heated. With a slight head shake, I replied, "Rip, we aren't even together."

His warm hands cupped my face, and he leaned down, his mouth inches from mine. It felt like the entire room was fixin' to drop out from under my feet.

"I told you I'd wait forever for you, Chloe."

His hot breath hit my face and made me dizzy. I needed him to kiss me, but a part of me wanted to stop him. As if he read my mind, he dropped his hands and took a step back. I felt the absence of his touch ripple through my entire body, leaving me feeling empty.

"The, um, the other bedrooms are about this big. They don't have the large picture window, though."

I blinked rapidly, trying to keep up with the way he changed subjects in a heartbeat.

"Do you want to see the barn?" he asked, walking around me and heading to the door.

"No."

He stopped and looked back at me. "No?"

I let out a gruff laugh. "You're just going to say all that to me, act like you're going to kiss me, and then ask me if I want to see the barn?"

"You said you needed time. I'm trying not to push you."

Burying my face in my hands, I let out a frustrated growl.

"Is that not what you said?"

My hands dropped to my sides, and I stared at him. "I did say that, but then you go off and do this."

He frowned. "Do what?"

"Do what?" I asked, my eyes widening. "Do what! Rip, you bought the house I said I wanted when we were fourteen. You told me it was for me. You're talking about a nursery, and all these plans and I'm... I'm..."

"You're what?"

I balled my fists and said the first thing that came to my mind. "Pissed!"

This time it was Rip's eyes that widened in shock. "You're pissed? Oh Jesus Christ, this is classic."

Rip shook his head and walked away. I heard him heading down the wooden steps, and it took me all of five seconds to go after him.

"Rip! Wait!" I called out as I rushed down the steps.

Chapter 22

Rip

CHLOE REACHED FOR my arm and pulled me to a stop.
"Rip, please wait."

I looked down at her. Those beautiful blue eyes looked so confused.

Well, she isn't the only one.

"I can't do this, Chloe. I keep trying to do the things I think will make you happy and all I'm doing is pissing you off. I don't know how to make you less angry with me. I know, I messed up, and there isn't a day that goes by I don't wish I could go back in time. But I can't. No matter how hard I pray, I can't."

I let out a frustrated sigh. "If you think for one minute I didn't want all those things, too... The kiss, the date, the first time I was with a woman. If you don't think I wanted *you* to be that woman, then I don't know what else I can do. It was all I ever dreamed of. Hell, the first girl I had sex with I fucking called her Chloe. I don't think I have to tell you how that turned out."

Chloe looked down at the floor.

"I know I'm confusing you because I bought this house when you were engaged to another man, but I knew deep down in my heart, I *knew* it would always be you and me. You're the only woman

I've ever loved. I bought this house for you because I love you more than I love the fucking air I need to breathe."

Her head popped up, and I nearly fell to my knees when I saw her tears.

"Goddamn it. All I can seem to do is make you cry."

Chloe shook her head and wiped her tears away before speaking. "Do you want to know the moment when I finally realized I couldn't marry Easton?"

I didn't answer because I didn't want to think about her saying yes to that asshole in the first place.

"I was standing in front of some mirrors looking at myself in a wedding dress."

My eyes stung with the threat of tears. I blinked rapidly to keep them at bay.

She saw the hurt in my eyes and paused for the briefest of moments before continuing. "And a memory hit me."

With a cracking voice, I asked, "Wh-what memory?"

More tears rolled down her cheeks as she placed her hand on the side of my face. In a reversal of our roles, her thumb wiped a tear from my cheek.

"Me sitting up on the swing under our tree. You were eating that stupid apple," she said with a half chuckle, half sob.

Smiling, I stepped closer and wiped the tears that kept falling down her cheeks.

"I'm...I'm going to m-marry you someday, Rip."

I closed my eyes as the familiar memory replayed in my head. When I looked down at her, her chin trembled as she tried desperately to stop crying.

Running my fingers through her hair, then down her neck to her jaw, I slowly rubbed my thumb over her soft lips and whispered, "Okay, but we have to get married here. At our tree."

Chloe fell into me and buried her face in my chest as she cried. I wrapped my arms around her and held her tightly.

"I love you, Chloe. God, I love you so much, and I swear to you I'll make up for all of it. I swear it. Just give me that chance."

She grabbed my t-shirt and cried harder as I held her against my body.

I had no idea how long we stood there. I'd have stayed in that house all night holding her, if she needed me to. When her body finally stopped shaking, she pulled back slightly, her gaze meeting mine.

Her lips pressed tightly before she spoke. "I love you, too. I wouldn't have done it." She was fighting hard not to cry, but her voice shook with each word. "I wouldn't have...m-married him. I need you... I need you to know that. It's always been you. It will *always* be you, Rip."

Cupping her face with my hands, I leaned down and kissed her. Chloe instantly wrapped her arms around my neck as we deepened the kiss. My entire body felt like it was floating above me. It felt like heaven and hell were mixing together. Heaven, because I was finally kissing her. Finally hearing her say the words I longed to hear. And hell because I hadn't done this four years earlier.

I'd never experienced a kiss like this with anyone before. I couldn't tell where I ended and Chloe began.

When she moaned slightly into my mouth, my heart felt like it was going to combust in my chest. I dug my fingers into her hair, pouring everything I had into this one kiss. The kiss I had dreamed about more times than I could count.

Slowly drawing our mouths apart, I leaned my forehead against hers. Our chests rose and fell with heavy breaths. "God, I've been dreaming of that kiss for a long time."

She smiled. "Me, too."

"Je t'aime, Chloe." Her eyes lit up and the tears seemed to slow.

"Je t'aime," she whispered.

I placed my hand on the side of her face, gently running my thumb over her tear-soaked cheeks. "I don't ever want to make you cry again, Chloe."

"What if these are happy tears?"

"Happy tears?"

Chloe nodded.

"It hurts my heart to see any tears."

Her blue eyes locked onto my gaze. I swallowed, trying to settle all the different emotions swimming around inside of me.

She licked her lips, her gaze falling back to my mouth. I wanted more of her, too. So much more. But not like this. Not on a day when we were both emotionally exhausted.

"There's a dance tomorrow night. Do you want to go with me?" I asked, watching her eyes slowly move back up to my face. Then she smiled, and my breath stalled in my lungs.

"Are you asking me on a date, Rip Myers?"

"I am."

Chloe's finger traced my jaw, then outlined my lips as she whispered, "Kiss me again."

"Is that a yes?"

"That is a forever yes."

"Chloe," I whispered before pulling her against me. I pressed my mouth to hers. The kiss was different from a few moments ago. This one was filled with passion. Longing. Our need for more of each other.

Lifting her up into my arms, Chloe wrapped her legs around me. I pressed her back against the wall. Her hands slid to my hair where she gently tugged. Pushing into her with my hard cock, Chloe pulled her mouth from mine to gasp.

"Rip."

"I'm sorry. I can't stop myself from wanting you, but this is not where our first time together is going to be, sweetheart."

She gave me a saucy grin. "The back of your truck?"

Laughing, I kissed the tip of her nose. "As much as I want that, no. Not our first time."

Chloe tilted her head to study me. "Why are you blushing?"

I let out a small laugh and answered her. "It's just, I've always had an idea of what our first time would be like. Where it would be. The things I would whisper into your ear when I first pushed inside you."

Her lips parted slightly, then she swallowed hard.

"It wasn't in an empty house against a wall."

The corners of her mouth lifted. "Where was it?"

It was my turn to smile. "If I told you, it wouldn't be as romantic."

"Romantic?" she said, her cheeks turning a soft pink.

"You deserve that, Chloe. After everything we've been through, you deserve that and more."

Her fingers ran through my hair as she let my words settle. "I'll be patient, as long as you promise not to make me wait very long."

I laughed. "Trust me, I won't."

Chloe's teeth dug into her lip, and I felt the strain against my pants. She must have also, because her brows rose.

"We should leave," she said in a breathless voice.

"Probably."

I set her down and kissed her gently on the lips once more.

"Rip?"

"Yeah?"

"Are you nervous? About this." She gestured between the two of us.

"No. Are you?"

The most beautiful smile I'd ever seen appeared on her face. "Not at all. It feels so right."

"Yes, it does."

Chloe laced her fingers with mine as we headed toward the front door.

"When do you close on the house again?" she asked as I was locking it.

"Wednesday. Do you think you could be there?"

"Sure. What time and where?"

"Frio River Title Company, three in the afternoon. We can drive together. I'll be working with your dad that morning."

My stomach flipped when she reached for my hand again. She had no idea why I wanted her at the closing, and I had no plan to tell her ahead of time. Once we got to my truck, I opened the door and held her hand as she climbed in.

I watched as she took another look at the old white house. I couldn't help the bubble of happiness growing inside my chest and noticed that that empty feeling was slowly fading away. When I told her I bought the house for her, I meant it. Now she was going to be a part of bringing it—and me—back to life.

And I couldn't wait to get started.

Chapter 23

Rip

ISAT ON the sofa while Steed and Paxton sat across from me. Steed stared at me with an intimidating glare. Paxton, on the other hand, was grinning from ear to ear.

"So, you're finally dating her," Steed said.

"Yes, sir."

He nodded.

"And you're going to the town dance tonight? How fun!" Paxton said, excitement in her voice.

With a smile, I replied, "I think it will be."

"What are your plans for after?" Steed asked.

"The dance?" I asked.

"Yes."

I shrugged. "We haven't really talked about it."

He tilted his head and looked at me as if I were lying out of my teeth. "Really?"

Paxton cleared her throat and spoke in a warning tone. "Steed Parker."

"What? I simply asked what they planned on doing after the dance. Is that a crime?"

I grinned.

Steed sighed. "Honestly son, I was getting worried there for a bit."

Rubbing the back of my neck, I replied, "So was I."

Paxton walked over to the bar area. "I would offer you a drink, Rip, but you're driving."

"Chloe told us you bought the old Durham house."

"Well, we close on it on Wednesday, so it's not official yet."

Paxton and Steed both looked at me with a curious look and said at the same time, "We?"

"Um, ah." I could tell it was taking everything out of them not to smile.

"You made her a promise once. I see you're sticking to it," Steed said. "Risky play on your part, considering she was engaged to doucheballs."

In an attempt not to laugh, I cleared my throat. "Yes, sir, I am, and yes, it was."

"Wait, what is going on?" Paxton asked, walking back over and handing Steed a drink.

"You both couldn't have been more than what, fifteen?"

"Fourteen," I said.

He nodded and let out a soft laugh. "Right. Fourteen years old."

"Who was fourteen?" Paxton asked, clearly eager to hear the story.

"Chloe and Rip. They were with me when I stopped by the Durham farm. Chloe was enchanted with the house, so much so that she made a declaration she was going to live in it someday."

Paxton sighed and placed her hand over her heart. "Oh dear, Rip Myers."

I could feel my cheeks heating.

"Rip here made her a promise he would buy it for her someday."

Shaking her head, Paxton leaned closer to me and squeezed my hand. "Rip, you had to put an offer in while she was engaged."

With a half shrug, I replied, "I would have finally gotten my head out of my ass and fought for her. And maybe the house was going to be a bit of a bribe, if I was being completely honest with myself."

They both laughed.

"She doesn't know, does she? That you're putting the house in both of your names?"

"No, sir. She doesn't."

Paxton sniffled, and I watched as she wiped a tear away. "That is the most romantic thing I've ever heard."

Steed faced his wife, his mouth gaping. "Excuse me? I've done some pretty damn romantic things."

She bit onto her lip. "Of course you have! It's just, well, Rip is buying our daughter her dream house. That's pretty big, Steed."

He rolled his eyes.

"Hey, what's going on?" Chloe asked as she walked into the room.

I stood and let my eyes take in every inch of her. "Hey," I managed.

Steed cleared his throat. "You might want to tone down the look of lust there, Rip. I am still standing right here, and she still is my little girl."

Chloe's cheeks turned pink as she walked up to me. She reached up on her toes and kissed me. It was quick, but it was on the lips...in front of her parents.

"Does anyone care I'm right here? Watching all of this? Anyone?" Steed asked.

Paxton and Chloe laughed.

"Of course, Daddy. Here is your kiss."

After she kissed her father on the cheek, he sent me a glare. "I used to get the first kiss when she walked into the room."

"I won't apologize for that," I stated.

A smile played at the corner of his lips. "You shouldn't. Now, you two go have fun tonight."

"Y'all aren't going?" Chloe asked.

Paxton and Steed followed us as we headed out of the living room and made our way to the front door.

"I think your mother and I are going to enjoy an evening to ourselves."

Paxton smiled as Steed opened the front door for us.

"Have fun tonight!" Paxton called as we walked down the front porch steps, hand in hand. "Oh, *finally* they are together," she added.

Chloe laughed and looked back at her parents. "Mom! I heard you!"

"It's about time, darn it!" Paxton yelled.

With a shake of her head, Chloe looked up at me. "I have a feeling we're going to be getting that a lot from folks."

I opened the truck door and helped her in. "I'm right there with you on that one. Tonight should be interesting."

Chloe chewed her lip. "Especially since some people will think I'm still engaged to Easton."

Leaning in, I kissed her. "They won't after tonight."

She sighed and leaned back in the seat. "Oh Lord, the prayer chain is gonna be put on high alert."

I laughed. The 'prayer chain' should have been renamed the gossip text. It would most certainly be lighting up tonight after Chloe and I showed up at the dance.

We walked into the dance hall, and Keith Urban's "Coming Home" was playing. I smiled and wrapped my arm around Chloe's waist.

"Okay, here we go!" Chloe said, looking up at me with a wide grin.

"I think we should give them something to talk about right off the bat."

She giggled as she leaned up and kissed me. When she broke the kiss, her eyes were locked on mine. "I love you."

"Oh baby, I love you more."

Her nose wrinkled. "Impossible."

"Good God, is this what we have to look forward to?" Mike said, reaching out to shake my hand. Alyssa wrapped Chloe in her arms and whispered something into her ear. Chloe blushed and said something back.

"Damn, dude, it was nice seeing the two of you walk in together like that," Mike said. "Fucking finally."

"Yeah, it feels right."

The song changed, and Chloe and I exchanged a look. "Want to dance?"

She nodded and reached for my hand.

"As much as I would love to stand here and shoot the shit with you, Mike, my girl wants to dance."

Mike laughed as Alyssa came up next to him.

Chloe practically ran onto the dance floor, dragging me behind her.

"Let's show them how this is done!" she shouted over the song playing.

I took her in my arms, and we took off two-stepping. Throw in a little bit of swing, and we soon had a group of people watching us. The smile on Chloe's face made my heart flip and flop in my chest. Especially after last night when I sat in in Patches' stall and she cried until she fell asleep. I had carried her to my truck and up to her house, where Steed brought her in. It had been an emotional day, and I was glad to see her smiling.

After a few more spins around the dance floor, Chloe and I made it over to the table where Mike and Alyssa were sitting.

"Beer?" Mike asked me.

"Nah, not tonight."

"I'll take one!" Chloe said.

I kissed her quickly on the cheek. "I'll go grab you one."

As I made my way up to the little bar by the dance hall, I was stopped a few times by people wanting to talk. Lori Rhodes was one of them. I tried to move on, but she grabbed my arm and pulled me to a stop.

"So how would Chloe's fiancé feel about the two of you being together like this? Folks are talking, Rip."

I laughed. "Let 'em talk, Lori. They don't know shit. Chloe is with me now."

Her eyes went wide. "She's not getting married?"

I smiled. "Oh, she's getting married. Someday. And the guy she'll marry is standing right in front of you. If you'll excuse me."

Lori's mouth dropped open, but I didn't give her another minute of my time. I ordered Chloe's beer and a bottle of water for myself. The way back to the table went faster. I kept my eyes focused on the beautiful woman in my sights, and pretty much ignored everyone else.

Chloe was finally mine. Nothing and no one would ever change that again.

Chapter 24

Chloe

THE SOUND OF my father and Gage arguing outside woke me up. I couldn't help the smile on my face. How long had it been since I'd started the day with a smile on face?

Forever.

I swung my legs over the side of the bed. Drawing in a deep breath, I stretched. My phone went off, and I reached for it.

Alyssa: You're on the prayer chain this morning after your appearance with Rip last night. Word is Rip beat up Easton and chased him away, eventually winning back your heart. It's like out of a damn romance novel.

Laughing, I typed my response.

Me: Well, it could be worse. I could be the cheating whore who suckered her best friend into an affair while her poor fiancé was clueless in Houston.
Alyssa: Yeah, that would have been much worse.
My phone went off again, and I saw his name. My stomach fluttered.

Rip: Morning, beautiful. How did you sleep last night?
Me: Like a baby. I had fun last night. Thank you.
Rip: I did too. How about a picnic this afternoon? I have the perfect spot.

With shaking fingers, I typed my response. Why in the world was I nervous?

Me: I would love to. What time and where?
Rip: I'll pick you up around noon? Sound good?

I couldn't wipe the silly grin off my face even if I tried to.

Me: Sounds perfect. I'll see you then.

He sent me back a heart emoji that said I love you.

Me: I love you so much more.

The knock on the door made me jump.

"Who is it?"

"Gage. Can I come in?"

I walked to the door, and smiled as I opened it. "What do I owe this little honor?"

"Folks are starting to talk about you, Chloe. Dad jumped all over me 'cause I came to your defense today in Lily's."

Lily's Place was one of the best cafés in town. It was on the square, and my folks had been going there since they were younger than Gage.

"What happened?" I asked.

Gage sighed. "Well, some asshole said you were sleeping around and cheating on your fiancé. I informed him you were not engaged to the douchebag, and he called me a liar. So I hit him."

I gasped. "You did what?"

"I had to! He was questioning your honor. Plus, I can't stand the guy, so it was a good excuse to take him out. Anyway, Dad found out about it and just chewed me out and said I needed to come up and apologize to you."

"Okay, first, don't be going around defending my honor. I don't need you to. I appreciate it, but it's not needed. Second, you don't need to apologize to me for anything."

He lifted his brows, stuck his hands in his pockets, and rocked on his boots.

"Oh no, what did you do?" I asked.

"Well, I sort of told everyone you and Rip have been in love for like...ever."

I smiled. "That's pretty much a true statement."

He shrugged. "I may have suggested you might be moving in together."

My eyes widened. "What?"

"It was an accident."

"An accident? Gage, why would you even say that?"

"'Cause Rip is buying a house, you love that house, Dad and Mom said you would probably be moving out soon. It slipped."

I sighed. "Well, I guess it's not that bad."

He avoided eye contact.

"What else?"

"Someone might have suggested you were pregnant and that sent everybody running to their phones. The prayer chain is on fire."

My shoulders slumped.

Then my phone went off with a text.

Alyssa: You might want to know, you're now pregnant with Rip's child, about six months along according to Karen down at the beauty shop. Rose said you're not pregnant, but Easton walked in on y'all in the barn... having sex...during your engagement party. He broke the engagement off.

"Six months pregnant! Sex in the barn! Are these people insane?"

"It's been a slow year for gossip," Gage replied with a smug grin.

I shot him a dirty look. "Do not defend me again. You caused all of this, Gage."

"Right. Got that message loud and clear from Dad."

After taking a shower and spending way too much time in my closet, I finally picked a cute little light blue sundress to wear on my picnic with Rip. Every time my phone went off, I groaned. It was either Alyssa updating me on the ever-changing gossip, or someone texting me to ask if the rumors were true. When my phone rang and I saw it was Rip, I sighed in relief.

"Hello?"

"Hey beautiful, how is it going?"

"Well, I've been fighting off rumors you and I are having a baby."

"Wow. Okay. We sure work fast. That should be considered some sort of miracle considering we've been on one date and haven't had sex yet. What's that called? Divine inoculation, immaculate emancipation, something like that?"

I laughed.

"If it helps, you beat up Easton in one of the rumors."

"I like that rumor. A lot."

"Between you, Daddy, and Gage...I swear. I'll be the talk of the town for months with the way things are going. How is your morning so far?"

"Busy. I'm going to be heading over your way soon. You might want to pack up a bag."

"A bag?" I asked, my cheeks burning slightly from grinning so big. "What kind of bag?"

"An overnight bag. Get a swimsuit, sneakers for hiking, couple changes of clothes."

"I'm intrigued, Mr. Myers. Are you taking me off somewhere?"

"Yes, ma'am. You better believe I am. I mean, unless you don't think we should. I don't want to push or rush."

"Ignore that comment I made the other night. I was emotional and then you kissed me. That pretty much sealed the deal."

Rip laughed, and it made my belly flip. "I'll see you soon, Chloe Cat."

"Au revoir!" I said and hit End.

With a giddiness in my step, I packed a bag. It seemed our picnic has turned into a bigger adventure.

Chapter 25

Chloe

AT TWELVE NOON on the dot, Rip was at my front door. I opened it and smiled at him. He was wearing Wrangler jeans, his brown cowboy boots he'd had forever, a white T-shirt, and a light brown cowboy hat.

Be. Still. My. Heart.

Lord, I'd never seen a man so good-looking as this one standing in front of me. My insides shook at the idea of simply having him touch me.

"Hey, beautiful."

"Hey, you're right on time."

"Like always. Well, except for maybe four years too late? But we won't mention that again." He smirked at his little joke.

I laughed, because it was true. Since I could remember, Rip Meyers could be counted on for being on time for everything. I, on the other hand, was always running late. For everything.

"You've got your overnight bag packed?"

My brows lifted. "I do, and are you going to tell me where we are going?"

The corner of his mouth rose into that flirtatious smile I fell in love with so many years ago. Then my stomach dropped as a strange zip of energy raced through my body. Overnight bag. Oh my gosh.

Oh. My. Gosh.

We were going to be...

I swallowed hard. "We're staying somewhere overnight?" This time you could hear the nerves in my voice.

"Unless you're not..."

"I am!" I practically yelled. Clearing my throat, I calmly added, "I mean, yes, I am. Give me two seconds to run back upstairs, I forgot something."

His smile grew bigger as he sat down on the sofa in the living room.

I ran past Gage and barely noticed him following me into my bedroom.

"So? Y'all are going somewhere overnight, huh?"

Digging through my closet, I came to a stop and glanced back at him. "Go away, Gage."

He laughed. "Did you forget something?"

I placed my hands on his chest and pushed him out of my bedroom. "Go. Away!"

"Fine. I'll just go downstairs and give Rip 'the talk.' You know, since Dad isn't here."

Jerking the door back open, I grabbed his arm. "If you do, I will never be on your side again when you need me to convince Mom and Dad of something. Never is a helluva long time, bro."

He looked thoughtful for a moment. "Fine. I'll just go talk baseball with him. You might want to leave before Dad gets home, though."

"Thank you! And why do we need to leave before Dad gets home?"

Gage laughed. "Okay, do you really think Dad is going to be like, 'Sure, Rip. Take my daughter away for few days and have sex with her.'"

I crinkled my nose at him. He shrugged. "Dad will ask a million questions about where y'all are going. Then he will give Rip the lecture. The last time he lectured Rip, he scared him away from you for years."

My eyes widened in shock. "Right."

Rushing back into my bedroom, I searched for something special to wear. I had nothing. A few pair of Victoria's Secret matching panty and bras, but nothing sexy. I grabbed what I thought would make Rip happy and put it in my bag.

I took in what I had. A bathing suit. A towel. Some changes of clothes. My favorite big sleeping T-shirt that was Rip's from high school football days, and a baseball cap for my hair. A few pair of sexy panties, a couple lace bras. Toothbrush, soap, and sneakers.

"Dad just called. They're at Waylynn and Jonathon's house and are about to head home!" Gage called out.

I grabbed my little stuffed goat that Rip bought me when we were eight years old. I had yet to sleep a night without him. I stuffed it in my bag, and I raced down the steps. Rip jumped up when I came tearing into the living room.

"We have to leave! Now!" I cried out, running past him and out the front door.

"Chloe?" Rip cried, following me down the porch steps to his truck.

"Have to hurry. If my father finds out we're spending the night together, he is going to flip out."

Rip had the oddest smile on his face. When he pushed his hands into his pockets, I stared at him.

I motioned for him to get into the truck as I said, "Rip. I don't think you understand the severity of this situation."

"Chloe, take a deep breath. I've already talked to your dad. He knows where we'll be."

My mouth dropped open. "So we're not having sex any time soon?"

His cheeks turned a deep red. I loved that he had that reaction to my outburst. Was he just as nervous as I was? I was scared shitless, truth be told.

"Well, it was on my radar to make love to you, but your father is not going to be coming and dragging me away, if that's what you're worried about."

I swooned when he said *make love.* That was so like Rip to describe our first time together in such a real and honest way.

"Okay. I trust you."

He nodded. "Good. Now stop worrying. Did you bring comfortable clothes?"

"Honestly, I'm not sure what I brought. I sort of freaked out and started grabbing things."

Rip laughed and kissed me on the lips. "Well, hopefully you'll be free of clothes for the next few days."

My lower stomach pulled, and I almost moaned. Wait, I did moan. Rip's eyes turned dark with desire.

"Come on. Let's go."

I climbed into the seat of his truck and watched him walk around the front. If he was nervous, it didn't show.

Once he headed down the driveway, I let out a sigh. Being alone with Rip was always one of my favorite pastimes. I felt like I could breathe and nothing on this Earth could bother me when he was with me. I never had to be on my guard or worry. He had always brought such a calm to my life.

"Where are we going?" I asked.

"We're going camping."

My face broke out into a grin. "Do you remember the last time we went camping?"

"Hell yes. I'll never forget it. You ended up having to sleep in my tent because the tent you were going to use was ripped open, and Alyssa and Mike refused to not sleep in the same tent."

I laughed. "I was so mad at her. Looking back, I think they were trying to force us together."

"Yeah, I'm sure they were. It was so damn hard to keep my hands off of you that night."

This time I knew my cheeks were red. "I laid there almost all night wishing you would touch me."

Rip looked my way, a hint of sadness in his eyes. "I'm sorry, Chloe Cat."

I shrugged. "How many times do you think we both wanted to do something and never did?"

175

"Something like touch each other?"

"Yeah, or kiss. Hug like we were more than friends. Wish that we could simply be willing to take the risk for something more?"

"Too many times on my part."

"Me, too."

"Do you remember when Justin was going to ask you to the senior prom, and I grabbed you and jumped into the river?"

"That was naughty of you."

"It was bullshit of him to ask. Anyway, when we were sitting on that rock, I almost told you how I felt about you. It was right there on the tip of my tongue. If Mike hadn't called us, I think I might have kissed you and finally confessed."

I smiled and looked down at my hands.

"I'm so sorry I didn't take the leap when you told me how you felt. I was so fucking afraid of losing you, Chloe. I didn't stop to think about how I would lose by not being with you."

With a sigh, I replied, "I'm sorry I wouldn't let you talk to me after it happened. We've both been stupid, but that's all in the past. I only want to think about our future, Rip. You and me and being together with no expectations."

He reached for my hand and brought it up to his mouth, placing a soft kiss on it. "I'm going to spend the rest of my life showing you how much you mean to me. I swear I will always be honest with you and never hold back."

I believed him.

"I promise you the same thing. I think if we are ever feeling anything we need to talk to one another. Not hold it in."

"Agreed."

"One thing I don't want to talk about, though, is past relationships. I don't want to know how many women you were with before me."

Rip looked at me. "How many women I've been with? You make it sound like I've slept around."

I shrugged. "I just figured that a guy as handsome as you probably had luck. I know you dated that girl Morgan."

Rip pulled onto the shoulder and brought the truck to a stop and put it in park. He drew in a deep breath, raked his fingers through his hair, then looked at me. "I'm not going to lie to you and say I don't want to ask questions about Easton. Deep down, that jealous asshole who was too afraid to tell you how he felt wants to know. But this guy right here in front of you wants to make up for all the lost time and hurt I caused you. As far as other women, Chloe, there weren't very many. Morgan? She was a mistake I made when I first came back to Oaks Springs."

"Just one time?" I heard myself asking.

"Yes. And there have only been two other girls."

"Heather?"

I nodded.

"It's only been two for me. Will and Easton."

My jaw clenched tight, and he looked at me intently.

"Ask me, Rip. Let's just get this all out there."

I closed my eyes. "Will you tell me one thing that's been bugging the hell out of me? Why did you agree to marry him?"

Glancing at my hands, I pulled in a deep breath. "When he asked me, a million memories flashed through my mind. All of them were about you."

"Me?" he asked, clearly taken aback.

"Yes. When we were little. Our senior prom. That day on the rock when I'm pretty sure we were both about to tell each other how we felt. All the times I longed to hear you tell me you loved me. The times I wanted to tell you but was too afraid. Then I remembered that day I told you I loved you, and I think the anger and hurt from your rejection fueled my answer. I thought if I said yes, I could forget the future I had dreamed about with you and move on with my life. Deep down, I knew I would never marry him. Even moments after he asked me I was crying, but they weren't the happy tears that he thought they were. They were all for you and for the future I was throwing to the side.

"I didn't want to leave Oak Springs. My future is here. Working with Daddy on the ranch. Being near family. Being near you. It all meant more to me than Easton. Once I came back, I was too stubborn to admit I had made a mistake. The more Easton talked about our future, the more I knew he wasn't the one I wanted my future to be with. I think he knew it too, but was pretending it would all be okay once we were hitched and living in the same city. It all hit me the day I was trying on wedding dresses, and I remembered you and me in our tree. I couldn't pretend anymore that I was happy with Easton.

"We hadn't been happy for a long time. We hadn't even slept together in three months or so. His proposal was his last shot at trying to win me over. The crazy thing is, I don't really think he was surprised when I told him I couldn't marry him. He tried to fight for it, but I could hear it in his voice. He was always so jealous of you. I knew it was because he saw what everyone else saw. Everyone but the two of us. Or maybe we did see it."

We looked at each other, and I went on. "I wasn't just mad at you that night I said yes. I was angry with myself."

"Why?" he asked.

"Because in my heart, I knew that it was supposed to be you asking me. I knew you loved me, and I knew those weeks after you first rejected me you wanted to tell me the truth. I was pissed off and I wouldn't let you explain. I don't know, maybe it was my way of trying to punish you for hurting me. Rip, I saw it every time you looked into my eyes. I felt it deep within my soul. We both gave up on each other, and I don't ever want to do that again."

He reached for my hand and squeezed it. "If it helps, I wasn't planning on letting you marry him. I'm sorry I decided to tell you the day Patches died. That was selfish, but the thought of him being there for you, hell, it nearly drove me mad."

I smiled weakly. "I want to put the past behind us now, Rip. I want this to be about you and me from this moment forward."

The corners of his mouth rose into that sexy smirk. "I'm glad you feel that way. Now that we got all of that out of the way, let's head to Wimberley."

"Wimberley?" I asked with a giggle. "Where in the world is there to camp in Wimberley?"

"Baby, I'm taking you Glamping!"

I wrinkled my nose. *Rip Myers Glamping? This I had to see.*

Chapter 26

Rip

I PULLED INTO the driveway and put the truck in park. Chloe was sound asleep, making the cutest little breathing sounds out of her mouth. Reaching over, I gently squeezed her leg.

"Chloe Cat, we're here."

She opened her eyes and stretched. "Oh, man. I can't believe I fell asleep."

It had been an emotionally exhausting few days, and I was looking forward to spending the next two days alone with Chloe. Nothing but nature and the two of us.

Looking around, Chloe faced me. "Where are we?"

"It's called Sinya. It's an authentic safari tent that sits on top of a hill overlooking Lone Man Creek."

"A safari tent! That sounds like fun!"

She had no idea.

"Come on, they're expecting us."

Chloe and I got out of the truck and made our way down a rock path.

A woman in her mid-to-late thirties came walking out to greet us. "Rip and Chloe, I take it."

Holding out my hand to her, I nodded. "Yes, ma'am. Rip Myers, this is Chloe Parker."

"It's a pleasure to meet you," Chloe said as her eyes took in the surrounding area.

"Pleasure is all mine. The name is Kim Evens. I'm the owner of Sinya, along with my husband, Ted. Everything you need, with the exception of food, is in your tent. There is a grocery store in Wimberley where you can find anything you need. The outdoor fire is already stocked with oak, and you've even got a s'mores kit if you'd like to use it. You will have complete privacy, so feel free to enjoy nature in its finest glory."

Chloe's cheeks turned pink.

"Are we celebrating anything?" Kim asked.

"Us," I replied.

Kim smiled. "I like that answer. I like it a lot. Let's get y'all all checked in, and I'll give you the key and send you to the trees."

Chloe looked at me, brow arched and a huge smile on her face.

Twenty minutes later we were walking up to the giant safari-style tent that was sitting on top of a wooden deck. You could walk completely around the tent on the deck and the views were out-of-this-world beautiful.

"Rip," Chloe gasped as we walked up the steps and looked down at a waterfall. Birds sang, water rushed over the rocks below, and a warm, soft breeze blew wisps of Chloe's hair around. It was June and the temperatures were starting to climb higher and higher, but the weather for the weekend called for mild to warm temperatures. I looked at Chloe. She looked beautiful. Her blue eyes almost giving the sky a run for its money.

"There are five outdoor spots for us to use."

"Five?" Chloe repeated, a slight giggle in her voice. "I don't think I want to leave this deck."

"Let's go inside."

I placed my hand on her lower back and guided her to the door. The tent was exactly that. A tent. With high-quality plastic windows that went all the way around, and canvas, lots of canvas.

The tent consisted of two giant rooms. The first was the living room, small kitchen, and bedroom. A sofa sat outside overlooking the amazing view.

Chloe looked down at the wood floors and then back up to me. "This stain...couldn't you see it in the farmhouse?"

My heart did a weird little jump because she was thinking about the farmhouse. And even more so, since she hadn't called it my farmhouse.

"I can. I'll ask them what the stain color is."

Dropping my hand, Chloe walked into the bedroom area.

"Rip! Oh, my goodness, look at this bed. I feel like we're at a five-star hotel!"

"Well, it did say upscale camping."

Spinning around to face me, she giggled. "This is not camping, Rip Myers."

I lifted a brow and walked over to her. "Do you really think the first time I made love to you was going to be in a tent, on the ground, with people only feet away at the next campsite?"

Her eyes sparkled. "You're buying a house, this must have cost a fortune."

I shrugged. "Your happiness is priceless to me, Chloe."

She lifted on her toes and kissed me. "I love you."

"Love you more."

Chloe pulled away and walked over to a sliding glass door. It led out to the veranda that also contained a hammock.

"I hope this faces west so we can watch the sunset," Chloe stated.

"Me too."

Like a flash, she was past me and walking into the bathroom. "Rip! Rip, come look at this claw-foot tub!"

Smiling, I walked into the bathroom.

"Oh, I love this so much."

I leaned against the door frame. "Big enough for two, and if it wasn't, there is a hot tub outside."

Her eyes widened in delight before she headed out onto the veranda. "No way!"

Not only was there a hot tub, but an outdoor shower, as well.

We walked onto the deck that held the outdoor bathroom, and my eyes caught the shower. I wanted to do naughty things to Chloe out here under the stars. Very. Naughty. Things.

"You look like you're thinking about something happy," Chloe said, placing her hand on the side of my face. Her thumb brushed over my unshaven jaw.

"Oh, trust me. What I'm thinking about makes me very happy."

Her teeth dug into her lip, and she blushed.

"I bet it's along the same lines as what I was thinking."

Closing my eyes, I moaned before looking down at her. "I sure as hell hope so."

Chloe smiled, and it seemed to even make the summer day brighter, if that was at all possible. "Rip, I never imagined a place like this. It's beautiful."

"Mike told me about it. A friend he knew from college brought his girlfriend here and asked her to marry him. I told him I needed a romantic place for our first time, he told me about this place. He's wanted to bring Alyssa here, but it's always booked."

"How in the world were you able to book it last minute?"

Running my fingers through my hair, I chuckled. "Pure freaking luck. I called to see if they had a list you could be put on for cancellations. Kim told me they had someone call up last minute and cancel. For tonight and tomorrow night. So that's why this went from an afternoon picnic to an overnight camping trip."

"You're kidding!"

"No!" I replied. "So, I booked it, and here we are."

Her tongue swept over her lips. "It's perfect, Rip."

"I thought so, too."

And it was perfect. I had dreamed about the day I would finally get to make love to Chloe Parker. And doing that among the trees, with nature singing us a love song, was the perfect way to make that dream come true.

Chapter 27

Rip

GIVING CHLOE A wink, I said, "Let's bring in our bags then make a list of what we want from the store. Once we come back, I don't plan on leaving until we check out."

"Agreed!"

An hour later, we had our stock of provisions put away and Chloe was changing into shorts and a T-shirt to walk down to the water.

"It's a bit of a hike, so make sure you wear your sneakers. I've got a couple of towels."

When she walked out of the bathroom in cut-off jean shorts and a Texas A&M T-shirt that I was positive used to be mine, I felt my entire body warm.

"Ready!"

I couldn't help but wonder if she had worn my T-shirts when she was with that douchebag Easton. A part of me hoped she had. No wonder the jerk didn't like me.

I smiled internally.

Chloe talked the entire way down the trail about the farmhouse. "I know I saw at least one claw-foot bathtub in the house. Do you think we can get it restored?"

I fucking loved that she said we.

"Yes, I'm positive we can."

She smiled, and we walked the rest of the way in silence. Chloe's eyes were everywhere. Taking in the beautiful countryside. The sounds the birds were making, the rays of sun dancing through the trees. All of it was stunning. Nothing compared to her beauty, though. Nothing.

Once we came to the river, she stripped out of her T-shirt and jeans and stood before me in a bikini. For once in my life, I took in every inch of that body and let her see me doing it.

"You're looking at me like you're hungry for something," Chloe purred.

"Chloe, you have no fucking idea. Eighteen years of pent-up energy here, darlin'."

She smiled and walked into the water, glancing over her shoulder and using her finger to motion for me to join her. I had never pulled a shirt over my head so fast.

With a laugh that sent shivers across my body, Chloe dropped into the water.

"It's cold!" she cried out as I joined her in the very chilly water.

Pulling her to me, she wrapped her legs around me and pressed her mouth to mine. It was heaven. Pure fucking heaven having my mouth on hers. Even with the countless times I had dreamed of kissing her, nothing could compare to the real thing. I knew I would never tire of it. It would be something I longed to do every single day for the rest of our lives.

"Rip," she whispered against my mouth when we stopped to catch our breath. Every part of me wanted her. Right there in that river. She pressed her center into me, and I moaned in pleasure.

Ripping my mouth free again, I looked into those sky-blue eyes of hers. "I want you so much, baby, but not here."

Her legs wrapped tighter. When she dug her fingers into my hair and pulled, I felt my resolve slipping. There was no way our first time was going to be in the damn river.

I'll save that for tomorrow.

Just as soon as she embraced me, though, she quickly pushed away and attempted to dunk me under the water. I let her, making her think she got the best of me. When I pulled her under with me, she came up coughing and laughing.

"Not fair! You're stronger, and I got water up my nose!"

"You pushed me under the water! Did you really think I wouldn't take you down with me?"

She laughed, and I felt my heartbeat pick up faster. The way this woman made me feel was unlike anything I had ever experienced before in my life. She was my everything. Always had been. Always would be.

We swam to a rock, and I climbed on first and then helped her up. Chloe tucked her body between my legs and ran her fingers up and down my skin. We sat in silence, taking in the beauty of the place. This felt so right. Not just that I was with Chloe, but the location itself. It felt so...calming. I should be nervous as hell. Soon I was going to be making love to the woman of my dreams, and I felt like it was my first time. I had to laugh inside at that one. It wasn't like I had been a manwhore. Hardly. I hadn't lied to Chloe. I had only ever been with a few girls. The girl I lost my virginity to, Heather, actually knew how I felt about Chloe. We both knew our time together was for fun, that it would never lead to anything serious. But she had taught me so much about not only my body, but a woman's body. What to do to make a girl feel good. To always put the woman first. I was so awkward the first time, and she knew from the get go I was a virgin. I hadn't actually told her, but she knew.

After Heather, I slept with two other women. Nothing serious. Mostly friends with benefits. Something to take my mind off of Chloe. It never worked, and I was an asshole to think that sleeping with another woman would ever make me forget about Chloe.

I had already learned from Mike—who told me everything Alyssa told him—that Chloe had only had two sexual partners. I felt bad for knowing, but like Chloe had said, the past was in the past. It was time to move forward.

"It's so quiet here."

Laughing, I replied, "What is your idea of quiet? I hear water, birds, and I'm pretty sure that is a cow in the distance."

She dropped her head against my chest and looked up at me. "That's what I mean. It's not College Station...or Houston. It's like home. The only things you can hear are nature. I love that so much."

I leaned down and kissed her forehead. "You're getting goosebumps. Want to head back up?"

Spinning around, Chloe faced me. Her eyes burned with desire, causing my body to heat in an instant. I no longer noticed the cold water.

"I want you, Rip. I honestly don't think I can wait another minute."

"Me either. Let's go."

We swam back to the shore and slowly walked out of the water. I wrapped a towel around Chloe, then quickly dried myself off and slipped my T-shirt back on. Chloe put on her sneakers, sans socks, and started up the pathway that led to the tent. As we walked up each step, my heart pounded harder and harder.

The sun wouldn't be setting for another hour or so, but it was sinking far enough that I could still turn on all the candles Lisa had placed out on the veranda. It would give the romantic feel I was hoping for when the moment struck.

Instead of going into the tent, Chloe made her way to the outdoor shower. I could feel my pulse everywhere in my body, not just my chest. I was positive that if she spoke I wouldn't be able to hear her through the roar in my ears.

Turning to face me, Chloe tossed her shorts and T-shirt to the side, then dropped the towel. My eyes roamed over her body. She was perfect in every single way. When she turned on the water, I kept my gaze on hers. Then she reached behind her back, and before I knew it, her top was on the floor at her feet. My knees wobbled, and I had to remind myself to breathe.

"Chloe," I warned.

She gave me a saucy grin and tilted her head as she slowly pushed her bottoms down.

Standing before me naked, she took a few steps back into the shower. I yanked my wet T-shirt over my head. She watched every single move I made. She was chewing on her lip, waiting for me to drop my drawers and show her how much I wanted her.

I gave her what she wanted. She gasped as her eyes locked onto my cock. I would have given a thousand dollars to know what that pretty little mind was thinking.

When I started toward her, her gaze swung up and met mine. I joined her under the showerhead, cupping her face in my hands and kissing her.

"You are mine," I spoke against her lips.

She whimpered her reply. "Yes. Always."

"Forever, Chloe. Mine."

My hand moved down to her heavy breast, loving the way it fit into my hand so perfectly. I rolled her nipple with my finger and thumb, causing her to suck in a breath.

"Jesus," she gasped, wrapping her hand around my dick. I jumped at her touch, and we both chuckled.

"If I come like this, I'm not talking to you for the rest of the night."

A smile spread across her face and her cheeks turned red.

"You're so...big."

I lifted a brow. "And I can't wait to fill you."

Her eyes lifted, and a dark, steamy haze fell over them. Her chest rose and fell as I kept rolling and pinching her nipple. If she wanted to play first, I could fucking play.

Leaning down, I took her other nipple in my mouth, and Chloe cried out my name. The sound of it being said in such a lust-induced way made my dick get harder.

With her other hand, she wove her fingers into my hair, little moans of pleasure coming from her as she slowly stroked me. She was about to make me come simply from touching me and moaning. Jesus, I needed to take control.

I dropped to my knees and lifted her leg. Chloe tensed, and I looked up at her. Holy shit, if she had never let Easton do this, I was going to be going to church twice on Sundays. "Have you never?"

She chewed on her lip. Her innocence sprayed across her cheeks. "No."

I closed my eyes and said a quick *Thank you, Jesus*. Then I looked up at her. "Do you not want me to?"

Swallowing hard, she finally found her voice. "I want you to. Desperately. But..."

I already knew what she was thinking. How many women had I given oral sex to? We had promised the past was in the past. "It's only me and you now, Chloe. If you want to know, I'll tell you."

For a few moments, she stared at me while she worked it out in her head. "More than one?" she finally asked.

"No."

The corners of her mouth lifted slightly. "One?" she asked in a timid voice.

I wasn't about to lie to her. It had been one of my many lessons from Heather. I had only done it one time with her. After that, I told her it was too personal of an act to share.

"Only one person, one time."

She licked her lips and slowly nodded. I kissed under her belly button and her entire body quivered. I loved that I did that to her.

"I want to taste you, Chloe," I whispered as I moved my mouth lower. With her leg over my shoulder, I grabbed her ass and licked slowly between her legs.

"Oh, God!"

I smiled. This was going to feel good for her. Repeating the action, I used my hand to spread her more, then slipped my fingers inside her. Her leg gave out some, and I worked at keeping her upright.

I focused on her clit while I massaged inside of her. Chloe's hips started to move, and her fingers were in my hair, pulling my face against her harder.

"Rip. Oh God, Rip."

Yes. The sound of my name coming from that sweet mouth was like music to my ears.

"What...oh...oh..."

My fingers moved as I flicked her clit faster with my tongue. Adding another finger and sucking on her clit threw her over the edge.

"Rip! Oh! I'm coming!"

Her body trembled as she rode her hips against my face. She repeated my name, as well as other words I couldn't understand. She held my head against her, taking what she wanted from me, and I loved it. I loved that she had waited for me to do this. Guilt slammed me in the middle of my chest that I hadn't done the same.

When she finally stopped trembling, I knew her orgasm had passed. I gently took her leg off my shoulder and stood. She wobbled for a moment but grabbed my arms.

Our eyes met, and I knew I couldn't wait another moment longer. Picking her up, I walked us into the tent, both soaking wet from the shower. Chloe was shaking in my arms, so I headed to the bathroom, grabbed a few towels and went back to the bed.

Slowly setting her down, I wrapped the towel around me and dried her off. The way she watched me with that heated expression had me picking up speed. I dried off and picked her up again, making her squeal in delight. I drew the covers back and laid her on the bed. Then I pulled the covers up and over her. She frowned and looked at me with a puzzled expression.

"I need to do something really quick, and I don't want you getting cold."

Chloe simply nodded and watched me move about the room. The candles were LEDs, which made it easier. I simply clicked them on. One by one, the room slowly took on the flicker of the lights. The horizon outside was starting to make its own romantic glow. Soft colors of orange and pink painted the sky's canvas. It couldn't have been a more perfect moment.

Walking to my bag, I took out a few condoms and set them on the side table. Chloe looked at them and then back up to me.

Smiling, I took a nipple into my mouth and moaned.

Using my other hand, I explored her while I sucked and pulled. Chloe did the same with her hands on my body. She moved slowly. Tracing every muscle, every scar. It was as if she was attempting to memorize each thing about me.

I moved my mouth up to meet hers. We were soon lost in a kiss as I settled between her legs. She rubbed against me, causing me to nearly come on the spot. I wasn't sure how I was able not to, truth be told.

"Rip, please. I want you inside me, and I can't wait another second."

Looking down at her, I winked. "Your wish is my command."

When I reached for the condom, she grabbed my arm and said the two words I didn't want to hear right now.

"Wait. Stop."

Chapter 28

Chloe

R IP STILLED WHEN I told him to stop. A look of utter panic moved over his face.

"I mean, I don't want to stop this, but I want to talk to you about using a condom."

He nodded. "I've always used them."

"Same here. I'm also on the pill and I..." My voice faded, and Rip looked at me like I had lost my mind.

"What's wrong?"

"Nothing's wrong. Everything is perfect. It's exactly like I always thought it would be, with the exception of one thing."

He lifted his brows. "What one thing?"

I chewed nervously on my lower lip. When Rip reached up and pulled it free from my teeth, I let out a nervous chuckle.

"Chloe Cat, talk to me."

I glanced at the condom, and then back to him. "I want to feel you, Rip. All of you. I want our first time to be connected."

He didn't say a word. When he finally smiled, I let out the breath I hadn't even realized I was holding in.

"No condom? Are you sure?"

I nodded.

"What if..."

"Then it was meant to be. I want to be with you...as one. Like we were always meant to be."

Rip moved back over me, resting his weight on his arms. "I love you so much."

I pushed my fingers through his short, light brown hair and replied, "I love you more."

He rubbed his nose against mine, and I felt him *there*. So close to pushing inside of me. "Impossible," I replied.

The tip of his dick rubbed against my clit, causing me to wiggle under him for more contact. He moved his fingers lightly down the side of my body then grabbed my leg, opening me more to him. When he had taken off his swim shorts before our shower, I nearly swallowed my own tongue. Rip Myers was well endowed. I knew I would be feeling our lovemaking for the next week, and I was perfectly fine with that. I wanted to move and be reminded of this closeness.

As he teased my entrance, I reached down and dug my fingers into his ass. He laughed, then slipped his fingers inside me instead. I knew he was making sure I was wet enough to take him in. Being wet was no problem. I was on the verge of having another orgasm simply from thinking of him making love to me.

"Rip, I'm so ready for you. Please."

"I like hearing you beg for me," he whispered against my lips. I smiled and lifted my hips to him.

His eyes met mine. "God, I love you."

My heart slammed frantically in my chest.

If this is a dream, I never want to wake up!

He positioned himself again as we held one another's gaze. When he pushed in slightly, I gasped, and he stopped.

"I only need a moment to adjust as you go in. Please don't stop."

"I don't want to hurt you." The sound of compassion in his voice caused tears to well up in my eyes. The two other men I had been with never treated me like this. They weren't harsh, by any means, but they never looked at me with so much love and care. When Rip said he didn't want to hurt me, I believed him. I not only saw it in his eyes, I heard it in his voice. Felt it in his touch.

This man loved me, and I loved him. Everything was exactly how it was supposed to be.

"Chloe," he softly said, kissing the tear that had slipped free. "Talk to me."

"The way you love me. I feel it so deep within my heart."

He smiled and pushed in farther. My breath hitched, and I arched upward. It felt heavenly. He felt heavenly.

"I do love you. More than you will ever know."

His mouth pressed to mine. My arms wrapped around his neck as he pushed deep inside me. When he stilled, our kiss deepened.

Rip slowly moved his hips and I could already feel my body reacting. Building to what I knew was going to be an overwhelming orgasm. I wondered if he felt the same.

He pulled his mouth from mine and buried his face in my neck. Wrapping my legs around his body, I silently urged him for more. I loved the sweetness of his lovemaking, but I needed more from him. Longed for more.

"Rip!" I cried out, digging my heels into him. "More."

He lifted his head and grinned the same way I'd first seen him smile so many years ago. Back then I had thought he was just a cute little boy offering me his swing. Now, that cute smile had a hint of naughty in it. I smiled back, and he gave me exactly what I asked for.

And so much more than that.

I was soon crying out his name as stars exploded behind my eyes. Rip's own moans of pleasure mixed with mine, along with my name falling from his mouth.

We came together. Both of us tumbled off the ledge at the same exact time. Like it was meant to be. Like it had always been meant to be.

Rip remained still for the longest time after he came inside me. I felt positive he was just as moved by the experience as I had been. My fingers moved lightly over his back while his breathing, and mine, settled to a more normal rhythm.

"It was better than any dream I have ever had," he said, his nose rubbing my jaw.

"Mmm, I agree." I was in a blissful bubble. The air in the room felt crisp and clean. The smell of flowers floated, and I looked to see the sky was the most beautiful shades of dark blue with just a hint of orange and pink from the sunset.

"I'll never forget this night for as long as I live," I said. I closed my eyes and committed every single moment to memory. It would be tucked alongside all the other amazing memories I shared with this man.

"It's only the beginning, Chloe Cat. I want to give you so many more nights like tonight."

His eyes caught mine, and we both smiled.

Rip started to pull out of me, but I hooked my leg around him and shook my head. "I'm not ready for you to leave me yet."

"Oh baby, I'm not ever leaving you. Ever."

Dear Lord, my heart couldn't take much more of this man. I'd just had him, he was still inside me, yet I found myself wanting more of him. Needing more of him. Wanting to make up for all the lost time we'd missed.

"Let me go grab a towel. We have to get dressed."

I jutted my lower lip into a pout. "Why on Earth would you suggest getting dressed?"

He winked and then he was standing. Leaving me feeling empty without him inside me.

"Dinner is being delivered soon."

Thud went my heart.

There he went again making me swoon.

"Have you been reading romance books?" I asked, lifting up on my elbows as I watched him retreat. He had a beautiful ass. A perfect ass. And it was mine.

I giggled at my silly behavior. I was ogling his ass, for crying out loud.

Rip walked back into the room with a washcloth. He sat on the bed and used his hand to spread my legs apart. The moment the warm washcloth touched between my legs, I moaned. No man had ever done anything like this for me before.

Looking back, I didn't know why I ever thought I was in love with Easton. After sex, he climbed out of the bed, pulled on his pants and kissed me goodbye on the forehead. It was never anything mind-blowing. I had blamed it, of course, on my love for Rip. Or the love I had refused to accept.

"Chloe, if you keep moaning like that, I'm going to make you come with my mouth again."

My eyes jerked open, and I turned to look at him. I was positive he saw the desire in my eyes.

"I'll save it for dessert. Get dressed, baby. They'll be here soon."

I didn't move. Instead, I watched as Rip pulled on a pair of jeans and a black T-shirt. He walked into the kitchen and looked around. Did he have any idea how incredibly sexy it was to watch him? Bare feet. Tight T-shirt. Just-fucked hair.

Ugh, Chloe. Stop and get up already.

Slipping out of the bed, I almost wrapped the sheet around my body, but decided I was never going to hide myself from the man I loved. This was new for me. Before this I would never have walked around naked after sex. Now everything had changed, just like I knew it would, but this time it was only for the better.

I felt the heat from Rip's eyes on me almost instantly. I may have added a bit more of a sway to my hips as I walked over to my bag, pulled out some sweatpants and Rip's T-shirt, then headed into the bathroom. When I heard him groan softly, I smiled and internally fist pumped.

Chapter 29

Rip

MY BODY HUMMED with pleasure as I found some tea and put it in the Keurig. Chloe wasn't a coffee drinker, but I knew she loved a cup of tea.

I glanced over my shoulder and saw her head to the bathroom. I noticed she'd almost wrapped her body up in the sheet but decided not to. I was glad she didn't. I never wanted her to hide that amazing body from me. Ever.

My phone buzzed on the coffee table and I walked over to it. I figured it was about dinner, but it was Mike.

Mike: This is just cruel. How is it going? Have y'all done it yet?

Me: Done it? What are we in grade school still?

Mike: I'm going to guess since you have ignored all of my phone calls, and Chloe isn't answering her phone either, y'all did it!

I laughed.

"What's funny?" Chloe asked, walking into the open room. I opened my mouth but couldn't seem to find any words.

Chloe looked down to the phone, then back at me. "What? What's wrong?"

Slowly, I shook my head. "You look...beautiful."

She glanced at her sweats and my old Oak Springs football T-shirt.

"What?" she asked with a giggle.

Her hair was pulled into a ponytail, and she had the most stunning blush on her cheeks. I wanted to pull her into my arms, kiss her fucking senseless, carry her back to the bed and make love to her all over again. And again. And again.

"Rip? What in the world is wrong with you? Why are you staring at me like that?"

I framed her face in my hands and kissed her. Chloe's body melted, and she moaned into my mouth. My hands went to her backside, and I pulled her up until her legs wrapped around me.

Her fingers sunk into my hair, and I was walking her back to the bed, when I heard someone call out.

"Hidey-ho!"

Chloe started to laugh as I groaned in frustration and let her slide down my body.

"Looks like dinner is here."

I rubbed the back of my neck as I made my way to the door. The delivery guy stood on the steps.

"Rip Myers?" he asked, giving me a jolly ol' happy smile.

"That would be me."

He reached out and handed me two bags. "I have your order from the Italian Garden."

"Oh, Italian!" Chloe said from behind me.

The delivery guy glanced her way and nodded. Chloe took one of the bags and walked to the table on the veranda.

"The tip should have been included when I paid."

"Yes, sir. Thank you for that."

"Of course. Thanks so much for being right on time."

Chloe tried not to chuckle, but she heard the sarcasm in my voice.

"No problem at all. Enjoy your dinner, and that view!"

"Thank you!" Chloe called out as I walked over to the table and set the other bag down.

"It smells like heaven. What did you order?" Chloe asked as she pulled out plastic plates and silverware, followed by a loaf of the most amazing smelling garlic bread.

"Your favorite. Chicken parmesan."

She closed her eyes and let out a moan that went straight to my dick. I attempted to ignore how much he liked that sound coming from her. "I almost lost control there for a second."

She helped me take out all the food. "What was that all about anyway?"

I shrugged. "You walked out of the bathroom and took my breath away. I wanted you again."

She chewed on her lip and a slight blush colored her cheeks.

I reached for her hand and squeezed it. "You look adorable as fuck in my old T-shirt with your hair up in a ponytail. I can't believe how lucky I am, and a part of me is really hoping like hell this isn't another dream."

"It's not a dream. I already pinched myself a few times in the bathroom."

We both laughed.

"Has Alyssa been trying to call?"

"Don't know. My phone is in my purse. I haven't even taken it out."

"Mike texted. He asked if we've, and I quote, 'done it' yet."

Chloe rolled her eyes and took a bite of bread. I handed her the salad. "What did you say?"

"I told him we weren't in grade school. Then you walked out, and I completely forgot about everything else but you."

The corners of her mouth rose. "You are a charmer, Mr. Myers."

"I try."

"This is all so delicious. I was thinking we might have to have beer and pretzels for dinner since we only bought lunch stuff and snacks."

"Nope. I've got dinner for tonight and tomorrow night planned out. I figured we wouldn't want to leave, so I'm having tomorrow night's meal delivered, too."

She gave me a sweet grin. "I think this is my new favorite way to camp."

"Mine too," I agreed with a slight chuckle.

Dinner was filled with the two of us talking about our lives. Chloe told me about how excited she was to be working with her dad. I told her about a project I was working with Jonathon on an old historical building in Johnson City.

Chloe talked about Patches. She missed him and that broke my heart. When she was about to get upset, she immediately changed the subject. "So, are you excited about the farmhouse?"

I paused for a moment, wondering if I should tell her what I did. Without her permission. "Um yeah, I am," I replied. "Are you?"

With a tilt of her head, she pulled in a deep breath and exhaled. "Rip, you're keeping something from me. Tell me what it is."

My eyes lifted to meet hers. "It's supposed to be a surprise, but I'm starting to wonder if I should give you a heads up. Your daddy warned me about you Parker women."

Her jaw dropped in shock before she giggled and threw a napkin at me.

I quickly batted it away but met her intense stare.

"I, um, you see... I told the title company your name was to be listed as one of the owners."

She kept staring at me. Not saying a word.

"I did, after all, promise you that I would buy you the house. I'm just hoping you'll want to share it with me."

Chloe swallowed hard, stood, then quickly walked to the railing that overlooked the dark countryside.

"Chloe? Are you angry with me?" I asked. The glow from the tent's inner lights lit her up.

She turned to face me, a look of disbelief on her face. "Angry? How could I be angry with you for doing something so...so sweet." Her voice cracked, and I knew she was trying not to cry.

"I planned on doing it the moment I found out it was for sale. That house is yours."

She shook her head and wrapped her arms around her body. My heart dropped to the floor.

"No, Rip. That house is *ours*. The place where I want to build our future. I'm just..."

I placed my hand on the side of her face. "You're what, princess?"

Her eyes lifted to meet mine. "I'm so happy. I never dreamed I could ever be this happy. You're making all my dreams come true, and I haven't done anything to deserve any of this."

My stomach lurched at her words. "What do you mean?"

She shrugged. "I don't know. I told another man I would marry him while you were planning on buying me a house. You didn't give up on us, and for a time I *did* give up. I don't deserve—"

I pressed my finger to her lips. "Chloe, look at me."

Her blue eyes sparkled from the flickering candles as she gazed up at me.

"Look deep, because you'll see right into my heart and know that you mean the world to me. Don't you see it?"

She nodded as I wiped her tears away with my thumbs.

"I would give up everything if it means making you happy. If you're not by my side in this life, I'm lost. I've been lost for far too long and I'm never looking back. We're on this journey together, and someday I'm going to marry you."

A sob slipped from her mouth, and she pressed her lips tightly together.

"I'm going to make every single dream of yours come true. Every one of them."

Her chin trembled as she placed her hands over mine. "Rip."

Leaning down, I captured her mouth with mine. The kiss was soft and slow. Dropping my hands from her face, I picked her up, carrying her into the house. We spent the rest of the night learning every single inch of each other's bodies.

Saturday, we spent the morning hiking, then took a dip in the river. The afternoon was spent back in bed until we needed to get up and dressed before dinner came.

"That was some of the best brisket I think I've ever had," Chloe said.

"You must have forgotten what my dad's brisket tastes like."

She crinkled her nose and giggled. "It's been so long since I had his!"

"Speaking of my parents, they want you to come over for dinner this week."

"I'd love to."

"It won't be weird, will it? Mom is probably going to cry. You know how she is."

Chloe wore a wide grin. "I don't think it will be weird. When you picked me up for the dance, and I kissed you in front of my folks, it felt so natural. This all feels so perfect."

"I'm sorry about the gossips in town."

With a heavy sigh, she waved her hands as if to brush it all off. "They'll be on to the next prayer chain drama in a day or so. Besides, who cares what they think?"

"Not me," I stated.

She smiled. "Me either."

"I think we need to make use of that hot tub tonight."

Chloe looked out over the dark hill country and then up at the star-filled sky. When she faced me again, she winked. "Looks like nighttime to me."

Chapter 30

Chloe

A MONTH HAD passed since that weekend in Wimberley. We had closed on the house and moved in enough furniture that was handed down from our folks to sleep, sit, and eat on. Rip and I tore things apart at night. During the day, I worked at the ranch full-time, and he worked part-time with Jonathon and part time at the ranch. My father was against us moving in together right away since we had just started dating. It didn't take me long to change his mind. Rip and I had always been inseparable. Now that we were a couple, it only made sense. Plus, we owned a house together.

A house.

I smiled as I thought about the farmhouse.

"Do I want to know what is making you smile like that?" My father's voice caused me to look up at him. "I know it's not the new marketing plan you're coming up with."

I leaned back in my office chair and tilted my head as I regarded him. "It just might be. I do love my job, Daddy."

"Right. I've seen that look before, and that is not an I-love-my-job dreamy look."

"Really? What sort of look is it?" I asked as he sat down in the chair before my desk.

"It's more like *I'm-in-love-and-can't-stop-thinking-about-my-man* look. I've seen it before on your mother's face."

I smiled. My parents were madly in love with each other. So much so that I would often catch the two of them staring when the other wasn't looking. It was a sweet, long-lasting love. One that I knew I had with Rip.

"I am in love with him, Daddy."

He nodded. "I know you are, sweetheart. You have been for some time. I have to give you credit for realizing that before you made a mistake with Easton."

"It wasn't just loving Rip that made me say no to Easton. It was you, the ranch, Momma, Gage, Grammy, and Grandpa. I couldn't leave all of this. Not for a man I didn't love the way he needed me to love him."

Daddy pulled in a deep breath and slowly exhaled. "How is the house coming along?"

I could feel myself beaming at that question.

"Good. We've gotten the entire kitchen gutted. I told Rip I wanted to start in there. Mike is already working on the cabinets."

"What have you gone with?" he asked.

"Knotty alder. Glass doors, I think."

"I like the sound of that." His phone rang, and when he took it out, I saw Rip's name on the screen. "Excuse me, darlin'. I need to take this."

I nodded.

"This is Steed."

Dad's eyes met mine. "I'm sitting in my daughter's office." He pulled the phone away while rolling his eyes but smiled. "He told me to tell you he loves you."

I could feel the soreness of my cheeks from smiling so hard. "Tell him I love him more."

"She said back at ya."

"Daddy!" I said with a laugh.

"Yes, I did hear from them. It's all been filed and taken care of. You're welcome, son. It was my pleasure."

I tilted my head, wondering what they were talking about. I decided to let it go while I looked back down at the marketing plan I had been working on. I had a meeting with Trevor, Mitchell, and my father to discuss my ideas about getting our ranch name out there on the horse breeding side of things. Yes, we were a cattle company, but Mitchell and Daddy had been toying around with breeding horses the last few years and had done a good job of it. It was an area I really felt like we could expand on. Uncle Trevor mainly dealt with the cattle, but ever since his daughter Aurora started to show an interest in horses, specifically raising and breeding them, Trevor started to pay more attention to that side of the business. If he thought he could rustle his little girl into the family ranch, he was going to do it.

"That could be a challenge, but I think we can handle it."

I looked up at him again.

"I'll take care of it. Don't worry. Talk soon."

He hung up and I asked, "What will be a challenge?"

Rubbing the back of his neck, he replied, "Mitchell thinks we need another barn, one near the south pasture. Rip's been looking over the financials."

"Is it not in the budget?"

"No, it is. I just want the boy to figure out how to do it. If he's going to be doing the books for this ranch, he needs to show me he's got what it takes."

"I have faith in him," I said, pride clearly in my voice.

"So do I, Chloe Cat. The boy has a good head on his shoulders. I guess if you were going to end up with someone, I'm glad it's him and not douchebag Easton."

"Dad!" I wanted to laugh, but somehow managed to hold it in.

"I'll let you get back to work, Chloe Cat. Just wanted to come in and say hi."

When he stood to walk out, I stood as well. "Dad?"

He stopped and faced me. "What's wrong?"

"Thank you."

"For what?"

Smiling, I said, "For letting me find the right path."

"Oh Chloe, it was so touch and go there for a bit. I almost had to kick the little asshole's ass, but I knew you'd find your way."

I tossed a pencil at him. "You never did like him."

"I didn't. Neither did your brother. As a matter of fact, the first time you brought him home and he got so sick, I'm almost positive Gage put something in his tea."

My mouth dropped open. "What!"

He winked and headed out of my office. I smiled and got back to work.

Later that evening, I stood in the middle of the farmhouse bedroom, stunned by what I was looking at.

"So? What do you think?"

My mouth opened, then shut. Then opened again. I couldn't seem to find any words.

"Do you not like it?" Rip asked, clearly concerned.

"It's...beautiful."

"I found it at an old antique shop in Johnson City. Jonathon brought it back to his shop, and I sanded it down and then repainted it white."

The old iron bedframe sat in the middle of the freshly painted master bedroom we had finished painting grey yesterday. It wasn't a dark grey, but a beautiful light grey with a touch of blue mixed in.

"It's perfect, Rip."

He wrapped his arms around me and kissed my neck, causing goosebumps to erupt across my body.

"Want to break it in?" he asked, his breath hot against my skin.

When his hands slipped under my shirt, I sucked in a breath. Slowly he worked his way up, cupping each breast while he laid soft kisses on my neck.

"Chloe," he whispered, pinching my nipples through my bra. My head dropped back against his chest, and I moaned in pleasure.

His other hand unclasped my bra before I could register what was happening. He turned me around and lifted my shirt over my head, tossing it to the floor.

My pulse raced in my ears when he took one nipple into his mouth. I needed more of him. Needed to feel his skin on mine.

I worked at getting his pants unbuttoned. When I finally gained access, I slipped my hand into his jeans. He was hard and ready, exactly how I wanted him. My body instantly heated with the need for him.

"God, your touch drives me mad with desire," Rip breathed out.

"I feel the same."

We quickly shed our remaining clothes and soon found ourselves in our new king-size bed. Rip rolled over so that I was straddling him. The heat of his hard dick pressed against me, teasing me as I moved to feel him.

Rip's hands went to my hips. He lifted me, and I positioned myself over him, slowly sinking onto him until I was fully seated.

"God, Chloe."

My head dropped back as I rested my hands on his chest. I moved slowly at first until I couldn't take it. My orgasm was so close. I rode him hard and fast. Feeling him under me was thrilling, the sense of power even more of a turn on. Each time Rip and I were together it felt more amazing than the last. I couldn't help but wonder if it would always be this way. We came together, and I dropped onto his chest.

Rip's fingers moved lightly up and down my arm as we stared out the window that overlooked our property.

Our property.

The thought that he had bought this farmhouse for us still made my stomach fill with butterflies. I loved this man so much. Life felt so perfect that it almost scared me. I was waiting for the floor to be ripped out from under us any day.

"How long do you want to wait before we have a baby?"

His question stunned me, and my body froze.

"Maybe I shouldn't have asked that out loud." He stared at me, gauging my reaction.

I sat up, pulling the sheet up and sitting with my legs crossed as I looked down at him. He had one arm behind his head, propping it up. His brown hair was messy, and I longed to run my fingers through it. Those soft brown eyes were staring up at me, concern clearly etched in them.

"A baby?"

He shrugged. "I mean, we don't have to do anything right now. We've only been together two months."

I laughed. "You do realize you're doing almost everything backwards, Rip Myers."

Rip sat up and put a pillow behind him. He gazed out the window. "I don't ever want to rush you on anything," he said. "I want to enjoy days like this where we can lie in bed and not do anything. Spending time with you the last couple of months has been like living in heaven."

Smiling, I took his hand. "I feel the same way. I would be lying if I said I hadn't already picked out what our kids' names would be."

A wide grin appeared on his face. "When did you first have the names picked out?"

Lifting my eyes as if in deep thought, I replied, "I'd say when I was about thirteen or so."

Rip laughed. "Tell me their names."

I could feel my cheeks burning with embarrassment. "Well, if we have a little boy, I wouldn't mind naming him Brady."

"Brady!"

"Yes! What is wrong with that name?" I asked, poking him in the side.

"I was thinking Cayden."

My brows lifted. "When did *you* come up with names?"

It was his turn to blush. "Sixteen, I think."

Oh my. My heart melted, and I wanted to kiss him. "Sixteen?"

He nodded. "You and I were sitting at a party outside on the edge of the pool talking. Hell, I don't even remember what we were talking about, but you mentioned something about when you had kids someday. I wondered if we would have a boy or a girl. Maybe both. Maybe even twins 'cause of your dad and Uncle Mitchell being twins."

I must have opened and closed my mouth six times before I spoke. "You thought about us having kids?"

"Yeah. Looking back now, I don't know why we didn't just tell each other how we felt. It was pretty damn obvious we were in love with each other, even then."

Tilting my head, I asked, "What was the girl's name?"

"You first."

"Let's say it at the same time!" I giggled.

"Okay. One, two, three."

"Emma."

My eyes widened in shock. "Did you say Emma?"

He nodded. "Yep."

"How did you know?"

Rip lifted a brow and gave me a look that said I should know the answer.

"I've said it before?"

"Yep. Prom night our senior year. We were dancing, and you mentioned you liked the name Emma. That if you ever had a little girl, you were naming her Emma."

Tears pricked in my eyes. "Do you remember everything I've ever said?"

He let out a soft chuckle. "No. Only the important things that mattered to you."

His words left me breathless.

"When I think I cannot possibly love you more, you say something like that and I fall even deeper."

Rip looked back out the window, lost in a moment of thought. "Will you go on a picnic with me tomorrow?"

"Yes! I'd go anywhere with you. Where did you want to go?"

"Let's explore our little piece of heaven here."

"I love that idea," I replied.

He turned his head and caught my gaze. "I love you, Chloe."

I couldn't help but wonder where he had gone off to in those few short moments. Wherever it was, I saw something on his face. Fear?

Worry? Something had him uneasy, and I didn't want him to ever doubt our love, our future, any of it.

"I love you too, Rip."

He motioned for me to come closer to him, so I did. Snuggled up to his side, I watched as the sun began its journey lower in the sky. The sound of Rip's heart beating in his chest relaxed me to the point where I was fighting to keep my eyes open. I'd never felt so loved or so safe in my entire life.

Chapter 31

Chloe

THE LIGHT KNOCK on my office door made me glance up. Gage stood there, a smile on his face.

"Hey!" I said, making my way across the room to meet him. "What's going on?"

"You've been so busy this summer I've hardly seen you."

He rubbed the back of his neck and sighed. "I know. There's not much time between helping out on the ranch and hanging with friends. You know, trying to get it all in before we all leave for school."

I nodded, walking us over to the two chairs in front of my desk. Something was bothering him.

"Come on, let's sit down."

He followed me, not saying a word. Once we sat down, I watched him stare out the large picture window that looked down the hill and to the main barn behind my grandparents' house.

"What's on your mind?"

He let out a big breath and his entire body sagged. He was stressed about something. Probably the idea of leaving for school in a few short weeks. Gage had been offered a football scholarship to Texas A&M. The Parker family was well-known at that school, for sure.

"I don't want to leave."

I smiled softly and took his hand again. "I know it's scary to leave for college, but once you get there, it's going to be okay, Gage."

"You don't get it, Chloe. I don't want to go to school at all."

My eyes widened, and I was positive I wore a stunned expression. "You mean...at all? Like never go to college? Ever?"

He let out a nervous chuckle. "Yeah. Never. I don't want to leave the ranch. I mean, I have been working here since I could practically walk. I've watched Trevor, Mitchell, Dad, Jonathon, hell even Granddaddy. I've watched all of them over the years work on this ranch. I've studied every book I could get my hands on in granddaddy's library. I know what it takes to make this a successful ranch simply by watching the people who have already done it. What am I going to learn at school? How to run a business? Hell, Chloe, that's your job. That's Rip's job someday when Dad steps down. I'm meant to be in the dirt. With the animals. I know what nutrients need to be in the soil from watching and listening to Uncle Wade."

Our Uncle Wade worked on the ranch and was married to my father's sister, Amelia. She had taken a step back from writing to raise our cousin John Jr, but now that he was in high school, she had gotten back into writing again. She was writing mostly historical romance books, her one true passion.

"I don't want to leave," Gage said.

I squeezed his hand. I actually got what he was saying. I hadn't wanted to leave this place to be with Easton. And everything Gage needed to learn about running the ranch, he already knew. He wasn't the least bit interested in the business end of things. Really, none of our other cousins showed much interest in working on the ranch.

"Have you talked to Mom and Dad about it?"

He scoffed. "Please, we both know they are going to force me to go."

"You don't know that, Gage. Be honest with them and tell them what you feel in here." I patted his chest. "I think you'll be surprised by what they might say."

"Do you really think so?"

"I know so. Do you want me to be with you when you talk to them?"

He swallowed and nodded.

"Rip is picking me up for lunch today. He said he has a surprise for me."

Gage's eyes lit up.

"Wait a minute. Do you know what the surprise is?" I asked.

"Me? No, but the guy is always surprising you. Hell, he bought you a house, for Pete's sake. I can only imagine what he has planned next."

I giggled. "He is pretty amazing, isn't he?"

"Chloe, I'm really happy y'all are together. It was meant to be."

I chewed on my lip. "I know it was."

He stood. "Okay, well, there's no time like the present. Mom is here with Grams in the kitchen."

"I'll go get her. You go wait in Daddy's office. Family meeting time."

Gage pulled in a deep breath and exhaled. "I hope you're right about this, Chloe."

Giving him a reassuring smile, I silently hoped I was right, too.

Gage headed to Daddy's office which was next to mine. I walked down the hall and into the main part of my grandparents' house. I could hear Mom and Grammy talking in the kitchen. I could also smell cookies baking. I took in a deep breath as I walked into the kitchen, ready for the scent to fill my senses with warm chocolatey goodness. Instead, it made me sick to my stomach. I covered my mouth and gagged.

Grammy and Mom both turned and looked at me.

"Chloe?" my mother said, rushing over. "What's wrong?"

I shook my head and lowered my hand as the wave of sickness passed. "I just got so sick to my stomach when I smelled the cookies baking."

Grammy pushed my mother out of the way. Her fingers pinched my chin, and she studied my face.

"What are you doing, Grammy?" I asked, letting a little giggle slip free.

"Oh. My. God," Grammy said.

Then it was my mother's turn to do the same thing. She studied my face, then let her gaze roam over my body. "How long has this nauseous feeling been hitting you?"

They were both so serious, I couldn't help but laugh. "Um, once?"

"One other time? Or just this once, Chloe Cat?" Grammy asked.

I shrugged. "I mean, I had an upset stomach last night, but I think it was the pizza we ate. It didn't agree with me."

"Are you using condoms when you have sex?" Grammy asked, causing not only me but my mother as well, to start choking.

"Wh-what? Why would you ask me that?" I sputtered.

"Paxton, do you remember the story about the chocolate chip cookies with Steed and Mitchell?"

Mom's face lit up. "Yes! Oh my God! Yes!"

They grabbed each other and started jumping and spinning around in the middle of the kitchen.

"Um, listen, I don't know what time the two of you started drinking today, but it's only like ten or so in the morning. You might want to pull back some."

My grandmother brushed me off with a wave of her hand before she focused on my mother. "Now, let's not get too excited. It could be nothing."

"Right. Nothing. Or it could be everything!"

They both started to jump again. I rolled my eyes. "Okay, well, Mom, I hate to break up your weird little celebration, but Gage needs to talk to you and Daddy. He's waiting for us in Daddy's office."

Turning to face me, my mother took a step closer. "Chloe, sweetheart. Smell this!"

She shoved a freshly baked chocolate chip cookie in my face.

"What the hell, Mom!" I cried out, knocking it out of her hand. Another wave hit me, and I covered my mouth. This time, it felt like I was going to get sick.

"I knew it! I knew it!" Grammy shouted.

My mother started to cry, and I was about to throw up all over the kitchen.

"I need to...oh, God."

Barely making it to the half-bathroom, I leaned over the toilet and threw up violently. I could feel the presence of my mother behind me. Suddenly, I was hyperaware of every single smell. I started to sweat and wished I had worn shorts to work today. It was mid-August in Texas and hot as hell. What was I thinking wearing dress pants and a dress shirt, especially knowing Rip wanted to eat outside?

"Mom, I think I have the stomach flu," I mumbled before throwing up again.

She rubbed my back lightly, instantly making me feel better.

"Oh Chloe Cat, this isn't the stomach flu."

"It's not?" I asked, raising up and taking the wet washcloth from her hands. She was wearing the biggest smile. How in the world could she be smiling when I just nearly puked up my lower intestines?

"No!" She was beaming. Placing her hand on the side of my face she said, "You're pregnant, sweetheart."

I let her words settle into my brain for a few moments. Then laughed. Then quickly stopped laughing.

"I'm on the pill." It was the only thing I could say. Even though I knew being on the birth control wasn't one-hundred percent effective, it was damn close to it.

"I'm pretty positive, sweet girl."

"Mom, you and Grammy deduced I was pregnant because I got sick from smelling a cookie?"

She nodded. "Not just any cookie. A chocolate cookie. When your grandmother was pregnant with your father and Mitchell, the smell of anything chocolate made her sick to her stomach. Especially cookies."

I laughed, but it sounded like an uncertain reaction to this little bit of information my mother just dropped on me.

"But. But. I'm not ready. I mean. Rip and I have only been together for two-and-a-half months. We're not even engaged! Mom, you're both wrong. I would feel it. I would know if I was pregnant."

She gave me a sweet smile and took my hands in hers. "Yes, you are so right. You would know it."

And like that, she dropped my hands and walked out of the tiny bathroom and back to the kitchen. I pulled in a deep breath and let it out, allowing myself to think back to when my last period fell.

Oh hell, when was *my last period?*

I stood and looked at myself in the mirror. My cheeks were pink, but that could be from being sick. Looking harder, I swore something was different. I'd noticed the rosy glow on my cheeks yesterday, and Alyssa had even asked if I had been out in the sun.

Placing my hands over my stomach, I closed my eyes. A wave of warmth swept over my body and I knew. Deep within my very soul, I knew.

I was pregnant.

Without even opening my eyes, I knew I was smiling.

"I'm pregnant."

My eyes popped open, and I looked at myself in the mirror. "Oh my goodness, I'm pregnant."

Turning on my heels, I walked back into the kitchen. Grammy glanced at me but didn't say anything. My mother cleared her throat and said, "Your father wants us for a family meeting."

She walked past me, and my eyes caught Grammy's once more. She winked, and I couldn't stop the smile that lit up my face. I followed my mother into my father's office. Gage and Daddy were talking about something happening in the south pasture. Construction of some kind.

"It's coming along nicely."

"What is?" I asked. I hadn't been aware of any construction on the south side of the ranch other than a barn Daddy had mentioned a few weeks back.

"A new barn, I told you about it, Chloe," my father stated.

"Yep, I remember you mentioned it."

"Trevor thought it would be best to have some sort of shelter since we've been noticing more cattle grazing that pasture land," Gage said.

"They'd better stay away from my tree!" I stated as I took a seat at the conference table. Everyone chucked. "What? I'm serious. I plan on getting married there someday."

Dad cleared his throat and looked at Gage. "You called the family meeting, so the floor is yours."

Family meetings in our house had been pretty common when Gage and I were younger. I had called the very first one. It was after my parents insisted Patches could no longer stay in my room with me for what I called bestie sleepovers. I must have been eight or nine. Gage was about three. He, of course, was easily swayed to be on my side. But my parents won out. They said Patches would have the best stall in the main barn among my grandfather's prized horses. I honestly believe Patches liked it in the barn better. He was subjected to me dressing him up if he slept inside the house.

"Right, so I think I'll just cut to the chase. I don't want to go to college, and before you both launch into the reasons why I need a degree, I want to say that this ranch has been my everything for as long as I can remember. I've learned everything I know from the best of the best. I've already proven my worth a few times. I've given suggestions to Trevor, who says that if he walked away tomorrow, he knows I would do the Parker family legacy right. I don't know what a degree is going to teach me. All it's going to do is keep me away from here for four years. I honestly don't think I could take it."

My mother and father calmly looked at each other and then back to Gage.

"What about football? I thought you wanted to play," Dad said.

"Not as much as I want to be here. Chloe's back now, and this feels right. I know I'm going to hate leaving. Football is great, but it's not what I'm interested in doing with the rest of my life. I already talked to Chloe about it."

All eyes landed on me. "I agree with Gage. He isn't interested in the business side of the ranch, and he probably knows more than the professors at school about the practical side. He's got his teachers here...at Frio River."

My mother attempted to hide the smile creeping up her face. Dad nodded thoughtfully and then looked off in the distance. He was letting everything Gage had said sink in. Finally, he took in a breath and exhaled. "I agree. If you don't feel like school is your thing, then you shouldn't go."

My jaw dropped, and it felt like it went all the way to the table. Gage stared at our father, dumbfounded.

"Paxton?" Steed asked. "Your thoughts."

"I'm with you on this one, sweetheart."

Blinking, I shook my head slightly. "Wait, you're both okay with Gage not going to college. Not getting a degree?"

"I mean, would I like for Gage to go and get a degree? Yes, I would. I also know my son." Dad focused on Gage. "Gage, anything you do in this life, if you do it with your heart and passion, we're going to support you. If this is the path you feel like you need to travel, I'm behind you one-hundred percent."

"We both are," Mom added.

"Gage, I'm so damn proud of you, son. You don't have anything you need to prove to us."

My eyes filled with tears as I looked at my parents. They both amazed me. They loved us unconditionally and always made sure they never pushed us one way or another. It was so important for them that we learned things on our own journey. Just like with Easton. They knew that would never work, yet they let me work through it.

Catching me looking at her, my mother smiled. Something passed between us. I placed my hand on my stomach, knowing that no one could see me beneath the table. Would I be as good a mother to my children as she was? I prayed so.

A light knock sounded on the office door. "Come on in," my father called out.

I didn't need to turn around to know it was Rip. A rush of tingles swept up my body and landed in the pit of my stomach. I stood and walked over to him, wrapping my arms around him. He hugged me back and whispered against my ear, "I missed you, Chloe Cat."

I giggled. "It's only been a few hours since I saw you last."

He winked and then looked past me to see everyone else. "Family meeting?"

Gage was still sitting in his chair, shocked. Dad made his way over to Rip, reaching out his hand and shaking it. "Good to see you, son. How are things with the house? Chloe said you're making good progress."

"We are. We've got the kitchen, one bathroom and our bedroom finished."

"Probably going to have to start working on the other bedrooms," I said absentmindedly.

"Floors are next. I'm glad we had the second floors sanded first. We still have to stain them."

Rip talked to my father about all the little projects in our adorable farmhouse. I looked up at Rip. Could he see the change in me, if I truly was pregnant? Maybe that was why he asked about kids the other day. I glanced over to my mom. She stood there intently listening to Rip. Gage had finally snapped out of shock and made his way over. He reached out his hand and shook Rip's.

"I can help with the floor staining."

"That would be great, but I don't think we'll be able to get to it for another week or two. You'll be gone by then."

Gage smiled. "I told them."

Rip's eyes jerked to my father. He simply nodded and that was that.

"You knew?" I asked Rip.

"Yeah, Gage came to me for advice. I told him to follow his heart."

"You went to Rip before you came to me!" I said, my hands on my hips.

Gage lifted his palms in defense. "I need to head on out. Trevor is expecting me."

I kissed Gage goodbye and my parents hugged him. I heard Gage say, "Thank you, Dad. I love you."

Dad told Gage he loved him, and Mom and Gage left Daddy's office together.

"You ready for that picnic?" Rip asked. "I thought we could go visit our spot on the ranch."

I looked at Daddy and smiled. He laughed and shook his head as I said, "Yes, I'm ready."

Chapter 32

Rip

ITRIED LIKE hell to keep my hands from shaking as I wrapped my fingers around Chloe's. We walked to my truck slowly.

"How's your morning been?" she asked.

"Busy. Jonathon's got a job here in Oak Springs, and I checked on it this morning."

"Oh? What kind of job?"

"It's a chapel."

She gasped. "A chapel! Oh wow, is it for a venue?"

"No, it's just a personal chapel, but could certainly be made into a venue."

"You know I heard once about a guy who built his wife a small white chapel on their property. It overlooked the hill country. She wanted a place to go and do her devotionals each day, so he had it built for their anniversary."

"That was nice of him," I said, turning to look at her as I drove down the gravel road to our tree in the south pasture. When we were younger, we would saddle up horses and ride out to our tree. Once I got my license, we drove one of the ranch Jeeps. For that tree being so damn important to us, I don't even remember how we stumbled upon it.

"Do you remember how we even found this tree?" I asked.

I could feel her eyes on me. When I peeked at Chloe, her mouth was gaping open.

"What?"

"You mean to tell me there is something that you don't remember! I can't believe it."

Laughing, I said, "Tell me the story."

"Gosh, we were little, maybe we had just turned six. Jonathon and Daddy brought us to the river to go swimming."

The memory hit me like a bolt of lightning. "That's right! We were in the water, and you pointed to the tree. I said it would make a great tree for a secret tree house."

She giggled. "Yes, and I said there was no way I was letting my daddy put nails in it."

"We asked your folks to bring us there so many times. Your dad finally put up the swing you kept asking for."

"Yeah. How many times do you think we've been to this spot?"

"Hundreds."

"We'll have to bring our kids here." Her voice cracked like she'd gotten emotional.

"You okay, Chloe Cat?"

She nodded as she looked at me and smiled. "It's been a crazy morning."

"I have to pull over really quick."

She drew her brows in and asked, "Why?"

Pulling out a handkerchief, I held it up.

Chloe's eyes went wide. "Are you into outdoor kinky sex?"

I laughed. "No, but I can be at a moment's notice if you're interested."

"Maybe on our property, not my family's."

"Turn around, I don't want you to see my surprise."

"Well, this must be some picnic if I need to be blindfolded."

"It's something special all right."

Once I had the blindfold on, I put the truck in drive and made my way around the bend. I had been onsite earlier. Jonathon had his best crew working on this project and I was shocked by how much they had gotten done. I was working on the inside along with Mike and Jonathon when I had spare time. Mike had insisted on doing the interior wood, and I was glad Jonathon had taken a chance on him after seeing the cabinets Mike built for the farmhouse.

I drove for a bit to give everyone time to get to the chapel. Jonathon had already made plans for the crew to cut out for a few hours and head into town to eat. It was just family and friends.

"We have to be almost there!" Chloe said.

When I came around the bend, I smiled at the sight before me. The large white chapel looked finished from the outside, but still had a way to go on the inside. The large, blue, antique doors were one of my favorite features, and I knew Chloe would love them, since she had unknowingly picked them out.

"Okay, we're here."

"I'll come around and help you," I said, opening my door as Chloe replied she wasn't going anywhere.

Everyone stood off to the side so that when I took the blindfold off, Chloe would only see the chapel first.

I walked her up to our tree with the swing we had swung on so many times.

"Ready for your surprise?" I whispered against her ear.

Chloe nodded and pulled in a breath. "Wait. Rip. I have something I need to tell you."

"Um, right now?" I asked, glancing over to the large group of people.

"Well, I'd rather look at you as I told you."

"That would really ruin my surprise, Chloe Cat."

She chewed on her lip. "Okay, right. Then I can wait."

I smiled and untied the blindfold. "Keep your eyes closed until I say to open them."

Chloe giggled. "Got it!"

Reaching into my pocket, I took out the ring my mother had given me. It was my great-grandmother's wedding ring, and since neither Jonathon nor my older brother Dalton wanted it, it went to me. It was an antique, and I knew Chloe would cherish it.

I didn't go down on one knee, I stood next to Chloe so I could see her reaction. The way my chest was squeezing, I felt like I couldn't breathe. I went to talk and nothing came out.

Clearing my throat, I whispered, "Open your eyes, sweetheart."

Chloe did and gasped at the sight. Both hands came up to her mouth, and she instantly started to cry. When she turned to face me, I got down on one knee and opened the well-worn, blue velvet box. When Chloe cried harder, I fought like hell to keep my own tears at bay.

"Chloe, I know we took the long way on this journey, and like you said the other day, we're doing it all backwards and we are moving at warp speed."

She laughed.

"But I've known, probably since I first pushed you on that swing, that I wanted to marry you. You happened to say it first, but I'm asking you first. Will you do me the honor of marrying me, Chloe Parker?"

Chloe dropped to her knees and threw herself into me.

"Yes! Yes, I'll marry you!"

Everyone cheered, but I was glad no one rushed right over.

Smiling, I took the ring out and slipped it onto her finger. I heard the photographer clicking photos. She let us be natural, which was something I had stressed. I wanted it all to play out first, and then she could pose us however she wanted.

I stood and pulled Chloe up with me. She wrapped her arms around my neck and I lifted her off the ground.

"I love you so much."

"Oh God, Rip. I love you too, and I really have to tell you something."

"Tell me anything!" I said, hearing the happiness in my voice.

"I think I might be pregnant," Chloe softly said, but not soft enough.

The photographer was close enough to hear and stopped taking pictures for the briefest of moments. Then I heard the camera going again.

Oh yeah, sure, capture my shocked-as-hell expression.

Chloe pulled back to look at me. I opened my mouth to say something but was cut off by the influx of family members.

Gage grabbed me and slapped me on the back. "Welcome to the family, brother!"

"Oh, Chloe!" Waylynn exclaimed. "You should have seen your face. It was beautiful."

Steed reached for my hand, then pulled me in for a hug, "Well done, son. Well done."

"Thank you, sir," I managed to reply.

Chloe was being tossed from one set of arms to another. Demands to see the ring were coming from all sides. Had Paxton put out the all-call for the entire Parker clan to show up?

John Sr, Chloe's grandfather, walked up to me and smiled. He was the monarch of the family and clearly the one with the most patience. With a firm handshake, he said, "Welcome to the family, my boy. You've always felt like a grandson to me."

A lump formed in my throat. "Thank you so much, sir."

Then he jerked my arm toward him and whispered, "You hurt her, and I will break both your arms."

I tried to form words in my suddenly dry mouth. Finally, I said, "I would never hurt her."

He lifted a brow. "I'm holding you to that."

Chloe's gaze caught mine. She looked desperate to talk to me.

I put my fingers in my mouth and whistled. Everyone's eyes were now on me. "I love that y'all were a part of this moment, but my fiancée needs to get some food in her. If y'all will excuse us."

Catcalls and claps were heard as a few people gave us their final congratulations and hugs goodbye. Alyssa and Mike were the last to leave. Alyssa held up the picnic basket as Mike handed Chloe the large quilt.

"Congratulations, y'all. It's about damn time!" Mike said.

"If y'all are up to it, want to hit Cord's Place tonight?" Alyssa asked.

"I'd love to, if Rip feels like it," Chloe said.

"Yeah, a night out would be nice. I feel like all we do is go home and work on the farmhouse."

Mike nodded. "I need a break from church pews and cabinets, anyway."

"You're making the church pews?" Chloe asked.

Pointing to the chapel behind him, Mike said, "You're gonna need places for your friends and family to sit when y'all tie the knot."

I could see the tears in Chloe's eyes building.

"We're going to head out. Y'all enjoy this beautiful day. It's unusually cool for mid-August. That little front moved down just in time to take the heat out of the air," Alyssa said, clearly aware that Chloe was holding back her emotions.

Chloe walked up and kissed her best friend on the cheek. "Thank you so much for the picnic stuff, Alyssa. Love you."

"Love you back. See y'all later tonight!" Alyssa called out as Mike took her hand and led them to his truck.

"See y'all!"

"Bye!" we said.

When Mike and Alyssa got in the truck, I turned to find Chloe laying out the quilt. I set the basket down and walked up to her, taking her in my arms and holding her. It didn't take her long to start crying.

"It's okay, baby. I swear to you, everything is beautifully okay."

She grabbed my T-shirt and attempted to stop crying but only made herself sob more intently.

Smiling, I kissed the top of her head and squeezed her closer to me. "A baby, huh?"

Chloe drew back. Those big ol' sky blue eyes sparkled as her gaze locked on mine. "I guess my confidence in the pill was slightly overrated."

Laughing, I cupped her face in my hands and kissed her with everything I had. Chloe moaned into my mouth as she held onto my arms. When I withdrew from her lips, I rested my forehead on hers.

"What are you thinking?" she softly asked.

"I'm wondering about the likelihood of you having twins."

Chloe busted out laughing. "Let's hope not too high."

I stepped back and took her hands in mine. "Tell me what you're thinking, Chloe."

"Well, I'm not sure. I could just have a stomach bug, but I feel different. I feel content. Happy. Overjoyed! We're getting married!"

Smiling, I placed my finger on her chin. "No matter what happens, if we're pregnant or not, I'm the happiest I've ever been in my entire life."

"Rip, you had a chapel built at our spot! When? How?" she asked with a chuckle.

I glanced at the white building. "About a week after we moved into the farmhouse, I got to thinking about our spot. I knew someday we'd be married here. We were at the antique store in Waco, and you were looking at those blue doors. You made a comment about how pretty they would look against a white building, like an old chapel. The idea struck me to build a little chapel here on the ranch. I remembered hearing you and your father talk about capitalizing on the ranch in other ways to bring in money. I talked to Trevor, Steed, and your grandparents about my idea for the chapel and suggested that it could be used for other events. Maybe even possibly a wedding venue if that was something they wanted to look at in the future."

"Rip, that's a great idea! And the cabin is not that far away from this spot. We might even be able to even put a few other cabins on the property. A bridal suite, somewhere the bridal party could get ready."

"That old barn around the bend could easily be restored as a reception hall. Hell, even the spring fling could be held there."

"Yes!" Chloe cried.

I could see her mind swirling with ideas.

"May I see the inside of the chapel?" she asked.

"Yes! It's not finished yet, but come on, I'll show you."

With her hand in mine, we walked over to the chapel.

"It's an open-air chapel. The sides will all have a heavy-duty vinyl that can be either lifted to let the breeze blow through, or drawn down to keep heat or air in. I wasn't sure what time of year you wanted to get married."

"Rip! Those are the same doors we saw in Waco!"

"They are indeed. The same ones that sparked this idea."

Chloe squealed next to me. "I told you they would look beautiful against white!"

I chuckled. "You were right."

Opening the doors, we walked into the large room. At the very end was a high rock wall with three cathedral windows. A small raised altar area sat under the windows. That would be where Chloe and I exchanged our vows.

"Those windows. They are beautiful."

"They are stunning. The vaulted, open ceiling adds to the large room and we will have ceiling fans as well as chandeliers."

Chloe looked up. Then around the room. "How many pews will fit in here?"

"Hopefully enough for the whole Parker clan."

She scoffed and hit me lightly on the stomach. "Fifteen long pews on each side. It will fit about three hundred people in here. The bell tower, will it hold a real bell?"

I smiled. "Do you want it to?"

"Yes!" she replied, excited. "As the married couples leave, they can ring the bell."

"That's a great idea."

"Rip, I know the perfect antique table that could fit under those windows. It could serve as an altar. It's long enough that it would fit under all three windows."

I nodded. "Chloe, do you want to dig into this project when we have the farmhouse remodel going on as well?"

She faced me. "Do I want to? I have to! This is where we're getting married! This is going to be the most beautiful place within a hundred miles for many couples *after* us to get married!"

Smiling, I asked, "So I take it you like it?"

"Like it? Rip Myers, I love it! Our baby, whenever we have one, we can have him or her baptized in here as well."

My arms wrapped around her. "I love that idea, Chloe."

Her head dropped to my chest. "Rip, this is the most beautiful gift anyone has ever given me. Thank you."

"Anything for you, Chloe. Anything."

Chapter 33

Rip

AFTER LOOKING THE chapel over from top to bottom, Chloe pulled out her phone and started making notes.

"Jonathon isn't going to be upset, is he?" she asked as I poured water into a plastic cup. We were sitting under our tree with the chapel to our left, and the view of the river farther down the pasture directly in front of us.

"Why would he be upset?"

She shrugged. "Well, I'm coming in and starting to toss around ideas."

"It's my project...*our* project. John and I hired Jonathon as the contractor."

"Granddaddy? Is he financing it all?"

I nodded. "When I told him my idea, he was the first to jump on board. Of course, I think the idea of his first grandchild getting married on the family ranch was good motivation."

"I imagine. Trevor was on board with it? I thought they were letting more cattle on this side of the ranch."

Rip pulled his brows in tight then he laughed. "Oh, the whole 'building a new barn' thing."

Chloe rolled her eyes. "That was a fib to throw me off!"

"Yes, ma'am, it was."

I took a bite of the egg salad sandwich Alyssa had made for us. Chloe followed my lead and then stared at the chapel.

"The old barn, how many square feet would you say it was?"

"Don't know. Maybe six thousand. It was one of the original barns on the ranch, Trevor said. It's pretty big on the inside. It would really make a great reception hall."

Chloe was deep in thought before she spoke. "I don't think we could have that done in time for our reception."

"When did you want to get married? You know there is no rush."

"I've waited nearly my entire life for you to ask me to marry you, and you want me to wait? You have heard about us Parker women, right?"

"Darlin', I'd marry you right now if you wanted to."

She tilted her head. "What about your chapel?"

I shrugged. "We can have two weddings."

Chloe's eyes seemed to light up. "If I said I wanted to run to the justice of the peace right now and get married, you'd do it?"

"Yes! Hell, Chloe, I've been waiting for the moment I could make you Mrs. Rip Myers."

Her cheeks flushed red. "How long would it take to get a marriage license?"

"Wait. Are you serious?"

"We've shared our entire journey with everyone on the outside looking in. Yes, I want to have a wedding with my parents and our families there, but a part of me wants it to be just you and me."

"And baby makes three?"

She grinned. "If that is the case, then yes."

"Today?"

"Right now."

"Right now. Then we can plan our perfect wedding here in our spot."

"You're crazy, Chloe."

"Crazy in love with you."

I looked at the chapel, then back to her. I stood and reached for her hands. "Let's do it."

An hour later, Dorothy Hilder in the county clerk's office stared at Chloe and me. "You want a marriage license today?"

"Yes," Chloe said with a polite smile. "We have an appointment with Judge Brody Brodbeck in an hour."

"To be married?" Dorothy whispered.

"Yes," Chloe and I replied at the same time.

Dorothy's eyes bounced between us. "Your parents are going to whip your behinds if they find out you eloped!"

"They won't, Dorothy. I mean, as long as you can keep a secret."

"We're having a wedding. We just want to take the pressure off," Chloe stated.

"I was not born yesterday, and I know the two of you have been itching to be with each other. Truth be told, Chloe, when we all heard you were engaged to a city boy...well, we wondered if he done hit you on the head and made you lose your memory."

Leaning in closer, I whispered, "I thought the same thing."

Chloe punched me in the arm. "Dorothy, please, can we get the license?"

With a long, loud sigh, she pushed back in her chair. "Well, I suppose. It is sort of romantic."

Wrapping her arm around mine, Chloe looked up at me, a wide grin on her beautiful face.

"You're sure about this?"

"We're practically married now. We live together. Own a house together."

Neither of us said what we were both thinking.

Could be having a baby together.

After a few minutes of waiting, Dorothy appeared with a piece of paper. "Here you kids go. Congratulations. I better be invited to the fake wedding."

With an excited giggle, Chloe took the paper and then threw herself into my arms.

As we walked out of the county clerk's office, I called Mike while Chloe called Alyssa. An hour later, the four of us stood in Judge Brodbeck's office. Mike was covered in sawdust from not having enough time to change. I was dressed in jeans and a black T-shirt with my favorite cowboy hat that had seen its best days back in high school. My shirt had the name of Jonathon's construction company on it, which added a nice family touch. Chloe wore dress pants and a dress shirt and was the only one who looked dressed for the occasion of an elopement at the justice of the peace. Alyssa had us all beat. She had gone home after I asked Chloe to marry me and changed into cut-off sweat pants with a white tank top that had purple paint dripped on it. And her hair was piled on her head with two pencils sticking out on either side.

Judge Brodbeck looked down the line at each of us. Then he lifted his brows and started the ceremony after clearing his throat.

My knees shook as I thought about what we were doing. I wasn't sure if Chloe had temporarily lost her mind, if she was worried she was pregnant, or she simply really wanted to be my wife. I was hoping it was the latter.

"Repeat after me, Rip. I, Rip Myers, in the presence of..." Judge Brodbeck looked at Mike then Alyssa. "Um, in the presence of these witnesses, do take you, Chloe Parker, to be my lawful wedded wife, to have and to hold, from this day forward, for better, for worse, for richer, for poorer, in sickness and in health, to love and cherish, till death do us part."

I stared at him. The only thing I could hear was the pounding of my heart in my ears.

Everyone turned and looked at me. "Wait, I don't remember a thing you just said."

Chloe giggled and Judge Brodbeck shook his head. "Son, have you been drinking?"

"No, sir. I honestly am so damn nervous that I can't remember what you said."

Squeezing my hand, Chloe lifted up on her toes and kissed me on the cheek. "Just say I do."

"I do. I do a million times over."

The judge smiled.

"Chloe, repeat after—"

"I do." Chloe blurted out. "Boy, howdy, do I ever."

Mike let out a small whoop as Alyssa said, "That's my girl! Get right to it!"

The judge let out a frustrated sigh. "Fine, you both do. I now pronounce you Mr. and Mrs. Rip Myers. You may kiss your bride."

Chloe and I faced each other. Then she started to laugh. "Oh my God! Rip, we just got married!"

"We did."

"Kiss me!" she demanded.

Framing her delicate face in my hands, I did exactly that. We were soon lost in the kiss, and I barely heard the judge speak.

"I'll need both witnesses to sign the marriage license, please."

When our lips parted, I looked into her eyes. "Hello, Mrs. Myers."

Her eyes were so blue they reminded me of what the sky looks like after a spring rain shower.

"Hey there, Mr. Myers."

"I cannot believe y'all got married the day you got engaged!" Alyssa said, hugging us both.

"Hell, I can. It's about damn time!" Mike said, bear hugging the three of us.

Chapter 34

Chloe

A WEEK HAD passed since Rip and I had secretly gotten married. We'd gone back to the farmhouse after we both took the afternoon off, consummated our marriage, then went out to Cord's Place and celebrated with our two best friends. I skipped on any alcohol, stating I was the designated driver. Rip nursed two beers all night.

I couldn't count how many times I glanced down at the twist of paper that was tied around my ring finger and tucked nicely against the antique oval diamond ring. It was our last-minute wedding band.

As far as my *stomach flu,* I still had it. And the smell of chocolate-anything still seemed to be the worst trigger. That and the smell of sweet tea. Sweet tea of all things. Every day Grammy brought me a large mug of it and set it on my desk. I somehow managed to keep the green from my face, and the moment she left, I dumped it out the window.

Rip had been bugging me to buy a pregnancy test, but I needed the blood test. I needed to be sure.

Today we would find out once and for all. I had stopped taking my birth control pills, just in case. Usually if I had even skipped a pill I would start my period, but that hadn't happened yet. I had a doctor's appointment in Uvalde with my gynecologist. Rip and I would get the answer to the question neither of us talked about, but both kept thinking about. Several times I had caught Rip standing in that middle bedroom, the one he had said would make a great nursery. I couldn't help but feel my heart nearly explode in my chest.

The knock on my office door pulled me from my deep thoughts. Glancing up, I saw those blue eyes that mirrored mine looking at me.

"Granddaddy! To what do I owe this honor?"

I stepped around the desk, giving him a hug.

"I have a special delivery of sweet tea for you."

My smile faltered slightly, but I was positive he didn't catch it. "Oh, great. I'm going to have to talk to Grammy about all the sweet tea she's giving me. I feel like I've gained ten pounds this week from drinking so much of it."

He nodded. "Yeah. That bush outside your window had been getting a hefty dose, as well."

My brows pulled in tight as my mouth gaped open. "How did you know?"

Laughing, he replied, "Your grandmother is like Old Faithful. She brews that tea the same time I go out for my morning walk. Each morning I've seen you open that window yonder and dump out the very full cup of tea. Then you cover your mouth and try not to gag."

A nervous laugh slipped from my lips. "Oh, I'm not gagging. It's, ah, the smell from the...mulch. Smells bad."

He nodded, clearly not believing the lie that didn't come out as smoothly as I thought it would. "You always were a bad liar, Chloe Cat. If you don't like your grandmother's tea, tell her."

My entire body sighed in relief.

Rip appeared at the door and tingles raced across my skin.

"Hi, John. How are you doing, sir?" Rip asked, shaking Granddaddy's hand.

"I'm well. You working here today?"

"Yes, sir. Helping Steed out with a new software program designed to help track the vaccinations."

"Fascinating," Granddaddy mused, clearly not the least bit interested. "I'm glad I retired when I did."

Rip and I both chuckled.

When Rip's gaze caught mine, I felt my cheeks warm. He always had a way of looking at me like he wanted to make love to me right there on the spot. "Hey, you ready to go?"

"Um, yeah, let me grab my purse."

As I made my way around the desk, Granddaddy asked, "Where you kids going?"

"Wedding shopping."

"Shopping for furniture."

Rip and I looked at each other.

"Well, a little bit of both," I quickly added.

My grandfather looked between the two of us, one brow raised.

Me.

Rip.

Me again.

Then back to Rip.

He pulled in a deep breath, smiled, and headed to the door. "No need to sneak. Let me know what the doctor says. I still feel too young to be a great-granddaddy, but I'm ready."

When he walked out the door, Rip swung around and looked at me.

"Furniture, Rip? That was a dead giveaway!"

"What?" I gaped. "We're remodeling a house. How is that a giveaway?"

I rolled my eyes.

We walked out of my office and out the back door. "Your grandmother probably told him."

"Where you kids going?"

Screaming, I covered my chest with my hand.

"Trevor! You scared me to death," I gasped.

"Why you two sneaking out of here whispering like you're up to something?"

"We are not sneaking! Why does everyone keep saying we are sneaking?"

A wide smile grew over my uncle's face. "Maybe it's because the two of you snuck off and got married."

Rip reached for the wall, and I almost did the same thing.

"How do you know that?" I whispered.

"Damn Dorothy! I *knew* she couldn't be trusted," Rip said. "I told you we should have sent her that beef jerky basket. The woman loves beef jerky."

"Who all knows?" I asked.

"Scarlett. She was at the county clerk's office that day visiting a friend she used to work with. She saw the two of you and was about to go say hi when she overheard y'all asking for a marriage license. She told me, and don't worry, no one knows. Your little secret is safe."

Rip and I both exhaled. "Thank you, Uncle Trevor. I don't want anyone's feelings being hurt."

"So, you couldn't wait, huh?"

With a smile, I leaned into Rip, and he wrapped his arm around me. "We waited long enough. I mean, we want the wedding with our family and friends, but first we wanted to do it just the two us."

"I get it, you don't owe anyone any explanations. What are you sneaking out in the middle of the morning for?"

Rip and I looked at each other and then back to my uncle.

"Furniture shopping."

"Going wedding shopping."

"Rip!"

"What! You got mad at me for saying furniture, so I said wedding! I can't keep up with the way your mind works."

Uncle Trevor put his hand on Rip's shoulder and slowly shook his head. "Son, don't even try. I'm telling you right now. Don't. Try."

"Chloe, please stop pacing."

"I can't help it. What is taking them so long?"

Rip sat calmly in a chair, looking through a book titled *What to Expect When You're Expecting.*

"This book has some pretty neat information in here. If you are pregnant, I think we should buy one."

I nodded. "Okay. But what if I'm not? What if that birth control jacked up my system and now I'm at risk of never having a period again!"

Rip lifted his eyes from the paperback and looked at me. "Would that be a bad thing?"

Grabbing the pillow off the examination table, I tossed it at him. There was a light knock on the door and I quickly jumped back up on the table. Doctor Buten walked in and gave Rip and me a polite smile.

"How is it going, you two?"

"The birth control you put me on...it's damaged me!"

My hand came up and stopped me from speaking.

Rip chuckled. "Apparently it's made her spontaneously yell out strange things in the last thirty minutes."

Doctor Buten tried not to laugh at Rip's joke and failed. "You know birth control is never one-hundred percent effective against pregnancy."

"I spotted a little bit a month or so ago, but I haven't had a period."

He nodded and looked at my chart. They had drawn blood *and* had me pee in a cup as soon as they brought me back to the room.

Looking up from the chart, he smiled. "The nurse said you haven't taken any at-home pregnancy tests. Is that correct?"

I nodded. Rip walked over to me.

"It also appears you got married. Congratulations."

"Thank you," Rip and I said at the same time, while looking at each other in that silly, lovesick way we couldn't help.

"Well, Mr. and Mrs. Myers, looks like you're going to not only be newlyweds, but new parents."

Tears pooled in my eyes. I slid off the table, and Rip wrapped me so tightly in his arms I almost couldn't breathe. Or maybe I was just overcome with emotion.

"We're having a baby."

A swirl of thoughts raced through mind. I was excited. Thrilled. Scared. Overjoyed. Then I swung back to definitely being scared.

"Oh my goodness, a baby."

Rip pulled back and studied my face. "Are you not happy?"

"Yes! I'm just shocked, I think. We were not planning on this. There is so much going on and..."

"Chloe, why don't you take a seat on the table," Doctor Buten said.

With a quick nod, I sat back. Rip held my hand for a few extra seconds before letting it go and sitting back down.

A new emotion rushed through my veins. Guilt. Rip looked beyond thrilled about the news and here I was trying to decide how I felt. The first thing I'd said was 'there was so much going on.'

I closed my eyes and willed myself not to cry. At least I knew why I could tear up at the drop of a dime these days.

"Let's go ahead and do a vaginal sonogram since you're pretty early on." He opened a drawer and took out a gown. "I'll step out and let the two of you take this all in. Take your time."

When he walked out the door, I got off the table and started to remove my pants. Rip gently took hold of my arm, causing me to stop and look at him.

"Talk to me, Chloe."

My chin trembled. "I don't know if I'm shocked, excited, scared, happy. I mean...I am happy. I think I've known, but for some reason I'm terrified suddenly. Is this too soon? We have hardly gotten to even be together."

He cupped my face within in hands. "Nothing about this changes the way I feel about you. It only makes me love you even more, if that is possible. Chloe, you and I are meant for each other, and if this baby is a part of our journey early on, then I say what an amazing journey we're starting off on."

A tear slipped down my cheek, and he kissed it. "If you're worried about me being upset, I'm fucking over the moon. The thought of our baby growing inside you..."

His voice trailed off, and he cleared his throat while he attempted to get his feelings under control. "I feel like the happiest man on

Earth right now. I'm secretly married to the love of my life, we're having a baby, and the cabinets for the master bathroom are finally done."

I started to laugh as I placed my hands on my stomach. "Oh wow, we're having a baby. A baby."

Rip kissed me. Not a sweet kiss that was meant to reassure me of everything, but a kiss that sent a rush of feelings through my body that screamed how much this man loved me. And just like that...only one emotion ran through me.

Love.

Love for Rip. Love for our child.

What an amazing feeling.

Chapter 35

Chloe

I STOOD IN the middle of the chapel and spun around.

Mike and Rip had found pews from an old church and had refinished them. They were stunning. The large chandelier over the altar hung down and captured the light from the sun as it peered into the large picture windows. Even the old antique table I had seen months ago in a store in Waco stood proudly under the large windows.

"It's beautiful," I whispered to myself as I rubbed my stomach.

I was now eleven weeks pregnant, and according to the book Rip was reading, the baby was the size of a large strawberry. He'd gotten into the habit of asking me how his little berry was doing. Once we found out, we got right to work planning our wedding. No one but Trevor and Scarlett and Alyssa and Mike knew we were already married, and I loved that Rip and I had these two little secrets of ours. Not that I wasn't excited to tell everyone. I was. The doctor had told us most people wait until the end of the first trimester. Rip and I had decided to wait until the wedding to tell everyone about the baby. The wedding was in three weeks, and we had decided to keep it a small event. Family and close friends. According to my Grammy, though, half of Oak Springs was like family.

"What do you think?"

The sound of Rip's voice made my entire body come to life. I turned as he walked down the aisle toward me. I couldn't help but giggle. That would be me in a few short weeks.

"What's so funny?" he asked, stopping and kissing me.

"Nothing. I was thinking how in a few weeks, I will be walking down the aisle."

"I can't wait to marry you," Rip spoke against my lips as he kissed me.

"Hate to break it to you, but you're already married to me."

He smiled. "I can't wait to marry you again. And put a real ring on your finger. I'm tired of tying things on your finger."

Holding up my left hand, I glanced at the string Rip had tied on last night. "I sort of like it."

"I'm pretty sure you're going to like the band even better. I had a few changes made to it."

My eyes lifted to his. The wedding set was an heirloom in his family, and I knew it meant so much to him to give it to me. I was honored to wear it.

"Really? Can I see it?"

Rip tossed his head back and laughed. "No! There are some things you will need to wait for."

I smiled. "We don't seem to be very good at waiting."

"That's because we did it for far too long."

"Agreed."

Jonathon made his way over to us, a smile on his face. "The final inspection is under way," Jonathon said. Rip and I laced our hands together.

"We built a chapel," Rip said.

"No, we built a dream."

My second experience wedding dress shopping was a complete one eighty of my first shopping trip. My mother and I flew to Dallas, just the two of us. We spent two nights and three days shopping, laughing, and enjoying each other's company. The first wedding boutique we stopped at was amazing and ended up being the place I found my dress. When they offered me a glass of champagne, I politely declined. With a raised brow, my mother looked at me, the glass, and then down to my stomach. Then she smiled.

Grammy knew I was pregnant, too. They'd called it from that first day in the kitchen when the cookies nearly sent me over the edge. I loved that they both respected the fact that Rip and I wanted this to ourselves. It felt like so much of our relationship, even before it existed, was on everyone's radar. These two secrets were ours to cherish. The baby and the marriage.

After I tried on five dresses, *the one* appeared in front of me. I didn't even have to try it on; I knew this was it. The bridal consultant, Virginia, held the dress up and I was stunned into silence. My mother grabbed my hand. She felt it, too.

Two thin straps held up the gown. The bodice was all lace with peek-a-boo lace on the sides. The neckline plunged low and I smiled thinking about how my already growing breasts would fill it nicely.

"How about this one?" Virginia asked.

"Yes!" my mother and I both said at the same time.

Virginia chuckled and motioned for me to back into the small suite. After I shimmied out of one dress and into the other, I had my back to the mirror. There was only one in the room, and as tempted as I was to look, I waited.

When I walked into the large room, my mother kept her back toward me.

"Mom? What are you doing?"

"Have you seen it yet?" she asked.

"No," I replied with a giggle.

"Let's look at the same time."

Virginia shrugged, and we walked up onto the platform, my back facing the mirrors. "On three, ladies. One. Two. Three."

While Virginia held the dress, I turned. Mom and I gasped at the same time.

It. Was. Perfect. The lace on the bodice trickled down into a white tulle fabric over satin. Beautiful lace designs edged the bottom of the tulle skirt. It wasn't too tight, yet was tight enough to hug my shape.

Tears pricked at the back of my eyes and I blinked. Virginia leaned in and said, "Stop fighting them."

I did, and tears quickly rolled down my face. My eyes caught my mother's, and she was fighting back her own tears.

"Oh, Chloe Cat." Her voice cracked. "You look beautiful."

Pressing my lips together, I tried to calm my rapid heart. The baby was probably wondering what in the heck I was doing. I placed my hand over my lower stomach and a sob slipped free.

Full. On. Pregnancy. Crying.

After I cried my heart out, I stood in front of the mirrors and beamed with happiness. "I love it."

"I do too, sweetheart. It was made for you."

"When would you need it by?"

"Today," I said, watching Virginia smile. "Well, it fits you like a glove. You might need to take the waist in a bit. When is the wedding?"

"Two weeks, and I'm pretty positive I won't need to take it in."

My gaze caught my mother's. She quickly dabbed at the corners of her eyes.

"Oh well, then. Let's get this off and get it run under the steamer and then you, my dear, have your dress."

Three hours later, Mom and I were sitting in my hotel room eating room service ice cream. Mom hadn't mentioned the baby, and truth be told, I was dying to talk to her about it.

"Mom?"

"Yes?" she asked, looking over at me while spooning vanilla ice cream into her mouth. She wanted chocolate, but I had been having a good two days of no morning sickness, so she opted for vanilla.

"What was it like being pregnant?"

She stared at me for the briefest moment, then smiled. It was as if a memory flashed by and something about it hurt her. "It was amazing. Beautiful. I loved being pregnant with Gage. He gave me a bit of hell in the beginning, like what you're going through, but not nearly as bad."

I smiled. "How did you and Grammy know?"

She shrugged. "Call it mother's intuition."

I chewed on my lip. "Were you afraid?"

Drawing in a deep breath, she exhaled and set her ice cream down.

"Very much so, at first. Chloe, your daddy and I never told you something. We were pregnant before you."

My mouth dropped open and I stared. Even though my mom, the one sitting across from me, wasn't my biological mother, I had no idea she and my father had a baby before me. I knew they had dated in high school. They reminded me a lot of Rip and myself. Maybe they had a great love at one point, and something had driven them apart, only for fate to bring them back together.

"I have another brother or sister?" My mind immediately thought that they must have put the baby up for adoption.

"No. We were seniors in high school, fixin' to graduate, and I lost the baby."

I sucked in a breath. "Oh Mom, I'm so sorry."

She smiled. "It's okay, honey. You didn't know. Your father and I have debated telling you and Gage, but it was so long ago. It was painful for me and things weren't good between your father and me back then. I think that's why it was so hard for him to sit back and watch you and Rip deny your feelings. When you've learned hard lessons in life, you just naturally want to pass those along to your kids. Some lessons, though, need to be learned on their own."

I nodded. "Were you very far along?"

"I was about a month."

Swallowing hard, I said, "I'm twelve weeks."

She pulled me into her arms and gently rocked me. I loved this. Loved that she still held me like her little girl. Still sent that warm feeling rushing through my body that said everything was okay. "Darling girl, you're going to be fine! Just fine."

"I know. I am feeling better and better every day. It is still something I worry about."

She shook her head and pushed a piece of my brown hair behind my ears. "When you were little you had such beautiful blonde hair. Those blue eyes of yours just stood out against all those curls. As you grew up and it turned darker, I remember your daddy saying, 'I can't pick her out in the crowd anymore. Those blonde curls were my marker.'"

I smiled.

"No matter how old your child is, you will worry. You're going to worry every time you feel a strange pain or panic if they don't move every single hour. It's all part of being a parent. No matter how young or old your baby is, you will always be worried about them."

"Are you secretly happy Gage is staying home?"

She winked at me. "I'll never tell."

"That is a yes!"

Mom shrugged and stood. "Come on. I'm taking you out to a fancy restaurant, and we are going to celebrate you saying yes to the dress and my little grandbaby."

"I love that idea!"

Chapter 36

Rip

I STOOD STARING at the baby goat in the pen. Steed stood next to me, a giant smile on his face.

"A goat?" I asked.

"Yep."

The little kid, who happened to be dressed in tiny pink pajamas, was currently bouncing all over the place. "A goat?"

"Yep. It will be the perfect wedding present."

My brows lifted. "Not to put your idea down or anything, sir, but I was thinking along the lines of some diamond and pearl earrings for Chloe."

Steed looked at me, then rolled his eyes. "Not from you! From me and Paxton."

Relief swept over me. *Thank God.*

"That makes more sense, I think."

"I know how much Chloe has been missing Patches, and I think she will love this idea. I was thinking we could have your little niece, Renee, walk the goat down the aisle with her."

My oldest sister Evie would totally think this was precious. Her daughter Renee was five and would be over the moon walking a goat down the aisle.

Between my two brothers and three sisters and Chloe's nine cousins, we had decided to only have Mike and Alyssa in the wedding party. Sort of like our actual wedding. Renee was the youngest in either family, so she was the natural pick for the flower girl.

"I'm sure she would love that," I agreed.

"The one with the pink sweater!" Steed called out.

"You'll keep it in Patches' old stall?" I asked as the farmer picked up the goat and put her in my hands.

"Yes. Then when you both come back from your honeymoon you can bring her home."

I forced a smile. "Great. Can't wait."

Steed looked at me and then busted out laughing.

As we walked to his truck, Steed started to talk. "Your mom and dad invited me and Paxton over for dinner tonight. That was sweet of them. You kids sure you want to spend the night before your wedding with your folks?"

"Of course we do."

What Steed didn't realize was that Chloe and I were going to tell our parents we were expecting a baby in March. We'd tell the rest of the family when we got back from France—which Chloe still didn't know was our honeymoon destination.

With the baby goat in the back seat of Steed's truck, we set off for Frio Cattle Ranch. When I looked back, I smiled. The goat was sound asleep in a peaceful slumber.

"Looks like we have the opposite of Patches," I mused.

"I love your optimism, Rip. It's one of your better qualities."

"Mom knows already," Chloe confessed in the truck on the way to my parents' house.

"I figured she knew from that day in your grandparents' kitchen."

Chloe looked at me sheepishly. "Well, in Dallas I sort of let it slip. Okay, it wasn't sort of. I really needed to talk to her. I was feeling scared and well…"

Taking her hand in mine, I squeezed it. "Chloe, you don't have to explain why you told your mom. That's your mom. It only makes sense you would tell her first."

"I just didn't want you to think I was playing favorites or anything."

I chuckled. "I would never think that."

When we pulled up, both sets of parents were waiting on the front porch. My folks shared the swing, while Paxton and Steed sat in the rockers.

"There they are!" My father walked down to greet us. "Chloe, you look beautiful as always."

Chloe blushed. "Thank you, Rip."

"RJ, how's that farmhouse coming?"

My father always called me RJ. Short for Rip, Jr. I was named after him. My three older siblings—Jonathon, Evie, and Hollie—were from our mother's first marriage. After she married my dad, Dalton, Hope, and myself came along.

"House is great. It had some really good bones, so it hasn't taken too much to fix it up."

"We need to come and see it again. You've made a lot of changes," my mom said. She kissed Chloe. "Hello, darling."

"Hi, Kristin. I can smell that roast from out here!" Chloe said. "Smells amazing."

My mother grinned. "Well, I know my roast was always your favorite."

Steed and Paxton hugged Chloe, then Steed shook my hand and Paxton followed up with a hug.

When we made our way into the house, Chloe glanced to all the boxes in the corner.

"Getting ready for Christmas, Kristin?" she called out.

"Don't you know it! I'd have it all up, but I was helping your momma and Melanie make some things for the reception tomorrow. I've got my outline all done and printed up."

"Laminated, of course," my father added.

"Each room color coded," Mom said with a wink.

Mom was the queen of Christmas. It was almost October and any normal year we would have at least two trees up in the house by now. Our wedding had thrown my mom off her game.

We stepped into the kitchen that also held a large table were we mainly ate together as a family.

"I made your favorite dessert, Chloe. Chocolate ganache with homemade ice cream."

"Oh no," Chloe whispered before slapping her hand over her mouth.

My mother had made Chloe's favorite dessert. Why hadn't it crossed my mind that she would make Chloe's favorite dessert? This was my first fail as a husband and upcoming father.

"Shit," I cried out as I ran past everyone, nearly knocking my mother into the chocolate ganache cake. I grabbed the trash can and rushed back to Chloe.

Opening the lid, I put it under Chloe who promptly leaned over and threw up.

I glanced over my shoulder to see four sets of eyes gawking. Steed and my dad looked like they were fixin' to have a sympathy throw up, while Paxton and my mother exchanged a knowing look.

"I've got some homemade peppermint tea in the fridge. That will settle your stomach," Mom said, rushing to get out the tea.

"I'm going to go ahead and take this cake on out of the room," Paxton said as she grabbed it and headed out the back door.

"Wait! Where are you taking the cake!" Steed cried out, following Paxton.

My father covered his mouth and raced out of the room. Once Chloe was finished being sick, I rubbed her back and then took the warm washcloth my mother had handed me. I sure as shit hoped I would be able to parent half as well as she did.

"Here, baby. This will feel better."

Chloe took the washcloth and then the tea from my mom.

"Is the cake gone?" Chloe asked, her eyes still watery from throwing up. This baby was giving her a run for her money.

"Yes. Sweetheart, I'm so sorry. Are you feeling okay?"

If my mother suspected anything, she wasn't letting on.

Chloe smiled. "I'm fine. I'm sorry about that."

We could hear my father from the hall bathroom. Mom rolled her eyes. "Good Lord, he's gonna need me. You'll soon see, Chloe, when a man gets sick in any sort of way, they all believe they're fixin' to die no matter how minor it is."

Giggling, Chloe took a sip of the tea.

When Mom walked out, our eyes met.

"Your mom had peppermint tea made up," she said.

I smiled. "I swear to you, I didn't tell her. She always has peppermint tea made."

Paxton and Steed walked back into the kitchen, and Steed was arguing with Paxton about why the cake had to stay outside.

"It's gonna melt!" Steed protested.

"You're fine, Rip. You had a little bit of sympathy throw up, for Pete's sake. Let's eat dinner, shall we?" Mom said as she walked into the kitchen. "Chloe, did you want to eat something?"

"Yes, please. I'm fine now."

"You sure?" Dad asked.

Chloe nodded. "Sorry about that, y'all."

Everyone quickly got busy filling their plates with roast and vegetables, then made their way to the table. Steed and my father quickly fell into a conversation about the barn that Chloe had suggested they transform into an event venue. Mom and Paxton went over last-minute things that needed to be done before tomorrow. The actual wedding ceremony was family only and a few close friends. The reception, on the other hand, was going to be held at Chloe's grandparents' house. It was the largest on the ranch, and Melanie had everything already to go since she hosted a spring charity event each year. The backyard was being transformed for the wedding reception. I had to admit it all came together pretty fast since I had first shown Chloe the chapel a month-and-a-half ago.

I glanced over at Chloe. She was staring at me. We both smiled at each other, and I cleared my throat.

"Um, since we have all four of you here, there is something Chloe and I would like you to know before the wedding tomorrow."

All eyes were on me. Looking at my beautiful bride, I motioned for her to take over.

"Rip and I are going to be making an announcement when we come back from our honeymoon, but we wanted y'all to know first."

"What is it, sweetheart?" my mom asked.

Chloe's eyes lit up and her face broke into a stunning smile. "Rip and I are expecting a baby. My due date is March 7."

I had to admit, I was nervous about what our folks would say. So far, no one had told us we were rushing into anything, especially since we had really only started dating in June. Now we were getting married and having a baby.

"A baby?" Mom said, standing up. "A baby! A baby!"

Paxton jumped up next. "A baby!"

My father was next. "We're having another grandbaby!"

My parents hugged while Paxton walked up to Chloe and wrapped her arms around her. I smiled as I took in the whole scene. When I got to Steed, my smile faded. He was sitting there, staring at Chloe.

"Daddy?"

Steed slowly shook his head and then stood. "Excuse me one moment."

He walked out of the kitchen. My heart dropped, and when I saw the tears forming in Chloe's eyes, I wanted to go after Steed and hit him.

Paxton moved to follow him. "I'll go see what's..."

"No, Mom, I need to go. If you'll excuse me." Chloe gave a polite grin and went in the direction Steed had disappeared.

"Paxton, is he not happy about this?" my mother asked.

"I'm sure he is in shock. I know he's happy." She looked at me. "He knows how much you love her. He probably wasn't expecting y'all to have a baby so soon."

"Well, we weren't either," I said. "I don't regret it for one moment."

"Of course you don't, RJ. Of course you don't," Mom said.

I glanced to where Chloe and Steed had walked out of the kitchen. Paxton reached for my hand. "Give them a few minutes, sweetheart. It's going to be fine."

"Of course it will," Dad added. "It's hard for a dad. You'll learn that someday, son, if you have a girl."

Doing the only thing I could, I nodded and sat back down at the table.

Chapter 37

Chloe

I FOUND MY father sitting on the front porch steps, staring out over the perfectly manicured lawn.

"Daddy?"

He looked over his shoulder and smiled. "Come sit down, pumpkin."

A warm rush of happiness washed over me. My father hadn't called me pumpkin in years. I sat down next to him.

"Are you disappointed in me?" I asked, barely above a whisper.

"What? God, no. I'm sorry I reacted that way. I needed to leave before I did something."

"Hit Rip?"

He jerked his head to look at me. "No! Why in the world would I hit the boy?"

I shrugged. "I dunno. You sat there with a deadpan expression, then got up and left."

Daddy chuckled. "Chloe, I was trying not to get upset. I can't be crying in front of Rip's daddy. I'll look like a pansy ass."

Grinning, I wrapped my arm around his and leaned my head on his shoulder. For a man in his forties, he was still muscular. I could easily remember these arms lifting me up and putting me on his shoulders for a ride.

"You're not mad?"

"Pumpkin, I'm so happy for you and Rip. I mean, I wish y'all would have waited just a bit longer, but I understand."

"It was an accident. My birth control failed. Big time."

He laughed. "I would say so. How are you feeling?"

"Well, anything chocolate makes me sick. I've had some light to moderate morning sickness. Except it comes at all times of the day so I'm not really sure why it is called morning sickness."

He laughed. "Rip taking good care of you?"

"Yes. He talks to my stomach every single morning and night and any time in between when we're alone. He's madly in love with this baby already."

"That's because he's been madly in love with the baby's momma for many years."

"Yeah." With a chuckle, I said, "He's reading this book, *What to Expect When You're Expecting.*"

"I read that. It's a good one."

I smiled. "He reminds me so much of you, Daddy. The way he loves me. Looks at me. It's how you look at Mom."

"Oh, pumpkin, that boy has been looking at you like that since y'all were about ten years old."

My cheeks flushed. We sat in silence for a few moments.

"I'm going to be a mom."

"I'm going to be a grandpa."

We both exhaled.

"I hope Rip and I are half as good as parents as you and Mom are."

He kissed my forehead. "You will be an amazing mother. I know you will. And Rip is going to be an amazing dad. He comes from a good family."

Squeezing his arm, I said, "We should go back in. I'm sure Rip is freaking out and worrying that you hate him."

Dad stood and then helped me to my feet. I was capable of getting up on my own, but Daddy was a true southern gentleman.

"Maybe I'll let him sweat it out for a bit before I make nice."

"Daddy!" I said, hitting him lightly on the arm. The front door opened, and Rip stood there. Looking every bit as worried as I knew he was.

"Steed, sir."

Holding up his hand, Daddy shook his head. "Son, I'm damn happy for both of you. I just needed a minute or two."

"He was fixin' to cry and didn't want to do it in front of your dad," I said, causing my father to glare.

Rip laughed, which made Daddy send the look to him, but he made it ten times scarier.

"Not funny. Got it," Rip stated.

As my father walked by, he held out one hand to shake while squeezing Rip's shoulder with the other. "Congratulations, son."

There was no way I could stop the flood of happiness that hit me. We spent the rest of the evening helping Kristin unpack some Christmas boxes and organize the decorations. It was a fun night, and it kept my mind off of tomorrow's wedding. I had no idea why I was nervous. I was already married. But this time we would be doing it in front of our family. And it wouldn't be just me and Rip. This time it was me, Rip, and our baby.

Renee ran around in a circle as she laughed. Shannon, one of my old college friends turned professional photographer, was snapping pictures. She'd gotten me before I got ready, as I got ready, and was now waiting for the big moment when I got on my horse, Lizzy, and rode over to the chapel.

"Chloe, lift your dress just a bit, let me see the tip of your cowboy boot."

I did as she said. A light knock on the door had my stomach dropping.

Aunt Scarlett popped her head in and smiled. "Rip and Mike are at the chapel. Are you, Alyssa, and Renee ready to go?"

Taking in a deep breath, I said, "Yes. Very ready."

Shannon gathered up all her stuff. She would be driving behind me in the ranch four-wheel drive Mule. Alyssa climbed up on her favorite horse here at the ranch, Pepsi.

With the help of Uncle Trevor, I got up on my horse. Shannon and Scarlett made sure my dress was laid out perfectly. No one would see me walking up to the chapel, since they would all be inside, but Shannon was snapping pictures.

"Ready?" Trevor asked, a giant smile on his face.

"Ready!" I glanced around. "Wait? Where is Renee?"

"She went on ahead with your Daddy. They'll be waiting outside the chapel," Scarlett said.

"Perfect. Let's go!" I said.

The ride to the chapel wasn't long, but it felt like it took forever to get there. Trevor, Scarlett, and Shannon went ahead so that they could get to their seats, and Shannon could get me and Alyssa coming up on our horses.

"Well, I guess now you get to finally call yourself Mrs. Rip Myers in public," Alyssa mused.

"Yes! Finally."

I looked her way. She was beaming. "Are you thinking about your own wedding?" I asked.

"Yeah, about that."

I almost brought my horse to a stop. "What do you mean...about that. Are y'all having problems?"

"What? No! Gosh, no. It's just, after seeing you and Rip elope like that, well, it got us thinking."

Nearly letting out a scream, I covered my mouth.

Alyssa giggled. "We're eloping."

"Shut up! Where?"

She shrugged. "We haven't thought about it just yet."

"What about the big wedding y'all were planning?"

"I don't want a big wedding. I want it to just be me, Mike, you and Rip."

"Oh, Alyssa! Where? When?"

She giggled. "We'll talk about it after you come back from your honeymoon. We have to work around your little baby."

The horses turned the bend, and I instantly heard the rush of water from the Frio River. In front of us was the little white chapel sitting in front of our tree. My stomach fluttered but not from nerves. Maybe it was excitement. Or maybe it was the baby. That thought nearly had me in tears. Was our little one making themselves known at our wedding?

As we got closer, I looked at the giant oak tree. It was all coming full circle today.

Once I stepped off that horse, everything changed. I walked up to the blue antique doors and stopped when I saw the sight in front of me. Renee stood there with a baby goat on a leash. My heart melted on the spot.

"Oh my God! A baby goat!"

"Do not get your dress dirty!" Alyssa warned.

The little goat jumped and twirled in the air. Renee and I both laughed. It reminded me of the day I got Patches.

"Do you like her?" Daddy asked.

"Is she mine?"

He nodded. "She's all yours."

I nearly jumped into my father's arms. "I love her so much! I'm going to name her Calamity Jane!"

My father laughed. "O-okay."

"Ready?" Alyssa asked as she stood at the doors.

Taking my arms, my father and I stood to the side with Renee and one very excited goat in front of us.

Two old high school buddies of Rip's, Colt and Bill, served as ushers, opening the big blue doors. Alyssa looked at me and winked before she started off into the chapel. Renee jumped up and down, which made Calamity Jane do the same.

"Ready?" I asked her.

She looked up at me and nodded as she held her basket of white rose petals. "Weady!"

"Go!" Daddy said in a soft voice. Renee walked through the doors and Calamity Jane followed.

Bill stood and watched as Alyssa and Renee walked down the aisle. He chuckled a few times and looked over at us. "The goat's eating the rose petals."

I covered my mouth and giggled. A part of me felt like Patches was here with me. My stomach fluttered again, and I took in a deep breath, forcing myself not to cry.

The wedding march started, and I looked up at my father. He gave me the sweetest smile. "I love you, pumpkin. You'll always be my little girl. Always."

"Oh, Daddy. Don't make me cry, my makeup will smudge, and I'll look a fright."

He leaned down and kissed my forehead. "Never in a million years. And it wouldn't matter. That boy waiting at the end of the chapel loves you with all his heart. I don't think he would care if you walked in wearing jeans and one of his old T-shirts."

I laughed. "He probably wouldn't care."

Bill motioned for us to start walking. When we turned the corner and entered the little chapel, everyone stood. That's when I saw him.

Rip.

He stood at the very end, dressed in crisp new jeans, his favorite cowboy boots, and a white shirt with a satin, light-tan formal vest and a brand-new white cowboy hat. My heart felt like it flipped in my chest. Mike stood next to him, dressed almost the same, but his vest was darker and matched Alyssa's dress.

Something caught my eye and I looked to see Calamity Jane jumping up to try and get onto Aunt Waylynn's lap.

"Are you kidding me right now?" Waylynn exclaimed as everyone started to laugh over the music.

"Shit, what are the odds?" my father said as I burst out laughing.

Calamity Jane decided she wanted to stick with Renee who had the rose petals and followed her up to the altar where Calamity Jane proceeded to lay down. The excitement of the aisle must have taken some energy out of her.

The long antique table behind the pastor was decorated with the most beautiful greenery and flowers. I had left it up to my mother to arrange the flowers in the chapel, and she had done an amazing job.

But my eyes kept going to Rip.

Stopping at the end of the aisle, Daddy leaned in and gave me a kiss. He placed my hand into Rip's when asked who was giving me away.

"I'm not giving her away. She is too rare and precious. I am, however, willing to share her with you."

Rip nodded, his emotions showing on his handsome face. Rip held my hand as I took the step up. We faced one another, and he looked me up and down.

When his eyes landed on mine, he whispered, "Les mots ne peuvent pas décrire mon amour pour toi."

Words cannot describe my love for you.

My eyes filled with tears, and Rip shook his head as he lifted his brow. "No tears."

"What if they're happy tears?"

Rip smiled, and the pastor started the service. I hardly heard a word as the man I had loved nearly my entire life looked lovingly into my eyes while he rubbed his thumbs over the back of my hands. My face was beginning to hurt from smiling so big. When it came time to exchange rings, I couldn't believe my eyes. The simple, white gold band Rip had shown me was now more elegant, covered in small diamonds and a decorative bead around the edges. It looked exactly like a ring I had seen years ago in a French magazine we were reading in high school.

My eyes jerked up to his. A tear slipped free, and he reached up and wiped it away.

"Do you forget anything?" I asked, my voice cracking.

Rip leaned in closer to whisper. "I ripped the page out of the magazine and have had it ever since. I had a jeweler in Johnson City make it out of my great-grandmother's band."

This man. Lord, this man.

Once the pastor had declared us man and wife, we kissed. Then I took my flowers and Calamity Jane's leash, and we made our way back down the aisle with a quick stop to ring the chapel bell. Our family and friends cheered as we walked out of the door.

The plan was to stay and take pictures while the wedding guests made their way up to the main house. It would give me and Rip a few moments alone together before we partied the night away with friends and family.

"Come here," Rip said, taking my hand in his.

Shannon followed our every move, snapping pictures as we walked across the grass to our tree. Rip held onto the swing as I sat down on it. He leaned his mouth to my ear.

"Je t'aime, Chloe."

"I love you, too."

His French made my stomach pull with desire. *Would anyone really miss us at the reception if we didn't show up?*

Pulling back, Rip let the swing go. I lifted my boots and laughed as I felt the breeze flowing through my hair. I had worn it half up and half down, knowing how much Rip loved my hair down.

"Stop the swing and kiss her, Rip!" Shannon said, snapping pictures as she spoke.

Rip stopped the swing, took off his cowboy hat, and hid our faces as he kissed me.

Shannon and I both laughed. The small flutter in my stomach told me this baby already thought her Daddy was so romantic and so funny.

Chapter 38

Chloe

RIP AND I walked hand in hand down a little alley in Paris. I should have known he was taking me to France from all his little hints. Talking to me in French at the wedding was one big tip off. Although he would often speak to me in French, especially when he was making love to me. I had never gotten the chance to study abroad, so this was Rip's way of making up for that lost trip.

We had been here for one week and had another week planned. Rip's wedding present to me was a set of beautiful earrings that we had found in an antique store here in France. I still had my gift to give him. Which I was about to do.

"It's so beautiful here," I said, taking in a deep breath. The weather had been perfect. Not too hot, and not too cold.

"It is," Rip agreed as we made our way out of the alley and stopped in front of a stunning park.

"Oh my gosh, look at the flowers!"

"Stunning. Look, there's a wedding about to happen! Let's go watch."

"Rip, we cannot go watch! It's someone's wedding."

"But we're dressed for a wedding in a park. And if they didn't want people to watch, why have it in a park?"

I glanced down at my soft pink sundress. Rip was dressed in jeans and a pullover. With a giggle, I said, "Okay! Let's go peek."

As we got closer, I strained to see what the groom looked like. From behind he looked exactly like Mike.

"That looks like..."

My voice trailed off as we drew closer.

"No! Are you kidding me?" I cried out as Mike turned and faced us. I rushed over to him and hugged him.

Rip was laughing behind me as he said, "We totally pulled it off!"

Mike returned the laughter and nodded. "That we did!"

"You're here! Where is Alyssa?" I asked, looking around. There was a small building off to the side where Mike pointed.

"She's in there, waiting for her maid of honor."

I screamed like a little silly school girl and took off toward the small building.

"Chloe, be careful running!" Rip cried out.

Throwing open the door, I came to a stop. There was my best friend dressed in a stunning chiffon gown holding a large bouquet of flowers, with a smaller one held out to me.

"I thought you were going to make me late to my own wedding."

Hugging her, I clenched my teeth to keep from crying. When I pulled back, I saw she was doing the same.

"We always said we wanted to go to France together. The four of us. When Rip presented us with the idea to just run off and get married and spend a week in France with y'all, we couldn't say no. We told our folks the plan, and they paid for this instead of the big fancy wedding in Oak Springs."

"I can't believe you're here. Will you stay longer than a week?" I asked.

"After y'all leave to go back home, Mike and I are going to Tuscany for a week."

My hands covered my mouth, and I started to jump around like a little girl.

The woman who had been standing next to Alyssa spoke in French, alerting her that the time was now.

"Let's do this!" Alyssa said, handing me the flowers.

As I walked down the little stone pathway toward Mike and Rip, I couldn't help the huge smile on my face.

Rip and I stared into each other's eyes the entire ceremony. Part of it was done in French, the rest in English. When it came time for them to kiss, I bit my lip and stared at Rip. He had been watching Mike and Alyssa but swung his gaze to meet mine.

We both smiled. And I felt it again, the little flutter in my stomach that I had been feeling every day since last week at our wedding when I first felt it. I placed my hand on my stomach and let out a half laugh, half sob. Rip instantly walked up to me.

"What's wrong?" he asked, placing his hand over mine.

Alyssa and Mike turned to face me.

"Nothing! Nothing is wrong. I'm just overcome with happiness."

I hugged Alyssa and then Mike. The photographer ushered them to stand for pictures while Rip and I moved to the side.

He glanced down at my hand on my belly.

"Our baby is moving, and I feel her."

His eyes went wide. "You feel the baby?"

I nodded. "I felt her last week. On our wedding day. At first, I thought it was nervous flutters, but I've been feeling it all week. She keeps letting me know she's here with us."

Rip cupped my face within his hands. "You keep saying *she*."

My smile was so wide that it made my cheeks ache. "That's because the baby is a girl."

Rip chuckled. "Is that so? And how do you know that?"

Reaching into the little pocket of my sun dress, I pulled out a piece of paper and handed it to him. I had asked Doctor Buten to do a blood test to find out the sex of the baby.

Rip opened it and instantly started to cry. He looked at me. "A girl? Our little Emma."

I nodded. "I hope you're happy. I know you probably wanted a little boy."

He shook his head and placed his hand on the back of my neck, bringing me into a kiss.

"I didn't care. I only want a happy baby."

Smiling, I placed his hand on my stomach. "I can't believe how much I love Emma already. Is it possible to keep falling more in love with her?"

Rip nodded. "I think so. And when I see her, I know I will fall even more in love with her at first sight. Just like I did with her mommy."

The End

Kelly Elliott is a *New York Times* and *USA Today* bestselling contemporary romance author. Since finishing her bestselling Wanted series, Kelly continues to spread her wings while remaining true to her roots and giving readers stories rich with hot protective men, strong women and beautiful surroundings.

Her bestselling works include, *Wanted, Broken, The Playbook, and Lost Love*, to name a few.

Kelly lives in central Texas with her husband, daughter, two pups, four cats, and endless wildlife creatures. When she's not writing, Kelly enjoys reading and spending time with her family.

To find out more about Kelly and her books, you can find her through her website.

www.kellyelliottauthor.com

Other Books by Kelly Elliott

Stand Alones
The Journey Home
Who We Were*
The Playbook*
Made for You*
*Available on audiobook

Cowboys and Angels Series
Lost Love
Love Profound
Tempting Love
Love Again
Blind Love
This Love
Reckless Love
*Series available on audiobook

Wanted Series
Wanted*
Saved*
Faithful*
Believe
Cherished*
A Forever Love*
The Wanted Short Stories
All They Wanted
*Available on audiobook

Love Wanted in Texas Series
Spin-off series to the WANTED Series
Without You
Saving You

Holding You
Finding You
Chasing You
Loving You
Entire series available on audiobook
*Please note *Loving You* combines the last book of the Broken and Love Wanted in Texas series.

Broken Series
*Broken**
*Broken Dreams**
*Broken Promises**
Broken Love
*Available on audiobook

The Journey of Love Series
Unconditional Love
Undeniable Love
Unforgettable Love
*Entire series available on audiobook

With Me Series
Stay With Me
Only With Me
*Series on audiobook

Speed Series
Ignite
Adrenaline

Boston Love Series
Searching for Harmony
Fighting for Love
*Series available on audiobook

Austin Singles Series
Seduce Me
Entice Me
Adore Me
*Series available on audiobook

YA Novels written under the pen name Ella Bordeaux
Beautiful
Forever Beautiful

Historical
Predestined Hearts by Kelly Elliott and Kristin Mayer

COMING SOON
Never Enough (Book one in a new series) December 2019

Southern Bride Series
Love at First Sight August 9, 2019
Delicate Promises October 2019
Divided Interests Early 2020

COLLABORATIONS
Predestined Hearts (co-written with Kristin Mayer)
Play Me (co-written with Kristin Mayer)*
Dangerous Temptations (co-written with Kristin Mayer)
September 30, 2019
Until There Was You (co-written with Kristin Mayer) Spring 2020
*Available on audiobook

Made in the USA
Monee, IL
18 November 2020